LOVE OUT OF SEASON

LOVE OUT OF SEASON

Ray Connolly

ISIS

LARGE PRINT

Oxford

First published in Great Britain 2008
by
Quercus

Published in Large Print 2008 by ISIS Publishing Ltd.,
7 Centremead, Osney Mead, Oxford OX2 0ES
by arrangement with
Quercus

British Library Cataloguing in Publication Data
Connolly, Ray, 1940–
    Love out of season. – Large print ed.
    1. Women novelists – English – Fiction
    2. Hotels – England – Devon – Fiction
    3. Love stories
    4. Large type books
    I. Title
    823.9'14 [F]

ISBN 978–0–7531–8022–8 (hb)
ISBN 978–0–7531–8023–5 (pb)

Printed and bound in Great Britain by
T. J. International Ltd., Padstow, Cornwall

To Plum.
Again.

'Love isn't just blind or strange. It's crazy, too, a mental illness which can lead perfectly sensible and intelligent people to behave in the most foolish and irrational of ways.

'Because of this it's also wonderful.'

— Amy Miller

CHAPTER
ONE

Given the choice, which would you prefer: that the person you love is making love to you and thinking about someone else, or that he, or she, is making love to someone else and thinking about you?

Amy considered the words on her screen. Was that an original thought or had she overheard it somewhere? She couldn't be sure. She hesitated for a moment, weighing up the risks of unintended plagiarism, and then continued anyway.

Why can't he, or she, be thinking about me as well as making love to me? you might ask.
But you never do.

She frowned now, then finally added:

You don't dare.

She stopped writing. Was this getting personal? Her finger dawdled on the *delete* button. Of course it was personal. Whatever else love was, a bunch of red roses, a metaphysical excuse for sex, a passing moment in human evolution, a confidence trick designed by nature, an accident, a song, a game, a poem or a pain, it was always personal. The telephone broke into her musings: a welcome distraction. "Amy!"

Her work frown dissolved at the voice. "Oh, *hello*! Nice surprise. I was just thinking about you! You were very good this morning with that . . ." she searched for the right words, "that pre-Raphaelite loony. What are you doing? Can you get away, come over . . .?" As she'd been speaking she'd been taking off her reading glasses.

"Amy, they're on to us." The famously mellifluent tones interrupted her.

"*What*? This is a joke! Right?"

"They may already be watching."

She wanted to laugh. That morning on television he'd been the epitome of the urbane, metropolitan man gently ribbing an over-dramatic, tumbling-haired actress whose view of the world ended at her mirror. Now his voice was as hushed as a conspirator. "Oh, come on! That's just paranoia," she scolded. "No one's watching us. I'd have noticed." And swivelling around on her typing chair she rolled on casters across the polished wooden floor to her study window and looked down through the black winter trees that lined the drive below. "There you are, noth —" she began, then stopped and stood up to get a better view.

"Yes?"

"Oh, my God!"

Two figures had emerged from the shadows of the bushes and were standing on the pavement, gazing up at her window. Seeing her, one of them appeared to say something to the other, then indicated her. Immediately a camera bearing a very large and long lens was pointed upwards.

She didn't need to hear the automatic shutter. As she dropped to the carpet she knew what the pictures would show — a fair, pretty-ish woman in her early thirties in a pale-blue working shirt and jeans, staring in dismay as the most exciting part of her life came to an abrupt end.

"Amy?"

She was on the floor, dragging the curtains across the window. "How did they find out? How did they *know*?" she gabbled into the phone. "We've been so careful."

"God knows! But don't worry. We'll sort it out."

"*Don't worry!* They'll roast us. You'll be skewered."

"Not if we do the right thing."

"But we've been doing the *wrong* thing!" She regretted saying that instantly. It wasn't supposed to sound like a wail, either. She didn't wail. She wasn't the type. But she knew that in that moment her life had changed. What she'd most dreaded, yet always half expected, had happened. "It's my fault," she said, lifting the hem of the curtains and trying to peep outside. But, as the camera was raised again, she pulled back. "We're being punished."

In truth, she wasn't sure she meant that either. In fact, she probably didn't, not being at all certain that she believed in a God who dealt so arbitrarily in rewards and punishments. But this wasn't the moment for reflections on the nature of divinity.

3

"Don't be silly. We've done nothing to be punished for. Don't panic," he calmed.

"I'm not panicking," she lied.

At the other end of the phone there was now a silence.

"Teddy?" she enquired at last. She recognized the sudden quiet. It worried her. He used it very effectively as a technique in his television interviews before asking outrageous questions.

"I was thinking . . ." he began. "Perhaps if you were to, you know, disappear . . .?" It came as a vague suggestion and question combined, but there was an emollient persuasion to the tone.

She was surprised. "You want me to go away?"

"Just for a few days. A holiday. You know, lie low. Go to ground, that sort of thing."

"You mean, go into hiding?"

"Well . . ."

"Like a criminal? On the run?"

"Amy!"

"But I'm working . . ."

"You can work anywhere."

This irritated. It wasn't true, but he wouldn't understand. He never did, and she'd given up trying to explain to him that writers work best at the same desk in the same room day after day. She'd been pathetic about that. Now she was giving in again. "Where would I go?" she heard herself ask, and realized she'd already agreed.

"Anywhere." He was coaxing now, cooing almost. "Somewhere anonymous and quiet until I can . . ." He stopped and corrected himself. "Until *we* can, you know, sort things out."

He's getting rid of me, she thought. I'm in the way. And, still on the floor, she gazed around her study walls at the silver-framed posters of the novels she'd written, the trophies that charted the somehow largely vicarious life she'd been living until she met him. Finally, her eyes came to rest on the blinking cursor of her computer, still waiting for her to finish her paragraph. She wouldn't be doing that tonight. Would she ever finish it? When it comes down to it, she thought, he's just a married man, a very famously, happily married man. And for a single woman, particularly one with a well-known name, to be in love with such a man had suddenly become an inconvenience he could do without.

Will Abbott contemplated the top-floor window of the apartment block. It would be an expensive place to own in such a fashionable area. But then she was a successful girl. Pity she'd spotted them so soon.

At his side, the photographer, cocooned in wet-weather gear, sniffed. He'd be complaining soon. Photographers always complained. But stake-outs weren't fun for anyone on a cold and wet February evening. Famous adulterers would be doing everybody a favour if they only let themselves be outed in the summer. Their pictures would come out better then, too.

Rubber brakes squeaked quietly behind them as a bicycle bumped on to the kerb and came to rest. A gawky girl in a school raincoat, a brace on her teeth and a *South Park* transfer on her helmet stood astride the pedals, watching them. "Her name's Amy Miller," the girl volunteered at last. "She writes romantic fiction."

We're so obvious, thought Abbott, the policemen of celebrity morals. The photographer wiped his lens, amused.

The girl indicated Amy's window. "I read one once. It wasn't bad. But the sex was a bit on the tepid side."

Abbott chose to ignore that observation. She was all of thirteen. "Have you . . . er . . . have you ever seen anyone visit her?" he asked. "Anyone famous, I mean."

The girl considered him without expression.

Reaching inside his overcoat for his wallet he withdrew a ten-pound note.

"More famous than that," she said scornfully. But now she smiled.

They settled at twenty, which he could later inflate to forty for his expenses. The girl's name was Polly.

"Yes, I've seen someone," she confided with quiet glee. "Teddy Farrow from *The Teddy Farrow Show*. He usually comes at night when I'm finishing my homework. He parks his car around the corner. It's a black BMW. Then he sneaks in . . . and . . . sneaks out again . . . much later!" She smirked knowingly when she said "much later", as though she had some personal experience of what occurred when Teddy Farrow came to call.

Abbott looked again at the sixth-floor window. There was now no sign of activity behind the drawn curtains, no shadows. "Do you live here?" he asked.

Polly nodded.

"And you know Amy Miller?"

"I've seen her. That's all."

He was pleased about that. It meant no loyalties would be compromised. He smiled at the girl, as though taking her into his confidence, flirting really, if one could flirt with a child. "You know, Polly, this may be really important. I don't know. But it might help if you could invite us into the building so that we could talk to the lady," he said.

Legally it would, he knew, still count as trespass, but as Amy Miller was now aware that they were there she could stay inside for days, and Teddy Farrow certainly wouldn't be coming around for a while. The old rules of reporting always applied. It was no use standing in the porch speaking into an intercom that could be slammed down at any moment. Until you actually knocked on the door and confronted your quarry eye to eye you never knew what reaction you might get.

She was racing. Dashing from bathroom to bedroom, she was quickly filling a large canvas bag with jeans, shirts, underclothes, shoes and sweaters. In her study she copied her work on to a disc and slid it into her laptop case. Then, turning off all the lights, she grabbed her coat and car keys, and, opening her front door, stepped out on to the landing.

Even before she'd finished locking the door she realized that the chase had entered the building. She could hear the hunters murmuring to each other about the swankiness of the place as they came up the stairs.

Tiptoeing along the landing she reached the lift. A red light read "Occupied". She winced. Her plan had been to take the lift down to the garage, and then drive out at speed, taking her tormentors by surprise. That was no longer an option.

"Next floor," she heard a man's voice echo in the stairwell.

Had her top-floor neighbour been at home she might have sought sanctuary in his flat. But this was professional London. Nobody was ever around when you needed them.

She glanced at her door. It was too late. She would be spotted now if she tried to get back.

Taking off her shoes, she shoved them into her coat pockets and crept silently up the stairs to the top landing. There was only one door. Pushing down the bar of the fire lock, she opened it and stepped out on to the flat roof of the apartment block.

He knew she hadn't gone down because Polly, the neighbourhood snitch, was earning an extra fiver in the lobby blocking the lift door with her bike. But she wasn't answering her door either. He rang the bell one more time. Nothing.

Kneeling down, the photographer tried to see through the letter box, then shook his head.

She could, of course, have been sitting inside the flat with the lights turned off, waiting for them to give up and leave. On the other hand . . . Abbott looked up the stairs to the top floor.

Holding on to the handrail, the other hand gripping her bag and laptop, she carefully felt her way down the iron steps of the fire escape. Soon she was passing the lighted, deckchair-curtained windows of flats lower down the block. Snatches of dialogue from *The Simpsons* and then *BBC News 24* followed her, voices welding together so that it sounded as though Homer was running the war on terror. She was already regretting her decision to leave, wondering what on earth she was doing, hating herself for being so easily persuaded. But to turn around now and face her pursuers was out of the question. People with nothing to hide didn't run, they'd say, and they'd be right. All the same, this was the most out of character thing she'd ever done. Teddy's anxieties had infected her.

From above she could hear footsteps and voices on the roof and instinctively she tried to make herself smaller. Pressing close against the wall, she realized she was peering into a sitting room. A couple of fifteen-year-olds were lolling on an island of large purple and yellow cushions, the girl watching a rock video on television around the side of the boy's hooded head while he snogged her, one hand up the back of her sweater trying to unfasten her bra.

Amy looked quickly away. This would be all she needed: a conviction as a peeping Tom. She half turned to continue down the steps, but further mutterings from above stopped her. She waited and, inevitably, almost magnetically, found herself looking back into the room.

With her eyes still on the television, the boy's mouth still stuck to hers, the girl now had both hands behind her back and was helpfully unfastening the clip of her bra.

Amy closed her eyes and waited for deliverance of some kind. There was none. When she opened them again it was worse. The boy was now putting an exploratory hand up the girl's cherry-red skirt.

Just then, perhaps disturbed by the boy's new approach, or just bored with the record playing, the girl peeled away from the television. Her eyes met Amy's gaze.

For a moment Amy just stared back, rooted with embarrassment. Dear God, they'll think I've gone mad, she thought. Perhaps I have. So be it. *Hello!* she mouthed with a wave and a smile, as though she always left the building by the fire escape. Then, disregarding the hounds above, she hurried on down the iron staircase.

The girl didn't move. The boy, more interestingly occupied, didn't notice.

Amy didn't even think about going back for her car. As her feet hit the garden she was already running through the rhododendrons towards the drive, the road and the yellow, for-hire light of an approaching taxi. She just had to get away before this night got any worse.

Abbott watched her from the roof. When he'd received the tip from the television researcher about Amy Miller and Teddy Farrow he'd been disinclined to believe it.

Farrow had built his daytime-TV career on an unblemished image as a family man, now with sensible, grown-up children and a clever, attractive wife. Amy Miller was the pretty bookworm who led a quiet, unreported life, didn't give interviews and sold, it was said, mountain ranges of books.

But now Abbott had no doubts. As the photographer cursed his luck at missing her getaway, and made his way back to the fire door, Abbott smiled to himself. The cute runaway author and the goody-goody TV star making the beast with two backs. It was going to be an interesting chase.

CHAPTER
TWO

"I'm sorry, sir, I'm getting no reply from 1507." The hotel operator was a middle aged, homely woman.

Tim Fairweather considered the rain splashing off his gutterless attic roof and running down his window pane, and wondered whether his home could take much more. February in London was a terrible, dismal month, and he could see a patch of damp plaster beginning to bubble and flake around the edge of the skylight above his head. "I see," he said. "By the way, what time is it in Denver now?"

"A quarter after two . . . in the morning." The operator stressed the last part. "Would you care to leave a message?"

"Well, perhaps you could just tell her that . . . Tim rang . . ."

"I'll do that, sir. 'Tim rang . . . *again!*' Goodnight now."

The connection went dead. Night in Denver, Colorado; morning in London. It was a pity the operator had added the "again" bit. If only Amanda would switch on her mobile. A text would do.

Putting the phone down, he considered a sequence of musical notes on the laptop screen attached to the

Yamaha keyboard that dominated his small living room. One-handed he played a short sequence, then stopped, unhappy.

He was a tall man of thirty-five, and his hair was dark, long, wavy and unkempt. This wasn't a shaving day. Not many were. He wore jeans and a navy blue shirt, and the room around him suggested the comfortable if frugal chaos of a musician who lived alone. Records and CDs rose in stacks like miniature housing projects across the faded Indian carpet, where music by Gershwin and Chopin inhabited the same neighbourhood as the Blind Boys of Alabama, the Eagles' Greatest Hits, Natalie Merchant, the Red Hot Chili Peppers, Dylan, favourite movie composers and hundreds of others. Sheets of discarded music manuscript lay abandoned across the furniture, while on the mantelpiece, along with the old letters, a postcard of Neil Young and various bills, was a partially obscured photograph showing an attractive, dark-haired, slim, determined-looking woman in a black mandarin outfit standing beside a battery of chimes.

Beside the photograph was a clock. Glancing at it, Tim swore quietly to himself. He was going to be late for his lesson. Pulling on his overcoat, he began to look quickly through a box of CDs. "Pie-Eyed Posse," he muttered to himself as he searched. "Where are you, Pie-Eyed . . .?" His fingers stopped as five young men stared accusingly at him from a plastic box. "Got you!"

And pushing the CD into his pocket he ran from his flat, down the echoing, uncarpeted stairs and out into the busy cacophony of a North Kensington street.

The school wasn't far away, a stern Victorian building with modern, once pastel but now graffiti-decorated wings, where, as he arrived, pupils were noisily mobbing their way from one lesson to the next. Pushing through, he made his way to the staff room, retrieved a portable CD player from his locker, and hurried to his classroom.

He would reflect later that 3M looked unusually pleased to see him as he entered. But, having told them at their last music lesson to expect something interesting today, he put it down to enthusiasm.

"Good morning. Sorry I'm late," he said as he stepped up on to the rostrum at the front of the room.

The thirty-strong class of fourteen-year-old boys and girls, who, for various reasons, few likely to be educational, had ticked the "music appreciation" box as their cultural activity choice, grinned back.

"As I said last week, I thought we'd listen to something new today to see if we can hear connections between different kinds of music," he went on. "So, I've brought along a record I know some of you at least will like — Pie-Eyed Posse . . ." As he'd been speaking he'd been taking the CD he'd brought out of its box and slipping it into the player.

"Oohh!" the class murmured sarcastically, mock impressed.

Tim smiled. He'd done the same when he'd been at school and young teachers had tried to earn some street cred. "Yes, even I've heard of Pie-Eyed Posse! And, despite their appearance," he said, happy to play for the ridicule he knew he'd get, "they're a clever group . . .

interesting rhythms, a bit of techno, hip-hop . . ." What he didn't say was that they'd been his pick for big things when he'd seen them at the Glastonbury Festival two years earlier. These weren't the sort of kids who had the opportunity to go to Glastonbury. It was probably time he stopped going.

At their desks the pupils exchanged exaggeratedly pained glances, humouring him. Desiree, a nervous, plump girl with braids who sat at the front of the room, bit her lip. Tim knew she liked him. The other kids mocked her for it.

"Anyway, let's give them a listen, shall we!" And, pressing the *play* button, he settled further back into a chair by the teacher's desk and looked around the class as he waited for the disc to engage. 3M were almost attentive now. Perhaps they weren't as bad as their reputation suggested after all.

They were. With a massive yelp of laughter there was a sudden explosion of derision. The music had started, but it was the wrong music, not the drum and bass of Pie-Eyed Posse, but the swell of a full symphony orchestra. Tim stood up, grabbing at the Pie-Eyed Posse CD container. Inwardly he groaned. He must have accidentally put the wrong disc in it when preparing for the class.

"I'm sorry," he said above the music and the laughter. "Tchaikovsky seems to have sneaked into the wrong box." There was more guffawing. "All right, calm down, calm down."

Eventually they did.

But what should he do now? Best to brazen it out, he decided. The music played on. "Well, as we can't really discuss the merits of Pie-Eyed Posse without hearing them, what do we know about Tchaikovsky?" he asked. "Anyone?"

Smiling, empty, young faces filled the room.

"Anything?"

"He was a poof, wasn't he?" The speaker was a shaven-headed, beatific-looking imp.

"Well, yes, I believe he might have been gay," Tim replied, hearing the creak of boredom in his voice. "He was also a composer."

"*Was* he?" the imp replied, pretend astounded, insolently straight-faced. There was more laughter.

Again, Tim waited for the mood to settle. "Yes, he was. One of the great, classical, Russian composers. Just listen to this. Does anybody recognize it?" And turning the music louder he sat down again and leaned back in his chair as he always did.

Perhaps, he would also think later, he should have suspected something when he noticed the quiet boy from Mogadishu, the one they called Jay-Jay, staring fixedly at the legs of his chair, but he didn't. The music had taken his attention, and he was wondering exactly how he was going to explain it to them. Pie-Eyed Posse would have been a lot easier.

"Well, we're listening to Tchaikovsky's music for the ballet *Romeo and Juliet*," he began, "and —"

He didn't finish. There was a sudden jolt as though a minor earthquake had occurred right under him. Then a shudder. And then with a crack he felt the back legs of his chair bend and snap sharply, first one then the other. Too late he put his hands out to protect himself, but there was nothing to grab hold of as he and the broken chair tumbled backwards off the rostrum, and, in a rush of gravity, the back of his head crashed onto the floor beneath him.

And as the class roared in triumph and hilarity at the success of their practical joke, he lost consciousness.

"*Romeo and Juliet*, you say. That was lucky." The young Egyptian doctor stared at the X-ray of Tim's skull on the light box.

"It was?" Tim put a hand gingerly to the lump on the back of his head. Gruesome, worrying moans were coming from the next A-and-E cubicle.

"Oh, yes. Think what they'd have done to the *1812 Overture*. Ingenious little buggers. Sawed through your chair legs, just for the fun of it?"

"They aren't all little. Some of them are bigger than you. But I don't think they meant to injure me."

"Well, try or not, they certainly did." The doctor smiled and unclipped the X-ray. "Luckily, you haven't fractured your skull or damaged your brain, so that's good news, just a deep cut and a coconut of a lump." He turned back to Tim. "How are you feeling?"

"Fine," Tim lied. He'd recovered consciousness before the ambulance had arrived at the school, but now he felt weak and, for some reason — probably shock — slightly tearful.

"I doubt it," the doctor contradicted, writing out a prescription. "Get these from the pharmacy on the way

17

out. Concussion can be tricky. You'll probably need a few days to get over it. Is there anyone at home who can keep an eye on you?"

"No. I live alone. And my girlfriend's in America. But I'm sure I'll be all right."

"Probably. But you never know. If I were you I'd go and stay with relations or friends for a few days."

Tim shook his head, then immediately regretted it. It felt heavy, and made his neck ache. "I can't do that," he said.

The doctor looked at him over his glasses, one of those professional expressions that conveys authority. "Well, you can't go back to school. And certainly not *that* school. The noise alone would probably kill you."

"Yes, but you see . . . I'm writing something . . . composing, I mean. Well, trying to . . ." Tim realized he was stammering, embarrassed, as he always was, by the word "composing". It sounded so pretentious. Besides, the continued groans emanating from beyond the screen made his problems seem so small. He felt like a cheat. He tried again. "I mean, the teaching bit is only part time. I play in a bar as well, actually several bars, but I write music, too. And as I've entered a competition for new works I'm really very busy at the moment."

"Doctor . . ." A harassed-looking nurse put her head inside the cubicle.

"So," the doctor finished writing his report, "what about a hotel? Go and spoil yourself."

Tim grimaced again.

The young doctor gave up. "Well, it's up to you. If you can't get away, you can't. It's a pity, though, because I would have thought a change might have helped your composing, especially somewhere quiet where you could be properly fed and looked after." He handed over a list of instructions. "Anyway, read this. Any headaches, blackouts, dizziness or nausea, come back here or call a doctor. You'll probably feel tired and a bit shaken at first. But that'll pass. Otherwise, a few days' peace and quiet and you should be as right as rain." And with that he hurried from the consulting cubicle, shedding one pair and pulling on another of surgical gloves as he went. "Now, what seems to be the trouble?" Tim heard from the next cubicle. The moans immediately stopped.

A second nurse, an ample, smiling woman holding a roll of elastic bandage, entered and peered at Tim's head. "Right," she said in a flat Glaswegian accent, "if you've ever fancied yourself as Che Guevara this is your day."

Amy hadn't slept well, not at all, until after four, the previous evening's events and her abrupt change of plans having tormented her.

She'd intended, in her first moments of panic, to seek sanctuary with one of her friends, but had quickly realized that that would have called for explanations which she just hadn't wanted to give. The affair had been that secret. So when, as the taxi driver had begun fretting after her second change of instructions, she'd spotted a blue neon vacancy light over the door of a small hotel near Paddington Station, its anonymity had beckoned. She'd needed time to think of a better idea.

Unfortunately, she hadn't been able to. Awoken by the racket of passing traffic she'd found herself in a narrow, cream room under a framed photograph of Princess Diana at the Taj Mahal, feeling locked out of her own life. As she looked down on the morning of a strange London street like a foreign tourist, today even the buses looked different.

Going without breakfast, because she really hadn't wanted to face anyone, she'd watched *The Teddy Farrow Show* on the television in her room, wagging her head admiringly at his skill in encouraging his guests to betray themselves so unwittingly. He was so good at getting exactly what he wanted from people. Sometimes when she'd watched the show at home she'd wondered whether he might send her a little message in code, and that had crossed her mind this morning, too. But when he hadn't she'd told herself she hadn't expected him to, anyway. He was, after all, renowned for his professionalism. Then she'd felt a fool for even entertaining such thoughts.

After the show had gone off the air, she'd taken a long bath, killing time. Only at eleven, and with some trepidation, did she put in a call to Teddy's mobile phone. It was switched off. Leaving a carefully worded message that would have meant nothing to anyone else, she'd then waited, afraid to leave the hotel because in her haste the previous night she'd left her own mobile on her desk.

Teddy hadn't returned the call, but then, she'd excused, he'd obviously have to schmooze with the guests after the programme, something he said he hated doing, after which there was always a production meeting to discuss the next show's line-up.

So she'd waited even longer, desperate for a word from him, yet, with every passing hour, hating herself more for being so bloody pathetic. How could she be behaving like this? No leading character in the novels she wrote would have put up with it. Her women were independent, witty creatures who knew exactly how to put a man in his place, the sort of girls whom reviewers in friendly newspapers described as "feisty". Yet here *she* was, totally *feistless*, if there were such a word. She was a fraud. And she remembered with some shame the intolerance she'd had to hide as she'd seen friends unroll themselves like doormats which turned into mattresses for the men they'd decided they loved.

A noon check-out time finally forced her to make a decision and, carrying her belongings, she made her way through the rain down the street, still unsure of what to do next. If she were to return home now, she wondered, would the Press leave her in peace?

A photograph staring out at her from a rack of newspapers on a corner news-stand answered her question. It was of her, caught the previous night, her fair hair looking as though it had become electrified in shock as she'd spotted the photographer's telephoto lens. A headline under the picture teased coyly:

ROMANCE FOR AMY — BUT WHO'S HER MYSTERY MAN?

(Turn to page 5)

It wasn't the lead item in the paper, obviously. It was worse. It was the human-interest celebrity story. The one everyone read. In despair she turned to page 5.

"Shorter," she said above the insistent hammer of a rapper on the radio who was, it seemed, threatening all kinds of mayhem if he didn't get a pay rise, some juicy sex and puddin' pie, and if his bitch didn't start respecting him more. She'd like to have said "Quieter", too, but that wasn't up to her.

"Shorter?" the young hairdresser with the ring and silver chain hanging from her belly button repeated. "Your friends won't recognize you."

"Promise me," Amy replied. This girl certainly didn't recognize her, but then Economy Cutz didn't look the sort of place where the reading of books, not even the books she wrote, would have been a priority.

With a downward movement of the corners of her mouth and the raising of her shoulders, which Amy interpreted as a "suit yourself" surrender, the girl continued to chop at Amy's hair. Already it lay around her like the jettisoned frills of a former, happy life.

Cautiously, as the stylist moved from one side of her to the other, Amy glanced at her newspaper, which was lying folded on a shelf below the mirror. The article on page five hadn't named the "mystery man". It couldn't. Get that wrong and it

22

could mean a serious and expensive libel. Instead, knowing hints about a new friendship with a "television family favourite" came free of risk.

"Something special in today, is there?" the girl asked as she noticed Amy's attention stray to the paper.

"What?" Amy quickly looked away. "Oh, no."

"No?"

"Well, just the usual."

"The usual?" This girl would make conversation with her client if it killed them both.

Amy tried a joke. "Yes, you know, *TWO SETS OF SIAMESE TWINS IN WIFE-SWAPPING MIX-UP.*"

"Really!" the stylist said seriously, concentrating on her job.

"Mmm. They took a bit of unravelling apparently."

"I bet," the girl came back, distractedly studying the lengths of two sheaves of hair. "It's the firemen I feel sorry for."

Amy didn't answer. There was no answer to that. And as the stylist went off to find a fresh pair of scissors she sighed inwardly and looked again at her newspaper. She hadn't noticed when she'd first read it, but at the bottom of the page about her was a two-inches-deep travel advertisement, an engraving of a large rambling house with balconies, ivy and a palm tree on the edge of a range of cliffs.

When you really want to get away from it all . . . the advertisement beckoned. *The North Devon Riviera Hotel.*

He'd fully intended to stay at home, work at his music and shiver in his mansard flat. But then the head teacher had called, and, relieved that Tim wasn't more seriously injured, had offered, on the school's behalf, to pay for a week's recuperation at a resort of his choice, "provided it's reasonably priced, of course".

The stain around the skylight decided him. If he stayed at home, watching it grow bigger by the day, he'd probably have to do something about it, which would inevitably turn into a displacement activity when the music became even more difficult, which in turn would defeat the whole object of staying at home. Besides, there was still no word from Amanda in Denver. So he thanked the headmaster for his solicitude and accepted the offer.

As it happened it turned out to be a resort of Valerie the school secretary's choice. She'd been there on holiday three years earlier with her mother and they'd had "a lovely time", she said when she called him with the details. "It was very quiet, with very nice people." It was called the North Devon Riviera Hotel.

So Valerie made the booking, and, after calling Razza, the manager of the Settle Bar in Muswell Hill and Harry at Ballantines in Victoria, to explain why he wouldn't be able to play for a week, Tim quickly packed his clothes and equipment and set off for Victoria Coach Station.

CHAPTER
THREE

They were all stiff with embarrassment. Standing on the Swindon station platform, waiting for the Intercity express, they could have been taken for a funeral party as much as a wedding celebration. Even Michael's new suit was dark grey. At his side, Eleanor, his wife of just three hours, her iron-coloured hair freshly cut and bouffant over-sprayed for this momentous day, gazed away across the tracks, avoiding all eyes.

They should have just slipped away and done it in secret, Michael told himself. What could have possessed them to think they could share their moment with others, when they could scarcely share it with each other? Was it guilt? Was it loyalty to those with whom they'd each lived their lives for so long? Or was it some kind of hope that they might finally find understanding and a blessing from these two unbending slabstones of the Church parochial, who, like warders seeing off prisoners at the end of their stretch, stood waiting with them equally lost for words? Only Sister Catherine, hardly more than a novice, and foolishly amused at the incongruity of the situation, seemed to be enjoying herself. She won't stay locked in holy orders, Michael thought. Not as long as Eleanor. Please God, not as long as he had done.

At last he heard the electric rattle and hum of their approaching train. Eleanor peered down the line, suddenly animated as above them the station announcer echoed his message of blessed relief. "The train approaching platform three is for Bristol and Taunton only."

"All aboard for the train of love," laughed Sister Catherine as the roar reached the platform, and then giggled at her own naughtiness.

The elderly nun pursed her lips. The old priest next to Michael pretended not to hear.

They'll take anybody these days, Michael thought, though not uncharitably because he liked Catherine. She'd been a constant source of amusement, if not exactly a confidante, for Eleanor in the convent. Turning to the priest at his side, he said, "Thanks for everything, Dermot, and for being, you know, so . . . so understanding." He offered that as a compliment, though it was a white lie. Understanding had never been celebrated as one of Fr Dermot's virtues. It was a joke in the parish that he could be a hard man to convince of contrition when hearing confession. Not that many went to confession any more.

"Isn't that all we priests ever do . . . understand?" Dermot growled back. "Though, God knows, it isn't always easy."

Michael didn't answer.

26

The elder nun was looking at Eleanor now. "All the sisters will be praying for you, Eleanor," she said, her eyes shining.

Eleanor smiled a thank-you.

"Every night at bedtime."

Now Eleanor looked at her feet and the new sensible, clunky, navy blue shoes she'd bought to match her wedding outfit. "Thank you, Mother," she said meekly.

"No need to call me mother now," corrected the nun.

Eleanor tried a wan little nod of agreement, but all Michael could see was a timid, middle-aged woman cowed by an authority greater than any of them, a centuries' old discipline. It's been harder for her than for me, he thought, and he loved her more than ever.

The train doors unfolded in front of them. It was a first-class carriage, the cost of the tickets being part of a wedding gift from the doctors and nurses in the hospital where he and Eleanor had met. He'd gone to administer the last rites to an elderly parishioner: she was pushing the library on wheels. Falling into conversation she'd allowed him to borrow a biography of Nelson Mandela, although as a non-patient that had, strictly speaking, been against the rules. After that, he'd made sure he borrowed a different book every week.

"Well, then," Michael said, picking up both suitcases, Eleanor's a brand-new blue one, his old and worn and from the Oxfam shop, and moving towards the train. Beaming, he indicated that Eleanor climb the steps ahead of him.

Without warning, the older nun suddenly softened: "Good luck. Both of you!" she called. Michael looked back at her. Behind her little round glasses her eyes were wet. "God bless you both."

"Thank you, Sister," he said.

Beyond her, the young nun, Sister Catherine, was laughing. "Don't do anything I wouldn't do," she hooted, almost hysterically, and tossed a last grenade of confetti over them.

That girl really wouldn't last long in the convent.

Quickly, amid a benediction of thanks and goodbyes and much waving, Michael shepherded Eleanor on to the train and into the carriage. With a *clunk*! the carriage door closed behind them, sealing, it seemed, their break with their pasts.

Cautious with each other, feeling as though they were on display for the world to watch, they searched for their seats. Mercifully they found they were on the opposite side of the carriage from the platform. There need be no more waving now. As Eleanor sat down, Michael lifted their suitcases on to the luggage rack.

Facing them was a young woman in her early thirties, her head covered in a hood, a laptop computer open on the table in front of her. With a polite smile, the young woman pulled the laptop closer to herself to make room for Eleanor's handbag.

Discreetly Michael picked a piece of confetti from the shoulders of his wife's new coat as Eleanor looked around the carriage.

"I've never travelled first class before," Eleanor whispered.

Michael smiled. "There's a first time for everything," he said, then wondering if that might, in the circumstances, be misconstrued, he hurried on, indicating the platform as the train began to slide away. "It was good of Dermot to come. I never expected to see him in a register office."

Eleanor was silent, thoughtful for a moment. "No." Then she added, "I don't suppose he ever expected to see you in one, either."

It had been a serious observation, but Michael smiled. "Well, no. But, what I meant is, the world's changing, and Dermot has difficulty with that. Old habits, you know . . ."

"I gave mine to Sister Catherine." Eleanor was looking down, holding the straps to her handbag.

"I'm sorry?"

Eleanor looked up, smiling now. "My old habit."

"Oh yes, I see." And Michael laughed rather too loudly as belatedly he got the joke. Eleanor liked her little jokes.

She blushed with pleasure. Then, turning to face him, she took the white carnation he was wearing in his button hole and put it into her handbag for a keep-safe.

She's such a kind and lovely woman, he thought. And she's given up so much for me. Please God, don't let me disappoint her.

Sitting across from them Amy studied her laptop. It wasn't her intention to eavesdrop the couple's conversation, but it was difficult not to overhear. She'd never seen such an anxious pair, the man, thin and grey

29

and mid-fifties, and the woman probably a couple of years younger. But, with an almost translucently pale and unlined skin, and only the faintest trace of lipstick, she almost had the complexion of a child.

And as the two talked quietly together, short, stilted, incidental sentences about the weather or the scenery or the frequent delays as the train struggled in fits and starts through England's monochrome, drenched winter, Amy's eyes wandered to the label on the new, blue suitcase stacked above them. *The North Devon Riviera Hotel*, it read in a neat, woman's handwriting.

Eventually as the couple's conversation lapsed into silence, not the comfortable quiet of familiarity, but a cul-de-sac of difficulty, neither seeming to know what to say next, Amy typed a note to herself into her laptop: *Blessed are the lovers*. And she remembered the story of Abelard and Héloïse, the twelfth-century monk and nun, who'd fallen in love. He'd come to a very sticky end.

He felt like a beach boy out of season as, with the bandage tied around his now throbbing head like a bandana and carrying his keyboard in its case over his shoulder like a surf-board, Tim made his way with his suitcase and laptop the few steps from the bus stop to the lifeboat station on the sea wall. This was where the hotel collected its guests, school secretary Valerie had told him: "I imagine they'll be waiting for you when you get there."

They weren't. Instead, a tall, solid girl of about eighteen sat huddled on a bench by the wall, her face turned against the wind and rain, her hair frizzy and rather too red and gripped by two large tortoiseshell butterfly clips. Wearing jeans ripped at the knees and scissored into slices at the hems, and an ancient angora coat tied around her waist with an old school tie as a belt, she was reading, by the light of the fluorescent street lamp, a book on hotel management, while all the time eating something from a Tupperware plastic container. At her feet lay a suitcase and a large cardboard box bearing a *Handle With Care* sticker. She ignored him as he approached.

"Excuse me."

The girl looked up with wide, pale, nonchalant eyes and carried on eating. She wasn't exactly pretty, her mouth was too wide, and her face looked slightly cock-eyed. But she was certainly striking.

"Are you waiting for the hotel car?"

She nodded, but again didn't answer.

Tim nodded in return. Teenage cool was something teachers understood well. "Right. Thank you," he said, and, turning away, made a point of considering a poster for a St Valentine's Ball stuck to the sea wall. *Music, romance and dancing at the North Devon Riviera Hotel from Lorna and the Doones*, beckoned the message. Valerie hadn't said anything about romance. But then she'd been with her mother.

Eventually glancing back towards the girl, Tim was just in time to see her take another morsel of food from her container. But this time, instead of eating it she slipped it inside her slightly open coat. Intrigued, he watched, only to realize that she was staring at him.

Quickly he looked away again and stared out to sea. There was nothing to be seen, but he didn't want her to think he'd been admiring her bosom. For God's sake, she wasn't much older than his pupils! That would amuse Amanda no end. For a moment he whistled to himself and stamped his feet to keep warm. It was biting cold down here.

"This looks like our lift," the girl suddenly said, and stood up as a pale green and blue people carrier headed towards them. "On the other hand, it could be a very large budgerigar. What d'you think?"

It had been very kind of the young lady to offer to give them a lift in her taxi, Eleanor told herself, as the car dropped down from the blackness of the moors towards the cliffs. It made sense if they were going to the same hotel, but the presence of a third party in their new life, especially one as quietly capable as this young woman, was unnerving. Michael, for his part, had been instantly jolly and enquiring, the way she'd seen him with patients on the wards when she knew he didn't really know what to say. He was actually a shy man, especially in the company of women.

"So, you're down here on . . . business . . . holiday?" he'd asked as the train had come to another of the many unscheduled stops along the way. Rainwater on the tracks was playing havoc with the timetable, the conductor had frequently apologized.

"Just a break," the young woman had replied, then, probably not wanting to appear unfriendly, had added,

"And you're on your . . . honeymoon?" She'd smiled congratulations.

Eleanor had felt her mouth tighten with embarrassment as it had that morning at the register office when she'd become aware of the gaze of their friends. "We were hoping to keep it quiet," she'd almost whispered back. The very word *honeymoon* suggested something fleshy and improper; the register office had been quite godless.

The young woman had backed off immediately. "Oh, yes, of course. It was just that I couldn't help but see you get on the train and . . ." Her voice had faded away as she must have thought better about exploring that line.

"They say February can be very clement in these parts," Michael had joined in, anxious to change the subject. "We're hoping to get some nice cliff walks in, if we ever get there!" He looked at his watch. "At this rate we're going to be very late arriving."

They were. Now, hours late, as the taxi slipped off the road and between pine woods and the lights of the hotel came into view, Eleanor felt the palms of her hands dampen.

Michael was all smiles. "At last!" he gushed nervously as the taxi came to a halt alongside a brightly coloured hotel people carrier. For a second, Eleanor looked at her husband as he held the door for her. He was such a well-meaning man.

Amy could see that in the summer it might be a pretty hotel, a white wedge of faded, late-nineteenth-century stucco caught between trees. But in the dark, in a February gale that sent rain and sleet scything up the Bristol Channel and swayed the lanterns that dinked on the trees around the car park, it hardly promised the warmest welcome. I should have stayed in London, she reproached herself yet again, then, waiting while the honeymooners took their suitcases from the back of the cab, she followed them up a couple of steps to the entrance. Would she have chosen this place for a honeymoon? Never. But then another thought interrupted. Would she ever have a honeymoon? And with this in mind, she stepped into the hotel.

She was immediately surprised. From the outside the building had suggested a traditional English conservatism. Inside, however, the modernizers and decorators had been to work. Once the hall would have been mock baronial, full of dark woods and heavy varnish. Now it was a cavalcade of seaside colours, few matching but all jolly, as though anticipating disappointment in the weather and already compensating for it. In these days of cheap flights to the sun in Croatia or Turkey, English resorts had to try that much harder.

Making her way across the lobby she joined a short queue at the reception desk where a tall man with a bandage around his head was checking in before a boy of about eighteen in an old-fashioned maroon porter's uniform. To one side of the man a tall, red-headed, bizarre-looking girl waited by a very large box.

"Fairweather," Amy heard the man say.

"You should see it in June," the boy porter replied, puzzled yet proud, his Devon accent undulating.

"No, I mean my name's Fairweather. I have a reservation."

The boy looked at him, then flustered. "Oh, yes, of course. Here we are. Fairweather, Timothy. A late booking. Sorry, Mr Fairweather."

The waiting girl listened, and almost giggled. The boy porter noticed and was embarrassed.

Suddenly a door at the back of the reception area opened and, with an excited yelping, a large black Labrador bounded into the lobby, closely followed by a stout, large-breasted, late-fortyish woman, her thin, mousy hair pulled back off a pink, pale, oval face. "Yes?" She smiled to the red-headed girl.

"I'm Shona. For the student placement. Work experience," the girl grinned, as now the dog dashed around the counter and began jumping up at her, sniffing her clothes excitedly. She tried to push it away.

"*Staff?*" the woman asked, her voice seeming to curl in derision.

"Yes!" The girl nodded, laughing, still trying to escape the attentions of the dog. "Hey, get down, that's rude," she giggled as the dog tried to push its wet snout under her coat and between the tops of her thighs.

At her side the man with the bandage watched, bemused.

"Darrell!" the older woman hissed, her large face twitching. "Put Giles outside." And, moving to one side, she abandoned the girl and took the boy porter's place as he dragged the dog away. In an instant, her features softened and her brow cleared for the guest with the bandage. "Ah, Mr Fairweather," she gushed, lifting her eyes sympathetically. "I'm so sorry Darrell was late picking you up. We're *so* pleased you chose the North Devon Riviera Hotel for your . . . convalescence?"

The man looked embarrassed and touched his bandage lightly, as though indicating that it was mainly decoration. "It's nothing, really. Just a bump."

The manager purred. "Brave soldier," she murmured, and with what looked to Amy like the slightest flutter of over-lacquered eyelashes, reached for a key from a strawberry-red board of pigeon-holes. "Darrell, the Exmoor Suite for Mr Fairweather," she ordered the returning boy, and passed him a key.

Dragging his eyes from the girl, the porter grabbed the man's bag and put it on to a trolley. Peripherally, Amy was aware that the man was turning to pick up a large oblong object propped against the desk, but as she did so her attention was drawn to a morning newspaper on the reception desk. Once again her own shocked face looked back at her:

ROMANCE FOR AMY — BUT WHO'S HER MYSTERY MAN?

For a second she froze, then afraid that someone would notice and she'd be recognized, she swung away, back towards the man just as he was passing the oblong object to the porter. She gasped as her head collided with it. "Ouch!" she exclaimed, more in surprise than injury.

"Oh, I'm so sorry!" the man with the bandage apologized.

"It's all right!" She wasn't hurt. "My fault."

"No, I was careless. It's my keyboard and . . . Are you sure . . .?" He put the keyboard down.

"Certain. You nearly missed me." She touched her head and shrugged. "It's nothing." Amy was smiling now, anxious to divert attention from the newspaper. Now that the man was facing her she saw that his bandage made his ears stick out at right angles, like little angel wings on the side of his head.

"That's a relief . . ." he began.

But at that moment Eleanor the honeymooner, who was waiting behind them and unwrapping her scarf, accidentally sent a shower of confetti over them both.

Embarrassment crowded the lobby.

"Oh, dear," Eleanor blushed.

Amy felt for her. If the couple's marriage had been a semi-secret when they'd arrived, that was no longer the case. "Don't worry," she consoled. "It looks like apple blossom."

The man with the bandage smiled and, bending down, picked up a few pieces.

"I'd better take that, if you don't mind," the young porter said, taking the keyboard from him and carefully sliding it on to a trolley alongside the bags and the large box.

Now it was the turn of the girl with red hair. "You'll be very careful with that box, won't you?" she insisted.

Amy watched. It was obvious already. The boy was smitten.

"I thought I'd take it up to your room for you," he said. "Something special in there, is there?"

"There might be. I'm not sure." The girl looked mysterious. "I was told it was Hitler's missing testicle, but it looks a bit swollen to me."

At her side Amy felt the keyboard man barely contain a chuckle. But the poor porter just stared and stared at the girl, blood surging to his face and ears.

"I'll show you to the Exmoor Suite, Mr Fairweather," he managed at last, and putting his head down over the trolley, hurried away towards the lift.

The girl, meanwhile, looked around with a merry, triumphant glint.

At the desk, the manager glowered at her. But then, in another triumph of muscle control, she transformed her face once more into a brilliant welcoming corporate smile as the honeymooners stepped forward. "Mr and . . . *Mrs* Nichols?" she teased.

The couple nodded, glum-faced now.

If the manager noticed their expressions she didn't let on. "Congratulations and welcome! I have some very good news for you. You've qualified for our complimentary North Devon Riviera Valentine's Weekend upgrading . . . to our Passion of the West Country honeymoon suite! What do you think about that?"

There was a stunned silence from the couple. Eleanor looked at her new shoes once more. At last Michael found the words. "Thank you very much," he said quietly.

It's going wrong for them already, Amy thought, watching Michael sign the hotel registration form, and remembering their quiet, shared excitement as she'd seen them get on the train at Swindon. Then as the manager slid a key across the desk, seeming to wonder why they were not more grateful, Amy looked away as, insisting they didn't need help with their luggage, the honeymooners trudged unhappily up the wide staircase to find their room.

"And what name would it be?" The manager's voice, now a little sharper, redirected Amy's thoughts.

She took out her credit card.

CHAPTER
FOUR

"Are you in a band?" Darrell asked, as, recovering from his embarrassment, he leaned the keyboard against a wall in the Exmoor Suite.

"No, but I know someone who is," Tim said, and smiled to himself, as he did whenever he teased Amanda by referring to her orchestra rehearsals as band practice.

"Anyone famous?" The boy porter looked hopeful.

Tim didn't have to hesitate. "Sorry," he said. Not even Amanda would think that being a late replacement percussionist with a touring symphony orchestra made her famous. "Do you play an instrument?"

"Oh no." Darrell almost laughed at the question. "I've no time for that sort of thing. My mum always says playing music's all right for those with nothing else to do with their hands."

"And is that what you think?"

"I don't know what I think," came the disarming reply. "But there's a chap down the village got a keyboard like yours. A Yamaha. It's a bit bigger, though. He's in a band. His mate's the singer. He doesn't play anything, but he gets all the girls."

Tim nodded. "That sounds about right. The players play the tunes but the bloke who can't play gets the girls. That's life."

"He's got a rotten voice, too. All croaky, like a crow squawking." And Darrell shook his head at the injustice of the world of music.

Despite the headache, which was now returning, Tim was amused. Darrell had a winning lack of guile. He was a thin, fair young man with a pudding-basin hair cut that was just growing out, giving him a step all around his head. It was probably the boy's single teenage attempt at being different, and it hadn't come off.

"Anyway, better be getting on . . ." Darrell made for the door, adding a porterly surprised, "Oh, thank you very much," as Tim pushed a tip into his hand.

Alone, Tim crossed to the window and looked out at a small, pink-tiled balcony on which a large puddle had formed. Then, turning back, he considered the Exmoor Suite, a grand name for a room that, though prettily decorated with water colours of wet-looking Exmoor ponies, was hardly palatial. Suddenly, he felt the sag of loneliness. Hotel rooms could do that.

Irritation followed as he unpacked. Having detached the legs of his keyboard in order to carry them, he realized he'd left them behind in his flat.

Going into the bathroom he dropped two of the painkillers he'd been given at the hospital pharmacy into a glass of water, frowning at his reflection and his Alice band of a bandage as he waited for them to dissolve. He wished the non-gangsta-rappers in his class had warned him he was about to get his skull cracked. Not that he blamed them. They had to go to school there.

All the same, a bashed skull wasn't the sort of thing to put a composer in a creative mood, he reflected, as he unzipped the plastic case, took out the keyboard and placed it across a small writing table. Then stopping, he immediately erased the word *composer* from his mind. Whatever Amanda might like to tell herself and her friends, he was really, so far, just a part-time music teacher and occasional bar pianist, a rainbow chaser and doodler with black-and-white notes. At college he'd played with a rock band, and had even mastered the organ to play at his friends' weddings. And there were, of course, his dreams, always unspoken. But whatever happened in the competition he was about to enter, should he ever finish his piece, that wouldn't make him a composer. Not in his mind, anyway.

But as he set to work plugging in his wires and headphones, allowing some Mark Knopfler to soothe his headache, he couldn't help but imagine a cross-faced Amanda shaking her head at his lack of ambition. He almost felt guilty.

Michael had never been in a hotel bedroom with a woman before. He and Eleanor had entered the room in silence, avoiding each other's eyes. Now he didn't know what to do. For months he'd wondered about this moment, anticipated it, and thought about how happy they would be — alone, together, married and close, in short, everything he'd wanted. But he'd never been able to imagine it in pictures, to see the expression on Eleanor's face, to guess what she might say. And all he saw now was fear. Even in the mirror.

Putting their suitcases down, they closed the door behind them and looked around. A white four-poster bed draped with lace dominated the room. It looked like an old-fashioned tabernacle on the altar at Easter, Michael thought suddenly, and wondered about the other sacrament that was expected here. Then quickly he tore his mind from the thought.

Together they crossed to the window, looked out at the balcony, tried all the lights with their romantic dimmers and then peeped into the bathroom. The bath was unlike any either had ever encountered.

"It looks very clean," Michael said at last, considering the heart-shaped whirlpool for two in the centre of the room. "I've read that water jets are very good for people with rheumatism."

"I'll make some tea," Eleanor murmured, and, quickly returning to the bedroom, she plugged in a kettle, which was on a Formica work surface.

Michael followed, opening a packet of digestive biscuits from the tray and offering her one. "Well, we're here," he said jauntily at last.

Eleanor took a biscuit. "Thank you." She hesitated, then added, "The tea's PG Tips. Is that all right?"

"Perfect!" Michael said, and wondered why it might not be.

Eleanor nodded to herself. Unable to think of what to say next, Michael began to re-examine the room. It was all voluptuously, expensively suggestive. A sofa had dimpled, pink cushions, on a hanging tapestry a shepherd boy and a sunny nymphet gambolled naked in clouds, while two dark chocolates in the form of a man and a woman lay together in a nest made of plastic straw on a table beside the bed.

"Yes, well, it's a very big room," he said at last, and snapped open his suitcase. "What do you think? Would you like to take the left or the right?" And he indicated the wardrobes on either side of the bed.

"Either is fine for me, Michael," Eleanor said. "You choose." Their politeness with each other was stifling.

"Right then, if you're sure, I'll take this side," he said and began to unpack. Behind him, he was aware that Eleanor was already discreetly slipping her underclothes from her case into the dressing-table drawers, as though hiding a secret. This isn't how it should be, a voice inside him shouted. But it was how it was.

"Eleanor." He put a hand out to her. It fell on her elbow. She stopped, her eyes staring into her suitcase. "Thank you for marrying me. You've made me very happy."

She tried to smile, she really did. He could see that. But then she bit her bottom lip. She was close to tears.

Putting an arm around her shoulders he tried to turn her towards him, but her body was stiff and awkward. For a moment they stood together, close yet hardly touching.

A knock on the door made them both part, guiltily. Michael hurried to open it.

Darrell was standing with a silver tray bearing a bottle of champagne, two glasses and a single red rose in a fluted glass. "Compliments of the management," he said with a smile as he entered. "Shall I open it now?"

"Er . . ." Michael looked to Eleanor for guidance. He got none. "Perhaps we'll have it later. Thank you very much."

Darrell left.

Eleanor put two teabags in the teapot. "The kettle's boiled," she said.

In the next room Amy, still wearing her coat and hood, sat on her bed as she called the voicemail on her home number.

Amy . . . what's all this in the paper? You didn't tell me!

She listened for a little while and then deleted the message.

It's Dill, Amy. What "Mystery Man"? Have you been holding out on us?

Again she deleted.

Amy . . . Helen! What did you mean "Speak later"? And where are you, anyway? Call me!

In the end she deleted all the messages. Why was there never the voice you most desperately wanted? she asked herself, then answered her own question: because if life and love were so predictable no one would ever be desperate for anything. Then, although all the way down on the train she'd sworn to herself she wouldn't do it, she called Teddy again. He still wasn't answering. She was disappointed and yet relieved. It saved her from at least some embarrassment. She left another message, anyway.

"Hello, it's me, the fugitive," she spoke into his message service. "Just to say, I'm here in North Devon's equivalent of Devil's Island . . ." She could hear the whining in her voice and hated it. Her eyes strayed to her photograph in the newspaper which was now lying on her bed. "I saw what they wrote. And what a photograph! They've made me look like a mad wraith." She hesitated. "Not any more, though. I've disguised myself . . . as a . . ." And for the first time since she left Economy Cutz that morning she pulled the hood of her coat fully off her head and examined herself in a mirror. ". . . Crikey, a platypus!"

She meant it. She scarcely recognized herself. She'd been fifteen and a Goth when she'd last had short hair. It had been black then. Now it was a strange shade of khaki and terrible, cropped at the back of her neck and longer at the sides. It just wasn't her at all.

"I hope you like platypuses," she began again, turning her head this way and that, gazing at herself in the mirror that stood above the small dressing table. The view didn't get any better whichever way she turned. Then suddenly, belatedly, aware that she might have sounded vulgar, she added: "Actually, I didn't intend that to sound quite so rude . . . asking you if you liked platypuses, I mean. If it did sound rude, that is." She stopped, sorry now that she'd even drawn his attention to the word. "Anyway," she finished, "if you get a minute . . . well, this is where you can find me." And, apologizing for having left her mobile at home, she read out the hotel name and phone number. Finally, as almost a postscript she whispered "Love you." Then hung up.

She immediately hated herself for that, for phoning him at all, in fact. She was hopeless, a desperate-to-please other woman, a younger bit on the side, a slice of nooky, a mistress, grateful for any scraps of attention that might be tossed casually from her lover's bed. And every day that it went on she demeaned herself further.

She stopped herself there, and, picking up a North Devon Riviera ballpoint pen from the bedroom desk, made a note on a postcard of Exeter Cathedral.

Love isn't just blind. It's mad. It's pure craziness. It's a mental illness which leads to irrational acts being committed by otherwise sensible and intelligent people. Love isn't strange, like it says in the song, it's insane.

CHAPTER
FIVE

"Amy Miller, yes that one. Not exactly one of your cliterati, so you probably haven't read any of her books, but they tell me the girls like them." As he spoke into his phone, Will Abbott's free hand rested on a small stack of Amy Miller paperbacks sitting on his desk. Behind them was a computer screen showing a faintly glamourized publicity photograph of the author.

He'd bought the books that morning on his way into the office, noticed the uniform, joky branding of their covers, all easily identifiable as Amy Miller novels, then casually dipped into them during the day, looking for lines and characters he thought might heighten or season his story with a little irony. Because when "one of the country's most popular romantic novelists", which was how Amy Miller's publishers described her, was having a secret, adulterous affair with the nation's favourite television Mr Clean, irony didn't come much sweeter — not in tabloid newspaper terms, anyway. Teddy Farrow was the main target, he was the hypocrite. But the titbit that the author was said to be currently writing a nonfiction book on the very nature of love was a detail the bitchy columnists in the up-market papers would happily smirk over for days. This story had angles for everybody.

There was, however, one flaw. Abbott couldn't yet *prove* the affair with Teddy Farrow, and without at least the semblance of an admission, short of catching the two in a compromising position, which wasn't going to happen, there was no story yet to write. And now, after the previous night's fiasco of a stake-out, the bloody woman had disappeared.

Increasingly he blamed himself for that, since a day working the internet and the phones, calling publishers, her bitch of an agent, neighbours, the Society of Authors and anyone else he thought might have had any contact with her had provided no clue as to where she might have run. Nor had the cuttings library been much use. Most authors begged to be interviewed when their books were published, leaving a paper trail of confessions about family fall-outs and past lovers in forests of printed profiles and trivia. Not so Amy Miller. From the beginning of her career, five best-selling books ago, she'd kept her privacy.

"So, who's she been doing it with then?" the voice on the other end of the phone line asked, not unexpectedly.

"Who said she's been under the sheets with anyone?" Abbott blocked. He was trying to buy information, not give it away. "All we want to know is when she last used her credit cards and where. Can you help?"

"I don't think so." The reply was cautious, whispered.

"We'll see you right if you can." The bribe extended its fingers. "More than right. You know that."

There was a pause, then: "I can't promise anything. It's bloody difficult these days. Just about impossible."

"Yes, I know. But there are ways, aren't there, Jerry?" Abbott left that lying. There were always ways.

Another silence followed, and then: "I'll let you know."

"Thanks, Jerry." Wearily, Abbott hung up. He was, he knew, asking his contact to risk an instant sacking, so it was hardly surprising the guy was cagey. But tabloid money could be very persuasive.

Wondering what to do next, he looked around the editorial floor. A freelance photographer he'd taken for a drink a few nights earlier, a pretty, lippy, pug-faced, streaky-blonde girl called Suzy in the tightest of jeans and a Russian army surplus anorak was hanging around the picture desk flirting with the guys. Everyone liked to flirt with Suzy.

After a moment or two she noticed him watching, gave him a long look, and then sauntered across the office, her camera bag slung over her shoulder, resting on her hip. "Are you watching me?" she asked.

"Yes."

"That's all right then." She smiled at him. Some girls knew just how to smile, how to hold on to a man's eyes without letting go.

"I think so," he said.

"I dreamed about you the other night," she said after a moment. "After having that drink, I dreamed about you."

50

"That's nice."

She laughed quietly. "It was for me."

"Yes?"

"Not half. I nearly fell out of the bloody bed." And she raised her eyebrows as she watched him interpret what she'd just said. "Anyway, see you again!" And with that, she walked on and out of the office, taking her time, a walk that said "I know you're *still* watching me, and I'm enjoying being watched".

Abbott looked after her. Well, well, he thought.

Silently a shirtsleeved man appeared at his side and stared at the photograph of Amy Miller on the computer screen. It was McKenzie, an assistant editor. "So where is she then, Will? What cozy little hideaway love nest is cheating the great British public of its right to know?"

Will Abbott reached into his drawer for a peppermint. "I'll find her," he promised. "Fancy a mint?"

CHAPTER
SIX

The trouble with love is that it's obviously governed by the same laws of physics as the see-saw, in that neither love nor see-saws are ever in total balance for more than a few moments. Put another way, no two people are ever in love with each other to the same degree of intensity at the same time . . . not after the first weeks of passion, anyway. And since that's usually just oxytocin-fuelled sex in two momentarily chemically clotted brains it hardly counts.

In the real world, the one everyone has to live in after those first few weeks, either he's on the up side of the see-saw and she's down, or vice versa. All of which can make things at the wrong end of the love plank . . . a bit like sitting on an emotional spike. Painful! No. Worse. Desperate!

Now, it seems to me that since this unfairness in the nature of love is a universally observed design fault, evident over millennia among all ages and at all stages of love, lovers and loved, it needs a name. Sod's Law would have been good, if it hadn't been used already and didn't carry with it at least one unsuitable and limiting association. So, instead, let's call it the Lovers' Law of the Eternal See-Saw.

Amy, cross-legged on her hotel bed, her computer in her lap, stopped typing. *The Lovers' Law of the Eternal See-Saw!* Was that a book title, or just a chapter heading? She didn't know. Her name was famous for spiky modern love stories. She enjoyed writing them. But this wasn't fiction and it made her uncertain.

"I want to write about the very *why* of love," she'd told her editor, Dill, some weeks earlier.

Dill's face hadn't quite crumpled at the suggestion, but it had been close. "Yes?" She sounded pained.

"I want to write about where it comes from, what it's for, what sex has to do with it and why it can hurt so much," she'd hurried on.

Dill hadn't quite yawned. She had, she said, thought they were meeting to discuss a new novel about a wealthy, successful, young woman barrister who'd been hired to defend a dishy, sexy con man who preys on wealthy and successful young women. That had sounded like fun, what Amy's readers expected from her, something jazzy and light, with some good jokes, not some misty-eyed cornucopia of kisses, dubious science and back-of-an-envelope psychology. Actually, she hadn't quite put it as bluntly as that, but that had been her general drift.

Amy hadn't been put off. "I'll come back to the barrister and the con man later," she'd promised. "Right now, I want a break from all that. I want to find out what love is."

"That's a pop song, isn't it?" Dill had laughed. "Foreigner or someone like that with a very high voice.

A singing eunuch, I imagine. God, Amy! Don't tell me some appalling man's finally got to you."

"As if . . ." Amy had fibbed. "No. I just want to think about love in the abstract for once and wonder why it runs so much of our lives, why I write about it and you publish it, and, yes, if you like, why we always like to sing about it."

Naturally, Dill had argued her publisher's point of view, that what the world really needed now was another Amy Miller romantic novel. But seeing that Amy wouldn't be moved she'd finally shrugged grudgingly. "Well, OK, if you must, but I wouldn't waste too much time on it if I were you," she warned. "The world and his goldfish have been asking what love is for the past five thousand years, but they never find out. And nothing sells as consistently as romantic fiction."

"But don't *you* ever wonder why?"

Dill had smiled like a one-armed bandit. "Not really. It would take the romance out of counting the money."

Amy now scratched her leg unhappily as she remembered the conversation. Dill had been right, of course. Teddy's entrance into her life had thrown her so much off balance she didn't want to make up love stories for the time being. She was living one . . . sometimes. The rest of the time she was waiting to live one.

There'd been other men, of course, and before them other boys. And some had seemed wonderful at the time, at school, at college and afterwards when she worked in the bookshop. She'd noticed then that boys liked bookshop girls, that their position in authority and knowledge at the desk behind the computer seemed to make them slightly starry. She enjoyed that. But there'd been no one as remotely overwhelming for her as Teddy, no one who'd left her so completely on the wrong end of the see-saw.

She was still re-reading what she'd written when the sound of a gong echoed around the hotel, summoning the hungry to dinner. About to close her laptop she suddenly remembered the girlfriends who'd left unanswered phone messages and emails for her, few of whom had enjoyed the stable, equal, loving relationship they believed they deserved.

Her fingers stabbed a final thought into her keyboard:

And if you don't believe in the Lovers' Law of the Eternal See-Saw, just take a look at any couple you know.

"That's a table for one, isn't it?" Darrell said, greeting Amy at the dining-room door.

She peeped inside. Everywhere the pall of quiet was broken only by the clinking of silver on crockery.

"This way, please." And the boy porter led her swiftly past islands of empty tables to a corner close to a large open fireplace where the few winter guests were collected.

Putting her bag down on a spare chair, Amy watched him hurry off for her water. Then, picking up the menu, she glanced around cautiously from behind it, mentally shivering. An English seaside hotel in February had its own peculiarly damp chill, as though staff and guests were afloat somewhere, cut off from the rest of the world.

A couple of tables from her a red-faced, sandy-haired man in a brown suit and an orange floral tie was eyeing her. He smiled when he saw that she'd noticed him. Nodding politely, she looked quickly away, past the tall, slightly scruffy man with the bandage, who'd bumped into her in the lobby, and Michael and Eleanor, who were now sitting tensely at the next table, both dressed smartly for dinner. Only in an alcove by the window did there appear to be any joy. There an old lady in a checked dress and blue cardigan was cheerfully ladling tomato soup into the mouth of a very old, disabled man in a wheelchair, occasionally wiping his chin with a napkin as he dribbled.

Pulling on her glasses Amy was beginning to consider the short menu when she suddenly found herself thinking about Teddy. Would he be having dinner, sitting with his colleagues in the studio executives' dining-room discussing the next day's show? No. That was quite unlikely. He hated the executives' dining-room. Perhaps he was at some power meeting then? Or was he sitting unhappily at home in Richmond making small talk with his wife, Gillian? Yes. That was where he would be.

But *would* they be making small talk? Surely not now. He'd be confronting the situation, owning up, making a confession, asking for the divorce he'd so often nearly talked about with her. Of course he would.

But then the question that had been pursuing her all day finally caught up: why hadn't he called?

She stopped herself. Such thoughts lead to paranoia.

She looked again around the dining-room. Shona, the college placement, now wearing a tight, short, black waitress's dress with a white pinafore, evidently cut for someone shorter and slimmer, was serving the elderly couple, chatting, apparently amusingly, to the old lady. Behind her, Darrell watched her as he manoeuvred his way across the floor with a tray of drinks. But as Shona passed him on her way back to the kitchen and his eyes met hers her smile withdrew into an expression of infinite indifference. Meekly Darrell lowered his glance.

"It must be good having someone new to help out," Amy said, indicating Shona, as he arrived at her table.

Darrell shook his head. "To be honest, I don't think she'll like it much here."

"No?"

"She keeps calling it Carbuncle-on-Sea."

Amy smothered a smile. "Oh, dear."

"And it's not fair. There's nowhere nicer in England." The local boy was puffed with indignation.

Amy considered the rain-lashed windows. "I'm sure," she said, and, addressing her menu, she made her choice.

Darrell hurried back to the kitchen.

Again Amy looked around the room, her eyes fixing now on a wiry-looking middle-aged Scottish-sounding couple who had entered the dining-room after her and who were now poring over maps and guides. Suddenly she envied them their companionship.

A murmur reached her from the next table:". . . and for that which we are about to receive, may the Lord make us truly thankful. Amen."

"Amen," responded Eleanor to Michael's grace.

Amy wished she couldn't hear, but every breath carried in this almost silent room.

"I'm feeling quite hungry now, aren't you?" she heard Michael say in his patient, even way.

There was no answer.

"Is everything all right, Eleanor?"

Perhaps there wouldn't be an answer.

There was. "Everyone knows, Michael." It was almost a sob from Eleanor.

"Well, yes, perhaps, but it doesn't matter, does it?"

"We're a spectacle."

"Now that isn't true."

Now Eleanor's voice cracked unhappily. "But what *is* true? Are we true . . . the priest and the nun who renounced their vows, and for what, Michael? For what?"

This time there was no reply from Michael, just the leaking wound of hurt and confusion.

"I'm sorry . . ." Eleanor was now whispering. "I'm so sorry. I didn't mean that."

Amy stared hard at the embroidered pattern that ran around the edge of her tablecloth. She really wished she hadn't heard.

"And how are we this evening? Head feeling better now?"

58

Across the room Tim looked up from a sheet of music manuscript he'd been considering. Immediately the musicians in his brain stopped playing, and the image of Amanda, which had been peering at him from behind those clever dark-rimmed glasses she wore, vanished. Instead, the heavily breasted manager of the North Devon Riviera Hotel was holding a bottle of red wine and glowing down on him. "Yes, thank you," he said.

"Excellent! We'll soon have you as right as rain again." It sounded more like a command than an encouragement.

Tim nodded a thank-you and watched as the manager uncorked the bottle.

"I expect you'll be looking forward to our Valentine's Ball," she said, slipping an invitation on to the table. "Free to all our guests, of course."

"Actually, I'm not much of a dancer," Tim came back, indicating that he wouldn't bother to taste the wine and that she could fill the glass. She did.

"No? Well . . ." She feigned surprise, then with a special smile, just for him, added, "Let's just see how the sap rises, shall we!" And putting the bottle down she left the table and set off across the room to nag at the new work-experience girl. "Table six, Shona! They're waiting!"

Tim considered the invitation to the ball. It was festooned with garish pink transfers of a woman's very full lips. Well, that would be one way he wouldn't be spending his Friday evening.

A few tables away a mobile phone rang an electronic opening to the *William Tell Overture*. The woman he'd bumped with his keyboard started for her bag, then stopped just as quickly as she realized the phone wasn't hers. Tim was glad about that. She didn't look like a *William Tell Overture* ring-tone sort of person.

He could see who was. It was the chap with the brown suit and orange tie near her who was telling his caller, in a jovial voice that carried across the dining-room, much to the obvious annoyance of the manager, that he was "ready, willing and able" for whatever was required.

Tim returned his gaze to the woman sitting alone. She was about his age, maybe a few years younger, with a copper-coloured bob of hair, and had now taken out a book to read while she waited for her dinner.

Slowly he sipped his wine, checked his watch and thought about Amanda in Denver, always a whirl of energy, her forehead permanently furrowed behind her black, sculpted, one-side-longer-than-the-other fringe. Would she now be at a morning orchestra rehearsal? And he pictured her at her cymbals and kettle drum. Or would she be still in bed, asleep, perhaps, after a late night? And he imagined how she looked when she was asleep, when that determined expression almost, if not quite, relaxed.

Then, as an unwelcome picture began to emerge, Amanda laughing and flirting, enjoying being the centre of attention, he turned away from it to watch the other guests, two latecomers, elderly women who were probably sisters, the brown-suited man who was now writing lists of figures in a notebook, the robust Scottish couple with the loud whispers who looked like serious walkers, and the old people by the window. There was no doubt about it. Dinner in an English hotel in a seaside resort in the off-season could be a pretty muted business.

Once again his eyes found the attractive woman with the copper hair, the one without the *William Tell Overture* on her mobile phone. He knew why he was there, but why would a woman like that be sitting alone?

Shona! Shona? What kind of name was Shona, anyway? Darrell fretted as together he and the new girl took away the dishes, served the guests coffee in the loggia, and, standing alongside each other, helped stack the large, industrial dishwasher in the kitchen. *Shona*! It sounded almost, but not quite, African, and sort of exotic. Posh, too. But then despite the clothes she'd arrived in, which made her look like a bag lady, and which she'd been told never to wear around the hotel again, Shona was the sort of girl who'd been to a private school, who had rich parents and who could say whatever she wanted because she was confident, clever and spoke nicely. He wished he spoke nicely. If he did he wouldn't have said the things Shona said, though. She shouldn't have called the North Devon Riviera a Carbuncle-on-Sea. That wasn't very clever. It was just mean: and snobbish. And untrue. He hated her for that. But he couldn't stop looking over at her, either. And, although he knew it was stupid, as together they reset the few tables for the following morning's breakfast, and she hummed "I Will Survive" rather too loudly to herself, he already felt possessive towards her.

When he'd first taken her into the kitchen for something to eat before the guests had had their dinner he'd noticed how Domingos, the handsome, black Brazilian chef had looked at her, not leering or anything like that, because Domingos was actually a very polite man, but with a kind of joky twinkle. Agnieszka, the triangular-faced Polish sous-chef, had noticed the twinkle, too, and frowned. She and Domingos just didn't get on. In fact, most of the time they didn't even bother to speak the same language to each other: Domingos always moaning at Agnieszka in Portuguese and Agnieszka snapping back in Polish. And that was just silly because they both spoke English perfectly well. But, as Darrell folded the last of the napkins and reflected on that twinkle and the babel of attrition that was more usually to be found in the kitchen, he offered a silent prayer that Domingos wouldn't forget about annoying Agnieszka and start getting on with Shona instead.

"Is that it for the night?" Shona asked after Darrell had checked the dining-room for the last time, and led the way back into the kitchen. "Am I finished? Because I have some very important things to do."

Darrell nodded. "We start at seven," he said, wondering what could possibly be so important. "If you like I'll knock on your door when I get up. Make sure you're awake like."

62

Shona raised her eyebrows. "You're such a gentleman, Darrell. Yes, please." And opening the door of the fridge, she took a large slice of lamb.

"Actually, we're not supposed to . . ." Darrell began to say. But Shona, her face illuminated into an eerie kookiness by the fridge light, fixed him with such a smile that the words died on his lips.

"Just in case I get peckish in the night," she explained. Then, wrapping the lamb in a sheet of paper towel, she added, "Do you ever get peckish in the night, Darrell? I bet you do. I bet you get peckerish, too, sometimes, don't you?" Again the smile shone from those pale, wide eyes.

Darrell felt himself blushing.

"Anyway, goodnight," she pouted. "God bless!" And away she marched back through the dining-room, her too-tight waitress's skirt clutched emphatically across her bottom, her bright, dyed, scarlet hair bouncing above her like a large red thistle.

Darrell didn't know what to think. He might hate her or he might not. She might be a snob or she might not. She might be teasing him or, again, she might not. She might even have been talking dirty. Yes, she'd definitely been talking dirty. Usually he didn't like girls who talked dirty or were suggestive, but tonight, well, he just couldn't wait for the following day.

She changed into her buttoned-to-the-neck, cotton nightdress and her powder-blue dressing gown in the bathroom, taking as long as possible to clean her teeth.

Staring at her reflection in the mirror she saw a young girl with the face of a middle-aged woman. She wanted to cry, but she was too strong for that. Besides, she didn't rightly know what she wanted to cry about. Opening the bathroom door she returned to the bedroom.

Michael was already in his pyjamas, also new, the Marks and Spencer cardboard and cellophane packing folded tidily in the bin by the mini-bar. He'd been looking out at the sea, the storm having now abated. A pale quarter moon lit up the coast. He turned and smiled when she entered the room. His eyes, she noticed, never left hers.

Together now they knelt on opposite sides of the bed to say their prayers, Eleanor hiding her face in a fold of the lace drapes, her eyes closed.

But there were no prayers to come. Instead, she found herself thinking of the year she'd spent working in the hospice when she'd left the convent, after she'd fallen in love with Michael. She'd had her own room there, beyond the laundry, her freedom for the first time since she'd been a teenager, and the only discipline that of her own making. Sometimes she'd longed to ask Michael back to her room, just for a cup of tea and a biscuit, perhaps, to show him how cosy she'd made her home, and how happy and agreeable she would make their life together. But she never had done. And he'd never suggested it. He wouldn't. He wasn't just a priest who had struggled with and then lost his vocation because of her. He was a shy, courteous sort of man, a man out of step with the modern march.

Sex. The word approached her slyly through her prayers. Yes, she'd thought about sex, often, and fought it, every time putting such thoughts and images aside for some future moment when they would be appropriate. She'd been told when she was young that impurity of thought was as grave a sin as an impure act if it was purposely entertained. And although she didn't quite believe that any more, the manacles of the life denied still gripped.

So, sex, yes, she'd thought about it, as some distant event when she would be a different person, a confident, successful, married woman, instead of the pale, frightened, foolish soul now missing the comfort of God's certainties.

Yes, sex, yes, she'd thought about it. And thought about it. But now, here in this honeymoon room, she didn't want to think about it.

Michael was waiting. She crossed herself and stood up. He was wearing the kindest of smiles. Taking off her dressing gown she folded it carefully over a chair and turned back towards the bed. He was watching her. She stopped as her fingers reached the sheets. She couldn't face him.

"It's all right, Eleanor," Michael said quietly after a long moment. "There's no hurry. We have the rest of our lives. Let's just go to sleep, shall we? We've had a busy day."

"I'm sorry, Michael."

"Don't be. Thank you for becoming my wife."

* ★ *

They slept together, but they didn't lie together. The bed was broad and they were slight, two lonely people clutching the outer edges of the mattress, leaving uninhabited the conjugal space between. And finally prayers came easily to Eleanor. She prayed for help.

Along the corridor, Amy considered the *Lovers' Law of the Eternal See-Saw* on her laptop and then watched a late-night movie starring Meg Ryan and Tom Hanks on television. She'd watched a lot of movies on TV since she'd met Teddy Farrow.

In the Exmoor Suite, Tim stared at his keyboard and calculated once again the time in Denver, Colorado.

CHAPTER
SEVEN

Looking down on the little port from her attic window, even Shona had to admit that as carbuncles went this was the prettiest she'd seen. Her view of the bay wasn't the best, rooms with that view being reserved for the guests. But standing on a chair in her bedroom above the hotel's old stables, now the staff quarters, she could see the merrily coloured fishing boats moored along the harbour wall, the sandy beach rinsed clean by last night's rain, and above the town the distorting shimmer of steam rising off the slate roofs of white- and buttercup-painted cottages. Even a winter sun as low as that in February made a world of difference.

She'd been awake for an hour, dressed and ready for work, waiting for the rest of the hotel to join her. She looked at her watch. A couple of minutes passed, then there was a knock on her door. She didn't answer. Then another knock, louder.

She yawned, as though struggling out of the deepest sleep. "What . . .?"

"It's seven o'clock." Darrell sounded nervous, as though not wishing to waken her too suddenly.

"Oh, God," she groaned theatrically. Then: "All right, thanks . . ."

From outside in the corridor she heard his footsteps make their way back to his own room; as from somewhere else came a morning trumpet of pipes quickly followed by a radio traffic report clicking on. Road works were already causing tailbacks on the M5 approach to Bristol.

She looked out at the day again. In the distance she could faintly hear the constant charging of a waterfall as the river dropped down from the moors and raced through wooded gorges to the sea. She'd listened to it half the night when, still crying, she couldn't sleep. "You've always been a disappointment to us, Shona. Your mother and I have done everything we can for you, but you just disappoint. Why you can't be more like your sisters, I don't know." Her father's words had pursued her, as so often, through a lonely night. Shona, the family disappointment.

Climbing down from her chair she considered herself in the mirror over her washbasin, for which she had to stoop to see herself.

"What do you think, Monty?" she said at last, her eyes smarting as she fitted her new contact lenses, which did so much to magnify her eyes, directing her voice at a large closed glass box standing on a unit of drawers. "And remember this is worth a million pounds. Am I the cleverest and the most beguilingly beautiful girl you've ever seen? Or am I just brilliant and stunning? And I'll be very hurt if you ask if you can phone a friend."

Then blinking her lenses into place, she hoisted her already despised maid's uniform up at the waist, thus

68

making the skirt even shorter, and set off for the day. "It's ten past seven. Knocking-up time," she mimicked with a broad Devon accent, as, passing Darrell's door, she hammered hard.

It didn't matter how well you knew someone, you rarely really recognized that person when they appeared on television, Amy reminded herself as she watched *The Teddy Farrow Show*. It wasn't just the pancake make-up, which ironed out the creases and created a pale orange tan, or the lights that seemed to rinse his grey hair a tint of blue. It was something to do with the way Teddy sat, artificially more upright, fondly patronizing the studio audience with his one-way friendliness, and that easy, instant, pally sincerity with today's guest, a football manager promoting an obviously ghost-written autobiography. But most of all, it was the fact that she knew she was watching a performance. Teddy wasn't like this in real life. He was confident, but nothing like so glib.

Before she'd got to know him, which had happened seven months earlier at a charity auction, her only opinion of him had been that his morning TV interviews were not for her. Four days a week at nine he would charm the celebrities of the moment into telling him more about themselves than they reasonably should. In return, they could plug whatever they were selling, be it books, records, films or cookery programmes. It was, like all of these programmes, pure television symbiosis. She'd rarely seen the show then, but when she had occasionally happened on it she'd marvelled at how promiscuous his guests were with their secrets. How did he get people to tell him this stuff? she'd wondered. Then she'd met him, and, casually invited to dinner as the auction ended, had quickly found herself laying bare the admittedly unremarkable details of her own life.

On reflection, what surprised her most was that she'd told him anything at all. Having, to her great surprise, found success with her first novel, she'd made the immediate decision that she wouldn't live her life in a media spotlight. Giving up her job in the bookshop, and not without some regret, so that she could write more, she'd remained a private, secretive person, behind a famous name — now a successful brand. But at dinner that night all she'd been aware of was the way he listened so very carefully, and how he made her feel good about herself. *So* good. She wouldn't go on his show, she insisted, laughing, absolutely no way, but when an invitation had come for her to join him for lunch a couple of weeks later she'd been pleased. Then there'd been another lunch and more requests for a TV interview. Then another dinner, always somewhere small and out of the way. And soon, somewhere between one invitation and the next, the suggestion that she should appear on *The Teddy Farrow Show* had stopped, and she'd realized she'd fallen in love.

She'd known from the beginning he was married. And happily. He'd made sure the entire nation knew. His was the perfect, long-distance, celebrity marriage, frequently blessed in the women's pages of the newspapers. Teddy the star, Gillian the beautiful, gracious homemaker, wife and mother. But as Amy had never expected to find herself in an affair, it had never seemed to matter that he was married. Then suddenly it was too late. They were in bed together, again and again.

Sometimes she tried to remember the exact moment when they'd gone from being friends to lovers. He'd dropped her off at her flat after lunch one day. It was raining. He had some time to kill. She'd invited him in. Had she realized then as they'd gone up in the lift together and she'd seen the expectation in his eyes where they were leading each other?

With the affair her life had changed. Now with guilt a factor they'd begun to go out together less, for fear of being spotted. He'd worried that his children might find out about her, explaining that he had to go slowly and prepare the ground. It couldn't be rushed, he'd said. She'd understood. And when he'd fretted that his public image was in peril she'd understood about that, too. She was in love. She understood everything. Of course she did.

And because she was in love and wanted only to be with him, she became used to staying in alone more than ever, hanging around her flat and getting on with her work, waiting until he came to her and never missing his programmes. Sometimes she even watched the late-night repeats of his old shows on the satellite channels. That's the kind of cringing wreck I've become, she would tell herself. But she still watched.

By nature studious, her work had always been her hobby, but as she'd sat in her study and written, waiting for those covert fleeting junctions of desire and happiness when they were together, she'd sensed her self-esteem sinking ever lower. She'd known why it was happening, but there'd been nothing she could do to prevent it that wouldn't have made her more unhappy.

Sitting up in bed on this Devon morning she watched now as Teddy joked with the football manager about the difficulties of keeping the late-night activities of young footballers out of the Sunday newspapers.

"My life would be a lot easier if more girls would just learn to say 'no'," laughed the manager to a round of applause. "And if the papers were less hypocritical."

Teddy shook his head sagely. "Come on, now, Billy," he jibbed. "Let's not blame the messenger when we don't like the message. The newspapers are only printing what we like to read, isn't that a fact, now?" And he smiled blithely into the camera as the show prepared to go to a commercial break. "Back in three minutes. Don't go away."

The newspapers are only printing what we like to read! Amy was puzzled. Was he deliberately mocking their pursuers?

A knock on the door broke into her ruminations. It was Darrell with the continental breakfast she'd requested the previous night. After dinner in the morgue, the cosiness of her room for breakfast had seemed infinitely preferable.

"Sorry I'm a bit late," the boy beamed, as, fastening her dressing gown, she let him in. "Breakfast in Paradise." And putting down the tray he drew back the curtains.

72

About to admire the view Darrell thought so heavenly, she stopped. There was a complimentary newspaper on the tray, and yet another photograph of her, this time in the contents box that ran down the side of the front page. **SO WHERE IS AMY? Page** 7, prompted a teaser.

Quickly she put the newspaper on the dressing table and joined Darrell at the window.

"It's a beautiful day." He seemed almost to be boasting, and she noticed that he'd washed his hair and shaved the dark floss from his top lip since the previous night. The scent of aftershave lotion lay on the air. Then, with a polite nod, he was gone again.

She returned to the newspaper, and, flicking to page 7, read a short gossipy piece about herself alongside an old photograph. *So who's the big secret, Amy?* it ended.

It was froth, nothing more. No revealing facts, no naming of Teddy, nothing libellous, nothing new at all, in fact, just a reminder that they were on to her. All the same, she hated it. It was *her* froth.

"God! You look like —" Shona blurted and then stopped.

Tim waited at his open door. "Like what?"

Suddenly Shona dropped, not accidentally, a napkin from the breakfast tray she was holding and bent down to pick it up. "I know what you're looking at," she snapped.

"I'm sorry?" Tim asked.

"No, not you," came back the girl, and, looking around, indicated Darrell who was passing and had glanced at her show of thigh. The boy hurried away as though bitten.

"So, what do I look like?" Tim continued, amused, as he let her into the room.

"Well, like, er, tired," Shona replied, less abrasive now.

"Is that all?" Tim pressed. She was a contradictory girl.

Shona set the tray down on a table. "I meant, you look as though you didn't sleep very well," she said.

"Fair enough." Tim touched his bandage. It was beginning to itch behind his ears. "But that wasn't what you were going to say, was it?"

Shona looked him in the eye, defiant now. "No. If you want to know, I was going to say you look like Death with a sick note." And she poured his coffee.

Tim didn't react. The girl puzzled him. "Why didn't you?"

She shrugged. "It seemed a bit unkind to say to someone with a bandage around his head."

"And a bit rude? Not really the sort of thing you should say to a guest, eh?" The teacher in Tim was emerging. He didn't like that.

Shona looked surprised. "If you like I'll apologize. But as I didn't actually say it, not until you asked me to, anyway, and wouldn't have done, I don't really think I've got anything to apologize for, do you? It was only a thought. We can't help our thoughts. And, anyway, it's

74

sort of true, in a nice way." Now she smiled, a wide-mouthed, crooked, slightly zany smile.

For a moment she seemed very young. Eighteen going on fifteen, in turns outrageous and then sweet, desperate to get a reaction and test how far she could go. Actually, Tim didn't care what she said or what she thought. He was used to much worse at school.

"Perhaps not." He grinned and took his coffee. Who knew why some kids tried to be chippy and draw attention to themselves? He spent his life avoiding confrontation, just getting on with his playing. Was that a better way to behave? Amanda didn't think so. "Maybe you're not cut out for the Samaritans after all, though," he teased as Shona went to the door.

"Thank God," she said, and left.

Sipping his coffee, Tim sat down at his keyboard and wearily considered what he'd written. She'd been right. He'd hardly slept. Putting on his headphones he played a few lines and then stopped, irritated. During the night his legless keyboard had developed a wobble on the table where he'd placed it. It was worse now. He tried playing again, then stopped.

An unrequested newspaper had arrived with the tray. Carefully folding it into two he wedged it between the keyboard and the table. The newspaper disappeared: the wobble ceased. Brilliant. Once more he began to play, but again not for long. Bored, he logged on to the internet and, eating a croissant, waited for his overnight email messages.

There were four. One from Harry at Ballantines asking him if he could suggest another pianist to stand in for him on Valentine's Night, two offering cut-price CDs, while the fourth looked like financial get-rich-quick spam. The email he'd hoped for, the one from Amanda, wasn't there. That was disappointing. So he wrote her one, a casual, chatty one, intended to show that he wasn't disappointed at all at not having heard from her.

Hi,

I've called once or twice, but Denver's obviously got you very busy. Good for you, I hope. Let me know what's happening. The head doesn't hurt much any more. Not as much anyway. Did you know that you do actually see stars when you get a bang on the head? Not stars like we see at night in the sky. What you get is more like a dimpled silver or aluminium plate, on which some dimples dazzle more than others. That's how it was for me, anyway.

He hesitated, then:

I'm a bit tired today because I worked all night on my new piece for the competition.

Another, pause, then:

To be honest, I really don't know about it. Give me a call if you have a minute. Miss you.
Love you,
Tim

Then pressing *Send*, he got up, opened the French windows and stepped out on to his balcony.

It was mild for February, with great calico clouds drifting across a blue sky, and going to the rail, he looked down across the hotel gardens where a tangle of rhododendrons, pines and creepers pushed upwards competing for light and life. To one side was a tennis court without a net, while beyond was a caged, presumably empty swimming pool, covered by a nylon sheet. A place out of season only ever looked half dressed.

The sound of a door opening prompted him to look further along the side of the hotel. The woman he'd bumped with his keyboard was coming out on to the next balcony but one. Politely, he smiled a good-morning. She nodded back, and, after looking at the view, went back into her room.

Tim turned back to look at the sea. The music wouldn't come. Not in London, not here. Not anywhere. For hours he'd sat at his keyboard, his ears filled with the sounds from his headphones while the rest of the hotel had known only creaks and silence. But it just wasn't working. Perhaps if Amanda were here she might offer some inspiration. Then he dismissed the idea. She wouldn't.

God loves a tryer, he told himself, and going back inside he reached once more for the headphones, accidentally catching the lead sharply on the corner of his bed as he did.

"Oops." He frowned as he unhooked them.

Then pulling them on, he pressed his fingers on the keys in front of him.

There was only silence. He tried again, then, puzzled, examined the lead from the headphones to the Yamaha. It didn't take long to find the fault. A wire had broken away at the headphones end.

"Bugger!" he said.

CHAPTER
EIGHT

What To Do and Where To Go on The North Devon Riviera!!! promised big, italic, red letters.

Pulling the flyer from the rack in the hotel lobby, Amy added it to her collection. She already had information on moor and cliff walking, riding, cycling and sailing, where to find the best cream teas, the best bird-watching sites, and where to book for Lorna Doone tours. None of these activities appealed, but now an advertisement caught her eye.

Madame Cora, it read, showing a spidery outline of an upturned hand. *Available daily for palm reading. First floor, Victoria Arcade.* Amy didn't believe in palmistry, but on an empty, lonely day in February it couldn't hurt to hear what the lady had to say. She could ask her about love-lines. At the very least it might make an amusing paragraph.

As she turned to leave, the man in the brown suit she'd seen at dinner the previous night approached, smiling like a Sunday. Today he was wearing a camel-coloured short overcoat, the kind people used to call car coats. "Morning," he cackled.

"Good morning." She forced a smile.

He looked at her clutch of brochures. "Thinking of seeing the sights, then?"

"Well . . . I thought I'd . . ."

"I could show you a few sights," he laughed, then quickly continued. "Devon's littered with them."

"Well, perhaps another day." Politely she tried to put him off.

It didn't work. "Right! You're on!" he relished. "Now, I'm sorry, but I have to dash. All play and no work makes Barry a poor boy." And he brayed loudly. "I'll see you later. All right!"

And before she could unscramble the misunderstanding, he was off towards the car park, samples of floor covering poking out from under the arm of his coat. At reception the manager scowled after him.

Amy shut him quickly from her mind as a fool, and, making for a side door, stepped out into the hotel garden. It was too good a day to stay in and work, but she needed to buy a new mobile phone if she was ever to escape her hotel room.

A steep, zig-zagged path, hewn out of the cliffs, made a short cut down to the sea. Sheltered by wind-broken Scots pines, and decorated by patches of early daffodils, it was a pretty walk. In other circumstances this could, after all, have been the right place for a romantic break, she reflected as she descended. Unfortunately, romance wasn't something to be enjoyed alone.

It was colder by the sea and she tied the belt of her coat more closely as she set off across the ribbed, damp sand, the only person on the beach. She wanted to think about Teddy, to bask in reveries of a future

80

different from the present, one in which she was permanently with him. But all thoughts of Teddy now came with worry lines.

For a while she walked slowly, pondering the waves breaking on the sand, wiping away the footprints she'd just made, as though continually deleting the past. Then, finally beginning to head towards the little port, she took a micro-recorder from her pocket, a gadget she usually used for dictating letters to readers when her part-time secretary came around one morning a week.

So, where was I? The Lovers' Law of the Eternal See-Saw, Part Two, she began, and, stopping again, drew a cartoon outline of a see-saw in the sand with her shoe.

Yes, well, as I was saying it seems to me that it doesn't matter how happy a relationship appears, or how well suited a couple, the truth is the two are very rarely in perfect equilibrium.

She walked on skirting a large sea-water puddle.

On the surface they may be a match. She likes sushi and fast cars. He drives a Mazda sports coupé. He's crazy about Mafia movies, she's got Joe Pesci's autograph. He has a thing about oral sex . . . she's an Ear, Nose and Throat consultant . . .

She hesitated at that, decided it was smart-arse and vulgar and not to include it when she typed up her notes, and then continued.

But that's just the packaging of their lives. It's the Eternal See-Saw that makes the rules. And emotionally you can be sure that at any given moment, one of them is soaring through the air having a terrific time and the most wonderful life, while the other is stuck, knees buckled on the ground. And if you're still not convinced, although you should be by now, just look in any mirror and ask yourself one question: at which end of the plank are you sitting?

She didn't see him, but Tim spotted her as he hurried down the cliff road to the town. A solitary figure on an empty beach, it occurred that she looked strangely romantic out there by the sea, like the traditional widow waiting hopelessly for her sailor to return. Then, overtaking her, he crossed over a short promenade and entered the town.

As a seaside resort it was tiny, a row of bathing huts behind the front, half a dozen defiant palm trees, a few white-fronted Regency houses, some shops, their windows boarded up for the winter, a tiny theatre still advertising last summer's attractions and, behind everything, a delta of pastel-coloured cottages bearing hopeful bed and breakfast signs.

The place he was looking for was close to the theatre, a short Victorian shopping arcade, the sort of wrought-iron and glass development usually bequeathed on such towns by local nineteenth-century philanthropists. The little electric and music shop Darrell had told him about was at its far end.

Quickly he found a new pair of headphones to replace the ones he'd broken, and he was heading back down the arcade when a bookshop a few doors along caught his attention. Some shops he just couldn't pass.

A green note had been stuck to the door of Madame Cora's Palmistry: *Closed — due to unforeseen circumstances*. So much for her predictive skills, Amy told herself, and, leaning on the first-floor balcony railing of the arcade, she looked around for a phone shop. She didn't see one. What she did see was a very large, black-and-white cut-out photograph. It was of her and it was in the mullioned window of a little bookshop across the arcade. She was surprised, flattered actually. Common sense suggested she ignore it. She was supposed to be in hiding. But she was an author and her books were obviously on sale in numbers here. One quick look couldn't hurt. And, with her short, sandy-coloured hair, she did look very different now.

Going down the spiral staircase she crossed the arcade and, pulling her hood closer around her new brown hair, she entered the bookshop. Inside there was another surprise. The cut-out was double-sided, so that it also gazed across the shop, right over a display of Amy Miller novels. You never got such promotion in London between books. The bookshop owner must either be an Amy Miller fan or had been made an offer of a job lot at some giveaway price.

She wasn't prepared to find out, but, keeping her face turned down, she moved towards the neat stacks of her books. Had they been there in those exact positions since the previous summer? She was a realist. Probably. Quickly she began to do some calculations. Twelve copies of *Porcupine*, seven of *The Garden Bench*, nine of *Figure Skating in the Dark*, but only one of —

"Hello!"

She swung around, startled. The man with the bandage was smiling, a sale copy of a book about film music in his hand.

"Oh! Yes. Hello!"

"Small world."

"Yes. Well, small town, anyway," she replied. Then, aware that she was standing exactly alongside the cut-out photograph of herself, she edged in front of it, blocking his view.

"You know, for a second, I thought you were . . ."

"Yes?" He'd recognized her, she was sure. She'd have to move on.

"Well . . . counting."

"Counting!" He hadn't recognized her?

"The books."

Relief. "Oh! Yes! Was I? That's a terrible old habit." She thought quickly. "I used to work in a bookshop. We had to count the stock every night to see how many had been stolen." Actually, that bit wasn't quite true.

"Oh, I see."

"*Teach Yourself Criminal Law* was favourite." Nervous, and playing for time, she embossed the lie.

He smiled. "Very useful, I'd have thought."

"Yes?"

"For book thieves."

"Absolutely!" She'd now begun to move him towards the door, but had to carry on talking to keep his eyes from the cut-out. "Closely followed by . . ." She glanced quickly around the shop for inspiration. A cover of a naked couple in an extraordinary position caught her

84

eye. The books they sold in these seaside resorts! "*Tantric Sex for . . . Kleptomaniacs.*" When you're in trouble make a joke, Teddy always said about live broadcasts.

"Perhaps more of a specialist volume," he came back, and then stopped walking and looked at the display of her books. "I can't imagine anyone wanting to steal Amy Miller books though, can you?"

That was a surprise. "You don't think?" she said, trying not to sound indignant. Obviously the idiot had never read any.

"Would you?" he asked easily.

"Probably not," she agreed, then quickly led the way out into the arcade.

She was prettier than he'd realized: a bit younger, too, but her face was half hidden by her hood so it was difficult to tell. For some reason he wanted their conversation to continue. "I saw you earlier," he said. "You were on the beach when I was passing."

"Ah, yes! I was taking the scenic route to Madame Cora's. I thought she might be able to tell my future," she said. "But she's not there." She indicated the palmist's booth on the balcony above them.

He shook his head. "Isn't that always the way?"

"What way would that be?" They were walking slowly down the arcade.

"You know, the future never being around when you most need it."

"Did I say I needed it?"

"Er, no. Do you?" He wasn't sure where this conversation was going.

She smiled now. "Don't you?"

"I think I'd rather wait and see what happens."

She dipped her head to one side as though accepting the point, but then said, "If you'd been able to predict the future you might not have that bandage around your head."

He was puzzled. She was teasing him and he was enjoying it. "That's true. But think of all the nice surprises I've had that wouldn't have been surprises if I'd known about them in advance. And all those still to come."

They'd reached a phone shop. She stopped walking. "But what about the disappointments?"

He shrugged. "We need those, too. Don't you think? They make the good days so much more special."

She seemed to think about that for a moment, as though it had some specific pertinence to her current mood. Then suddenly she became practical. "Perhaps. Anyway, it's been nice meeting you. But I have some shopping to do."

"And I should be working," he replied. "I'm Tim, by the way."

"Tim, right."

He waited for her to exchange her name. She didn't. Inwardly he shrugged. No matter. "Well, anyway, I'd better be off. Bye."

Strange woman, he thought, as he made his way back towards the sea. She'd been reserved then joky, chatty then not. Not that it mattered. Reaching the harbour he began walking back up the steep hill towards the hotel. Dark clouds had pushed in from the west, and, like pieces of jigsaw, had filled in the blue sky while he'd been in the arcade. Now the first drops of a new squall began snapping at his face. All the same, the North Devon Riviera didn't seem quite so alien any more.

Michael and Eleanor saw him go by as they sat in the window of the Old Tea Rooms, which stood on an elevated pavement above the promenade. After breakfast they'd toured the hotel grounds, agreed with each other on how much more advanced the plants were down here compared to those in Wiltshire, and then, wearing wellingtons and anoraks, set off for a walk around the town. They agreed with each other about that, too. It really was the prettiest of places, and the surrounding cliffs and hills much more wooded than they'd expected. In fact, they told each other, they couldn't imagine why this part of the world wasn't more famous. But then, as they'd settled into their tea and scones in the tea shop and watched the occasional passer-by, their conversation had frozen.

"Isn't that the young man . . .?" Michael began as they saw Tim. Then he stopped. Tim was so obviously the fellow guest from the hotel it wasn't worth saying.

Eleanor nodded.

They were the only customers in the Tea Rooms and neither spoke for a few more moments, so Michael refilled their cups. "Perhaps if it clears up again we could try a walk up the gorge this afternoon," he suggested.

"That would be nice."

"Yes." After that he couldn't think of anything to add. A bonnie-faced waitress came and went, just checking that they were all right.

It was Eleanor who finally broke the silence. "I'm sorry that I'm spoiling your honeymoon, Michael," she said.

Michael touched her hand. "Don't be silly. You are my honeymoon. I'm having a lovely time just being with you."

"You know what I mean," she pursued.

He was embarrassed. "Sex isn't everything, Eleanor," he consoled.

She looked at him. "How do you know?"

He gazed out at the rain again.

Amy bought a new mobile phone and chose a new number. Then, because it wasn't yet charged, she phoned Teddy from a pay-phone in the arcade. She got his answering service once more, which was, of course, what she'd expected, and which was again both a disappointment and a relief. Then she left a message with her new number. She felt better after that. Now she need never miss a call when he wanted to talk.

But as she packed her new phone safely inside her coat pocket a murmur inside her stirred: Pathetic, it said.

He was half way back up the hill when the people carrier drew alongside him. A window wound down.

"I thought it was you. Pneumonia next stop. Hop in." It was the hotel manager, her round face beaming.

For just a moment Tim considered declining. But the rain was getting heavier. "Thank you," he said and climbed into the car.

Immediately the manager giggled. "I'm sorry. My name's Jane, by the way, and you've just plonked your bottom on my pink mushy heart."

He'd accidentally sat on something, of that he was certain.

Jane hadn't finished: "And you're squashing my darling pussy-face," she hooted as she put the car into drive.

Tim was wishing he'd chosen the rain. "Sorry!" he said, pulling a brown paper bag from under him. A collection of red, satin-hearted Valentine decorations fell into his lap. *My darling pussy-face*, read one. He tried to smile.

"Don't worry. Just throw them in the back with the rest. They're gifts and decorations for our Valentine's Ball on Friday night."

Obediently he put the bag on the back seat alongside boxes of balloons and rolls of crêpe paper.

"You're a musician, aren't you! A composer, yes?" She was probing now.

"Actually, I'm a music teacher mainly."

"Don't be so modest. The room maid said she couldn't help but notice. Quavering crotchets all over the bed." She giggled loudly.

Miserably, Tim pictured his room, wishing he'd picked up the rejected sheets of manuscript. "I wasn't tired last night," he explained.

Jane was hardly listening. "I don't think we've had a composer stay with us before. We had a magician, I remember. Very clever. Tried to magic his way out of paying his bar bill. Didn't succeed. And a mortician . . . sticky fingers all over the pillow slips." She pulled a face. "You must be a very quiet composer. We haven't heard a single note."

"Oh, no. You won't hear anything. The only sound is in my headphones." And he opened the bag he was carrying to show her the new set he'd bought.

"But we'd *love* to hear something!" Jane gushed. "What about a little concert? Just to give us an idea of what you're working on up there."

Tim pulled a face. "I really don't think . . ."

But now she was coaxing. "We have a beautiful piano in the Tiverton sitting room. It's Korean. With rosewood inlays. Shall we say teatime?"

Tim felt as though he'd missed a chapter. "Today?"

"It needn't be very long."

"I'm afraid I always work in the afternoons."

Jane smiled triumphantly. "Tonight it is, then. Splendid!"

"I didn't mean . . ."

Jane wasn't listening. "What a wonderful birthday present."

"You don't understand . . ." he began. But he stopped. "It's your birthday?"

She ignored the question. "A musical soirée at the North Devon Riviera Hotel. How marvellous! Thank you *very* much."

90

Already they were pulling up by the front of the hotel. Tim stared unhappily at the new headphones in his hands, imagining Amanda's snort of derision when he told her how easily he'd been talked into playing. Better not to tell her, he decided. "I really don't think your other guests will like my music," he said finally, unhappily, as they crossed the car park.

Jane ignored that, too. "They'll be bilious with envy at the Grand," she murmured and went inside.

Somehow Tim doubted that.

Jane went straight to her small flat at the back of the hotel when she got in. Already she was regretting the sexy double entendres she'd used in the car. She'd behaved foolishly. He was nearly a generation too young for her, for heaven's sake, too attractive, and probably too talented, not to mention that he was a guest, and head office in Bristol had strict regulations that staff and guests did not mix socially. What the rule really meant was "Staff must not sleep with guests", a stricture mainly aimed at junior members, not senior managers, and one which, in her experience, was universally ignored.

Not that she would have had a chance with this chap, anyway, she reflected, as she re-touched her make-up, adding some blush to her pallid cheeks as she did two or three times every day. She knew that. She knew what she looked like. She'd known since school. "Moon Face," some of the other children had called her. Big and bossy, that was her. When you were a plain and single woman of forty-nine-plus you'd accumulated enough scars and rejections, and regrets, too, to at least know that much about yourself. Though it didn't stop you wanting or hurting and sometimes making a fool of yourself.

Then, with her front restored, she set off for the kitchens. Domingos, the chef, had been complaining about a temperamental fault with the main oven again, and, typically, Bristol still hadn't sent anyone to take a look at it.

CHAPTER
NINE

Will Abbott couldn't imagine why he hadn't realized it sooner. He'd spent the entire previous day researching and seeking a character as thin as a ghost. The books may show a pretty author on the back covers, and the Underground stations may have photos of the same woman up and down the escalators whenever a new one was published. But for all he could discover, Amy Miller appeared to have had little past before she began writing. The biography offered by her publisher's website was skeletal. *Born in London . . . university in Edinburgh . . . Amy Miller wrote her first novel,* Porcupine, *while working in a London bookshop. She has since written four other novels.* That was more or less it, and now, since she'd disappeared, she had no present either. No one who knew her professionally would, or perhaps could, tell him where she'd gone. In fact, no one who knew her well was even prepared to talk to him about her, beyond demanding to know why his newspaper was hounding her. Naturally, he couldn't tell them that. He admired their loyalty, but in Abbott's school of journalism questions only went one way.

Then his phone had gone. "Have you found her yet, Will?" It was Polly, the schoolgirl snitch, calling in her lunch hour.

"Hi, Polly. How's school today?" He'd asked her to let him know if Amy Miller came home again, but she'd called three times yesterday and was becoming a pest. She was developing a crush on him, he suspected, or at least on the idea of the exciting life of the tabloid journalist, and he regretted giving her his private extension.

"School is school," Polly came back dismissively. "But I was thinking about our friend Amy in English today and wondering if she'd lived when George Eliot did whether she would have had to have a *nom de plume*, too."

"A *nom de plume*?"

"That means a pen name that writers use sometimes when they don't want to use their own names."

"I do know that, Polly," Abbott replied. She might want to one day become one, but at the moment she clearly had a low view of the educational standards of reporters. Yet . . . a *nom de plume*! Why hadn't he thought of that? Already he was reaching for another phone.

"Oh, right, well, George Eliot was really a woman called Mary Ann Evans and she looked like a horse without a bridle and no one fancied her. Anyway, she had to change her name because at that time only men wrote novels and . . ." Polly was continuing, and was well into the plot of *Silas Marner* before he could get her off the line with a promise to show her the editorial floor when he was less busy.

"Amy Miller . . ." he said into his second phone to a young foot soldier trainee across the office. "You wouldn't like to check with the latest electoral roll and find out if that's her real name, would you?"

As he put the phone down, a familiar scent drew close. Suzy leaned over his shoulder, her camera case sliding on to his desk. "How are you today?" she murmured, the top of a denimed thigh touching his shirtsleeve.

Was that by accident? he wondered. He knew it wasn't. She wasn't a bad photographer either.

CHAPTER
TEN

Mommy, what's adultery?

As the television studio audience whooped with a hilarity the line didn't deserve, Amy's finger hesitated on the remote. She'd been lying on her hotel bed, devising races for raindrops, as huge, horizontally flying globules of water hit her window, exploded and ran at a forty-five degree angle down the pane to the finishing line of the window frame, when she'd finally given up and turned on the television. On her bedside table her shining new mobile phone, still charging, awaited its first call.

At home, watching television in the afternoon would have seemed degenerate. But she wasn't at home. Time lounged uselessly around her and only the prospect of door-stepping paparazzi had dissuaded her from catching the next train back to London.

She'd worked, of course. Sitting with her laptop, she'd wondered fancifully for a while whether the length of Cleopatra's nose might be described as a historical observation of the chaos theory put to love and war. But she'd given up on that when she'd come across a piece on the internet pointing out that Cleopatra was said to have serviced a thousand Roman legionnaires in one night. She was no mathematician, but even supposing a generous twelve-hour Egyptian night, she had trouble with that statistic. "That makes it . . . forty-three point two seconds each!" she calculated. "Some girl! But, I don't think so!"

She'd made herself some tea at four o'clock, smiled to herself as she'd recalled the chap with the bandage being so disparaging about Amy Miller novels in the bookshop that morning, and then casually begun flicking through the TV channels, past news, movies, a situation comedy, reality shows, sport and into another situation comedy. That was when she'd stopped to watch. That was when she'd heard: *Mommy, what's adultery?*

The scene featured a girl of about ten having breakfast in a dazzling Hollywood kitchen the size of a small gymnasium while her mother prepared an *Incredibles* lunch box for her. The mother, an unlikely, long-legged, tanned, svelte, blonde and beautiful woman in just-pressed jeans and shirt, stopped at the question, her mouth comically half-open as she stared into a vast and fully stocked refrigerator.

Is it like Monopoly? the child persisted.

This brought a roar from the audience.

Her mouth now fully open in comic surprise, the TV mother emerged from the fridge holding a carton of orange. *Actually, it's the exact opposite of Monopoly,* she answered.

But it is a game, isn't it?

Well . . .

Amy was beginning to feel awkward. It didn't matter that the child looked older than she was playing and was too smart with her questions to be believable, she could see where the scene was heading.

I mean, is it a good game? asked the girl.

There was more laughter from the audience.

I don't think good comes into it, wisecracked the mother.

So, it isn't a good game?

The mother snapped the lunch box closed on the table. *I guess that depends on who you play it with.*

The laughter turned to confirming applause at that. Amy wanted to change channels, but she didn't. For a second she wondered if Teddy's wife, Gillian, was watching. She hoped not.

Come on, eat! You'll miss the bus, the TV mother harried.

Can I play adultery? the girl now asked as the tempo of exchanges increased.

No, you can't.

Why not?

Why not! Because . . . it's for grown-ups only.

You mean it's an adults' game.

Well, sort of . . .

Is that why it's called Adult-ery?

The audience loved this. They hooted and clapped. Amy hated it. She hated the word.

Probably. I don't know. Come on, let's go. By now, the mother was pulling the child from the table.

But the script hadn't finished. There was more to be milked. *Does Daddy play Adultery?* the little girl persisted.

The mother's impossibly pretty face closed like a trap. *I would say . . . whenever he gets the chance*, she virtually spat.

As the audience guffawed again the child seemed satisfied. But this was television. There had to be a final exchange to end the scene. And as the mother put the lunch box into the schoolbag and the pair made towards the door, the girl had one more question. *Mommy, do people cheat when they play Adultery?*

The mother sighed. *As I understand it, honey, that's the entire point of the game*, she moaned, and led her daughter out of the kitchen door to a round of exaggerated applause.

Amy switched off the television. All right, she knew that in other circumstances she might have been amused, too. But at this moment she couldn't see anything funny about adultery. It might inspire any number of jokes for those not involved — the cuckold's horns, the husband returning home unexpectedly with the lover hiding in the closet, the older man who has a heart attack in the bed of his young mistress, "The Reeve's Tale". But when you were on the wrong side of love, when you were just waiting and hoping, feeling permanently bad about yourself, blocking out thoughts of your lover having sex with his wife, living a secret, and feeling somehow left out of the world, it wasn't a game at all. It wasn't much of a life either.

★　★　★

Tim spent the afternoon distracted by thoughts of Amanda. Sitting at his keyboard, with just a tuna sandwich brought up for his lunch by a noticeably more polite Shona, he found himself continually playing his way into dead ends, his mind veering off repeatedly as he pictured her, dressed as always in black, joking with the orchestra, that winning little grin emerging every time she knew she'd come in too loud or too late. She'd been excited, effervescent, when she got the late call as a replacement for the tour of America after the resident percussionist had sprained a wrist. She liked touring and she liked the camaraderie of an orchestra. Pretty girls often did.

He'd met her at a festival in Bamberg in Germany. She'd been involved in some modern workshop productions, while he'd been helping with a children's orchestra from South London, as much a minder as a teacher. Amanda's group had come third in the John Cage Prize, which was honourable; two of his charges had been sent home having been caught peddling marijuana, which wasn't.

For most of the festival he'd been aware of her only from a distance. At first, he'd thought she was Italian or Spanish, so black and shiny was her hair, so vibrant her personality, so cherry red her lipstick. He'd also been unaware that she'd even noticed him, so surrounded was she by admirers. Then, on the penultimate night of the festival, he'd been sitting alone in the refectory when she'd asked if she might join him. He'd discovered later that the rather dashing conductor with whom he'd mostly seen her, a man prone to wearing colourful scarves even on quite warm days, had publicly criticized her playing. She'd been devastated. He learned much later, because she told him, that they'd been sleeping together.

They'd got on immediately, Tim being a good listener. And on the next night, the last night of the festival, they'd become lovers, somewhat to his surprise, although sex and music were hardly strangers. He'd expected that they'd lose touch once back in London, his life and his music being quite unlike hers. Amanda had thought differently. They hadn't moved in together, but their relationship had taken root. She was social, vivacious, driven, and he was flattered that she found him such good company.

"You're like an old, blue-jeaned hippy, you know," she would joke sometimes, looking around his cluttered flat, while running a hand through the waves of his almost shoulder-length hair. It was true. But, though he thanked her when she bought him a black velvet jacket for the smart events she liked to take him to, that was as far as his make-over went.

What puzzled her most about him, she would say, was his lack of ambition. That hurt, although he hid it. She never quite said it but he knew that success for Amanda would be red carpets and public, artistic and, most of all, avant-garde approval. She liked people on the edge. Tim wasn't so sure. Most of the people on the edge looked to him like poseurs who should be given a gentle shove. *Poseurs* was his polite word for them, anyway. For him ambition fulfilled meant contentment in what he was doing. And it wasn't the same. They didn't argue about it, but little by little he'd felt the pressure to do things her way.

He'd always composed, or fiddled around with tunes, as he thought of it. Now he did it for her. She had plans for them both. She liked to quote a lyric from an old Carly Simon song at him, "*You said that we made such a pretty pair*," and would sing it whenever they were going out somewhere she considered exciting. Actually, it was Amanda who said they made a pretty pair. She liked the idea of that, of being half of a good-looking, artistic couple. He went along with the notion. He didn't want to let her down.

But did she let him down, this beautiful social woman who enjoyed going on tour so much? She'd let other lovers down. She'd told him. He knew about her past and all her other lovers and he'd been jealous of them. How much of her present did he know about?

Outside, the eternal rain of a West Country winter afternoon hammered against his window.

"Get off, you pest! Get off!"

The voice was amused as much as angry, but it was enough for Darrell. He'd been in the office checking the food and drink orders for the Valentine's Ball, trying to balance the amounts with the numbers expected, but now something much more urgent needed his attention. He hurried into the dining-room.

"Go away!" It was Shona, of course. Giles, the dog, had reared up on his hind legs and was pushing his wet nose into her stomach and sniffing hungrily. Shona was half laughing, trying to hold the dog off, its front paws

102

resting almost on her bosoms. She saw Darrell coming, but pretended not to. "Now stop that! Do you hear me? It's illegal in this country. Even for a dog. Even in bloody Devon!"

Darrell grabbed hold of the dog under his front legs and pulled him away. He felt almost gallant, though, in truth, Giles was the softest guard dog. "I'm sorry. He shouldn't be in here," he apologized, grateful for their moment alone together. Shona had hardly spoken a word to him all day, and when she had it had only been to mock his country accent and unfortunate haircut. But in the day she'd been at the hotel his entire waking life had been transfigured.

"He's a mad thing," she said, pretending to be affronted, and brushing imaginary paw marks off her uniform. "You didn't find him on the moors, did you? He isn't the Hound of the Baskervilles in disguise, is he?"

"He's just friendly. Pleased to see you. He must like you. I've never seen him like this with anyone else."

"Really?"

"It must be the way you smell."

"Thank you. I'm smelly now, am I?"

"Oh, no. I just meant he's taken a right shine to you."

"Ah! I see. Good. That's nice." Shona smiled. "And what about you, Darrell?"

"Oh, he likes me, too," he replied. "Don't you, boy?" And holding the excited dog's collar he dragged him out of the dining-room, and into the office.

It was only as he returned to his calculations and mentally re-ran over and again their short conversation that it occurred to him he might have misinterpreted what Shona had been asking. But then, he really couldn't be sure. She came from Sussex.

CHAPTER
ELEVEN

Tim considered the Korean piano and its rosewood inlays, then played a few bars. The keys were stiff and a tuning was overdue, but it was better than many of the pianos he regularly played in lounges around London. He tried a little ragtime to warm up and then stopped.

Amanda had always been dismissive of his evening cash job. Sitting behind a piano at the end of a noisy bar in Covent Garden, or behind a baby grand in one of the West End's hotels wasn't her idea of being an artist. Nor his. Indoor busking he'd sometimes call it, which would annoy her no end. She could be very intense. Actually, he quite enjoyed being a bar pianist, wandering from tune to tune as the feeling took him, playing Stevie Wonder or George Gershwin in the style of Chopin or Liszt just for the fun of it, watching everyone while hardly anyone watched him. As a bar pianist he was either ignored or tolerated, the only time he was really noticed being when he was resented by those who didn't want a musical soundtrack to their conversation.

Tonight would be different. Tonight the people would be coming just to hear him play, virtually a captive, probably a captured, audience.

He looked around the sitting room as the old lady wheeled her husband into the room. The two elderly sisters were already there along with the Scottish hiking couple, without their maps for once. From outside in the lobby he could hear Jane, the manager, trilling away, waylaying anyone who tried to escape to their rooms. "This way for the concert. Starting soon. Musical treats for all!"

Jesus! He grimaced to himself.

"Quiet down this way in February," a conversation opened at his side. It was the chap with the brown suit, tonight wearing a button-down, open-necked, pea-green shirt with it, and he was leaning on the piano, viewing the guests as they entered. He was overweight, in his mid-forties, with thinning hair and a freckled forehead.

"That's what I came for," Tim replied.

"You wouldn't like August then. The name's Barry, by the way, Barry Harrison." And he put a half-full glass of beer down on the piano.

"Probably not," Tim said, mildly irritated, beginning to look through his music. It had happened hundreds of times before, but he always resented it when a piano was used as a bar. It was a musical instrument, for God's sake. He would play soon and get the whole silly episode over.

"It's sex on tap in August," Barry went on matter-of-factly.

Tim didn't need to know this. "Really? Water shortage, is there?" he said quietly and drily to himself, and then watched as the honeymoon couple entered and found two places in a crescent of chairs facing the piano. In front of them was an open space.

Barry hadn't registered Tim's sarcasm. "A lobster isn't safe in her pot in August around here," he went on, picking up his glass.

"But this is February!" Tim countered.

Barry's face now brightened for the punch-line he was about to deliver. "Well, if you don't tell her, I won't." And, cackling loudly, he downed his beer.

Tim smiled politely at the joke. Through the open door to the lobby he could see Jane stopping a final guest. It was the young woman he'd met that morning in the bookshop. Everything about the woman's body language suggested that she would rather continue on her way to her room, or just about anywhere, but Jane, as he knew, could be persuasive. At last, with a look at best of bored surrender, the woman entered the sitting room and found a seat. Suddenly Tim realized that he was pleased to see her there.

Standing alongside the piano, Barry watched her closely. "See this," he bragged quietly. "I'm on a promise here."

It shouldn't have mattered to Tim, but for some reason it did. "Really?"

"Gagging for it. Alone in a hotel! A woman like that! Why else would she be here?"

Tim looked back at the woman. She was sitting holding a notebook, slight and neat in jeans and sweater. She nodded at him, with just half a smile of recognition when she saw him looking. "Probably the same reason as you and me," he replied.

Which gave Barry the opening for another riposte. "And why d'you think I'm here?" And this time he brayed so loudly that everyone in the room turned to look.

Tim smiled out of politeness then stared at his piano and waited as the last of the audience arrived, Darrell and Shona, followed by a young man and woman in chefs outfits. Obviously the hotel staff who lived locally had had better excuses and left for the day.

At last, satisfied that no one would miss this moment, Jane moved to the centre of the open space in front of the piano wearing an expression that somehow managed to simultaneously convey gratitude and discipline. "Thank you so much for coming, everyone. It's so nice to see such an enthusiastic audience." And she shone her smile around, as though she really hadn't had to twist any arms at all.

Darrell virtually nodded, Shona looked scornful and the elderly lady rested her hand on the shoulder of her husband in his wheelchair.

"As regular guests will know, the North Devon Riviera Hotel has long been recognized as a fortress of culture . . ."

"The Colditz of the arts . . ." sniggered Barry, just loud enough for her to hear.

Jane shot him a glance of pure contempt, then continued. "So tonight we're especially thrilled to be able to bring you our own composer in residence . . ." She beamed at Tim. "Mr Timothy Fairweather . . . who will now play the opening movement for a composition he is still, I believe, working on. So, if all mobile phones could be kindly switched off . . ."

In the audience a crease crossed the brow of the young woman from the bookshop as she complied. Tim noticed.

Jane turned to him again. "Mr Fairweather . . ." And she stretched out her arm. The room was his.

Tim contemplated the piano keys. He was angry with this silly woman, but crosser with himself. He should have just refused. He'd been a pushover and he disliked himself for it. But here he was again, too nice for his own good, as Amanda would say.

Well, maybe not. This would give them something to think about. And, after waiting until one of the elderly sisters had finished clearing her throat, he began to play.

A tumour had been the bait to draw Amy into the room. "I'm sorry, I really don't feel in the mood . . ." she'd begun as Jane had stopped her in the lobby.

But then that little extra moment of pressure. "He's been told it's probably benign, but . . ."

And Amy had followed Jane's eyes to Tim's bandage. Oh, God! What had she said that morning?

Now she was sitting with the other guests in a semi-circle around the piano totally perplexed. Notes were being played, but had the recital begun yet? She couldn't tell. Nothing of what she was hearing made sense to her. If there was a pattern she couldn't follow it, if there was a tune, she couldn't hear it.

Yet there in front of her the bandaged composer was concentrating hard on his hand-written manuscript. Singly, in clusters and in runs, what sounded to Amy like discordant chords and random notes followed one another. As the pianist turned a page, a loose sheet of paper floated down to the floor. In their consternation no one moved to pick it up.

Amy looked furtively around the room. Just behind the piano the horrible Barry was frozen, his pint glass half way to his mouth, while next to her the honeymoon couple were listening, anxious, as always, as though not wanting to get anything else wrong. By the door the two kitchen staff looked bored already, while Darrell wore the dismayed expression of a boy who'd bought a DVD in a pub only to discover it was in Cantonese. To the other side of the piano sat the manager, her expression now going through the seasons of change, from expectation to confusion, impatience and now betrayal.

As though aware of the growing confusion around him, the pianist now began to increase the tempo. It still sounded awful, but suddenly a giggle erupted from the old man in his wheelchair. Behind him his wife, far from being embarrassed, smiled happily, and as the old man began to tap his foot as though trying to keep time with the ever-changing rhythm, she began to rock his wheelchair backwards and forwards.

This must have amused Shona, because, leaning against a wall, she, too, began to rock on her heels, as if imagining the rhythm that wasn't really there. The seriousness of the piano recital was becoming a joke.

110

Across the room the manager's face was a cleft of disappointment. Amy had to smile.

At that moment the pianist looked up and saw her. Immediately she was sorry. "I'm not laughing at your music," she wanted to shout out, little though she understood it. But surprisingly he smiled back, and then, without pausing, segued into a slow rock version of "Smoke Gets In Your Eyes".

Immediately the mood changed. By the window the two elderly sisters soundlessly applauded in relief, while the old lady standing by her husband's wheelchair now began to move from one foot to the other in a slow foxtrot, quickly followed by Shona who, rocking slightly, showily, in front of Darrell, began a little shuffle display. Darrell looked past her, not knowing how to react.

Amy relaxed as the weight of embarrassment in the room lifted.

"Come on, then, it's a party! Up you get," a loud voice noisily announced above her. And, without warning, she found herself being pulled from her seat into a burp of beer fumes, as Barry took her in the arms of his brown suit, and began a slow smooch around the room. "*So I smile and say, when a lovely flame dies, smoke gets in your eyes,*" he crooned, nothing like The Platters.

With great effort Amy attempted to hold her body away from his, her face set in the rictus of a smile. If he noticed he ignored her response and pushed a knee between hers as they danced. Now she frowned. She could feel a lot more of him than she wanted to. With

111

her eyes fixed over his shoulder, and still holding her notebook in one hand, she could see the expressions of astonishment in the eyes of the staff and other guests. Even Shona had stopped tormenting Darrell to watch. The chef was shaking his large head, while his assistant, still wearing her soft white cap, was pulling her face in a look of unmistakeable repulsion. That was when it got worse. Holding her ever tighter as they revolved slowly on the spot, a fat, podgy, brown-suited thigh began to rub between her legs. In desperation she looked towards the piano.

The pianist saw the plea. Instantly the music changed again, the rhythm increasing to a fast, marching disco beat. *I'm so excited, and I just can't hide it* . . . The lyrics of the song, absolutely appropriate for her partner, bubbled into her mind. For a moment Harrison tried to hold on to his smooch, but already Amy was pushing him off, bobbing away, forcing him to do the same. Reluctantly, the crooning stopped and the arms disengaged.

She was free. Quickly she half danced her way to the sanctuary of the piano, leaving her partner stranded alone on the loggia floor.

Then, with a flourish, the pianist finished the recital-that-never-really-was.

The guests applauded, of course, it would have been impolite not to have done, and then quickly made for the door, as though half afraid that this was only an interval and there would be more terrible music to follow. Jane slipped silently, unhappily, from the room.

Amy turned to her rescuer, still at the piano. "I owe you a drink," she said.

He nodded. "I need one."

"But not here," she said quickly.

He laughed. "*Anywhere* but here."

CHAPTER
TWELVE

They walked down the hill into the town together, laughing with relief. It had stopped raining now, and the lights of the promenade and jetty were mazily reflected in the shifting sea, which at high tide was now washing heavily along the beach. It sounded noisier at night.

Near the beginning of the harbour wall was a former customs cottage now painted white. Inside it had been heritaged with antique copper pieces and sea charts and turned into a pub. It was almost empty. Sitting in an old red banquette with a table between them, they dawdled over their drinks.

"You mean, you haven't got a tumour? Not even a benign one? There's been no probing investigation under that bandage?" Her face was a query of amused indignation.

Tim laughed. Obviously his version of why he'd come to the North Devon Riviera in the middle of winter hadn't quite matched the story put out by the hotel manager. "Sorry. Concussion at the worst."

"So, she lied to me to get me in?"

"She was selling tickets, or at least trying to give them away. In music circles that doesn't count as a lie.

Besides she probably lied to me, too, to get me to play. It can't be easy entertaining guests down here in the middle of winter."

Amy shook her head. "But you *are* a composer?"

Tim pretended to look hurt. "It was that bad?"

"Oh, no. No. It was . . . it was the audience," she stammered.

"You mean you liked it?"

"Oh . . . yes. Yes."

"Ah, good." He looked at her. She became prettier each time he saw her. He hadn't noticed before how small her nose was. It had been pink with cold from the walk down the hill, but now her whole face was rosy in the light from the open fireplace. "Was it the melody you liked . . . or . . .?" he teased.

"Er . . . and the rhythm." She was so anxious not to offend.

"Right," he mused. "You didn't think you'd perhaps heard it somewhere before?"

"Somewhere else, you mean?"

"Mmm. Because, you know, that's every composer's nightmare. That they accidentally rewrite or steal Beethoven's Fifth."

She smiled now. "Your tune is definitely not Beethoven's Fifth."

"No? Good. What about Grieg's Piano Concerto?"

She was laughing at herself for having been taken in. "That didn't spring to mind either."

"Nothing by Chopin? Or Schubert?"

"I don't think so." Beside her, the wood fire hissed and popped.

"Ravel, perhaps?" Tim continued. "Or what about Gershwin, Stockhausen, the Blind Boys of Alabama . . .? I like them."

"I don't think I know anything by Stockhausen," she said.

"Well, that's a relief. He's a bugger to hum along to."

Giggling, she pushed strands of hair behind her ears. He watched her, enjoying her company so much it amazed him.

"I know it isn't easy . . . musically," he said at last, slightly more seriously now. Then seeing that she didn't know what to say next, he joked, "It isn't easy for me, either. No wonder I've had a headache."

"I'm sure Beethoven had his off days," she threw back. It was her turn.

"Probably. But he was deaf. He didn't have to listen to what he was playing."

Self-mockery came easily and she laughed out loud at that. This woman, who had looked quite sophisticated when he'd accidentally bumped into her with his keyboard, was suddenly so approachable. "You haven't told me your name yet," he said.

She hesitated for a moment. "Er . . . Millie."

"*Er* . . . Millie! Is that supposed to be with a hyphen, or was it just a dramatic hesitation?"

"Millie."

"Well, thanks for your support tonight, Millie. It was very much appreciated."

For a moment they sat quietly together, one of those laybys in life when a new arrangement has just been

116

made and time has to be taken to reflect on the situation and plot the way forward.

In the end they broke the silence almost together. "It's an unusual place to come in February . . ." he began, but gave way as she began to speak.

"Perhaps I shouldn't ask this, but . . . if you really find your music so difficult, why do you write it?"

He winced inwardly, but didn't answer.

"I'm sorry. That was rude?"

He shook his head. "No, not at all. It's just that there is a sense to it, you know, though perhaps I was being a bit spiteful trying it out on the hotel guests. Actually, very spiteful. I knew they'd hate it."

"Oh, I don't think they hated . . ." she began.

He stopped her, mulling over her question. "Why do I write it? Why do I do it?" Why *did* he do it? He tried to answer. "Well, there is a sense of exploration going on, of finding out where music can go, what can be done with it . . ." He stopped. He was beginning to sound like one of Amanda's poseur pals. He shrugged and tried again. "I mean, not *everyone* hates that sort of stuff. Some people quite like it."

She looked at him. "Yes. I'm sure. Of course." But then: "Someone special?"

He was amused. She was intrepid. But he was flattered by her interest, too. "Well, yes, I suppose . . ."

Now she smiled. "Can I ask who it is? A girlfriend? Wife . . .? Or boyfriend, perhaps?"

He stopped her there. "It isn't a boyfriend," he said with a smile.

She was feeling guilty. She'd told him her name was Millie. No one had called her Millie since she'd been a little girl. It had been her grandmother's name for her, another diminutive of Amelia, her full name. Her mother had deemed Millie old fashioned, so Amy she'd become — until this moment. Now, although they were talking about his music, she was still half-worrying about the little lie she'd told. She wasn't a good liar. She didn't want him to ask any more questions. She might let something slip. In fact, she really didn't want to talk about herself at all. "So the piece you played . . . the one you're working on . . . your girlfriend likes it?"

He looked dubious. "I'm not sure yet. It's for a competition. Let's see how it goes. I hope she will, when it's finished."

"I'm sure she will," she encouraged. "What's her name?"

"Amanda. She's on tour in America with an orchestra at the moment, while . . ."

". . . you're here writing your great opus."

He smiled. "Until I got mugged, I was. It might help, you never know. Perhaps a creative clout was what I needed."

"And Amanda, is she a pianist, too?"

"Actually, she's a percussionist."

"Oh, right. You mean she likes banging things."

He seemed not to see the joke. "I think there may be a bit more to it than that," he answered.

"Yes, obviously. Sorry. I'm a musical moron. I even like opera."

118

That made him laugh. "You haven't told me what you do yet?" he said.

She'd left a gap in the inquisition and it was his turn to be curious. "Oh, nothing too exciting . . ." she said lamely, which was actually true on a day-to-day basis.

"Such as?" he persisted.

She thought quickly. "Well . . . paper," she explained. "I work in the paper distribution business." Technically speaking, at least, that wasn't another lie.

But it *was* a dead end. "Oh right . . . yes. And you're here for . . .?"

"Just taking a break. Time to think," she said. Then, glancing out of the window and seeing squalls of rain blowing past a light on the quay, she added, "And . . . right now, I think it's raining again. You're going to have to cover your bandage on the way back to the hotel. And I'm going to need some more wet-weather clothes if I'm to survive down here much longer."

"*Welcome to the Hotel Passion Killer, such a lousy place, such a lousy place*," sang Shona to the tune of "Hotel California", as, balancing on a stepladder, she neatly pinned a large pink *Welcome* heart to the lobby notice board. "*Bring your own Viagra to the Hotel Passion Killer, you're going to need it here, for your entire career . . .*"

Darrell considered her from behind a pile of decorations on the desk. Jane, in a huff, had dropped them there after the failed piano recital, demanded abruptly that he and Shona begin hanging them, and then disappeared to her flat. She could be a bossy,

119

sharp-tongued woman, Darrell had thought as he'd watched her go, but she was fair with him. The hotel was her first as manager and she was desperate to make a success of it. Sometimes it was nearly possible to feel sorry for her.

How he felt about Shona he couldn't tell. One minute she wanted him to dance with her, the next she was ridiculing him and everything the North Devon Riviera stood for. He'd never been so confused. "Our Valentine Ball's a big thing down these parts," he said loyally as she continued to sing.

Shona climbed off the stepladder and put her head to one side to view the heart, the way she'd accidentally hung it. "A big thing down which parts, Darrell?" she teased.

He ignored the question. "People come from miles around. Taunton, Bampton, Shillingford. All over the place."

Shona raised her eyebrows wickedly, which Darrell now noticed were pencilled and arched like brackets. "Get away!" she taunted. "Not Shillingford, too. Well, whatever next!"

Again, Darrell felt the curdle of being a country bumpkin, and he looked at her, hurt into silence. Perhaps Shona noticed, too, because she was eyeing him carefully, as though baiting him into snapping back, but at that moment he became aware of one of the guests watching them from the hotel bar. It was Barry Harrison and he was signalling for another drink.

Darrell hurried through. Harrison wasn't a bad sort, but a bit on the vulgar side, which didn't always go down well with Jane, because, July and August apart, this really was quite a refined hotel. "Same again, Mr Harrison?"

Harrison nodded. He'd been very quiet since the dancing incident. He had, it was believed, a small company that laid floors and he was using the hotel as a base while he worked the entire North Devon coast looking for business. He'd already done Cornwall and the Torquay area. But the gossip was that his company wasn't doing very well. Darrell was under strict instructions from Jane not to let him run up a large bar bill.

Harrison took the new whisky and soda, rattled the ice in the glass, then, looking past Darrell, he indicated Shona who was now back on the stepladder adjusting the heart. "You want to get stuck in there, boy," he said.

Darrell was embarrassed. "She's not my type," he replied quietly, afraid that Shona might have heard, and not at all sure that he even had a type.

"Come on, it's winking at you," Harrison smirked. "Did you know that the heart-shape Valentine symbol, the thing that Cupid shoots his arrow through, isn't that shape because the ancient doctors thought a heart looked like that. They knew what hearts looked like, all right. The heart was originally drawn that shape because it was meant to represent a woman's you know what. Did you know that?"

Darrell could feel himself blushing. No, he didn't know that. And he didn't want to hear it. It was embarrassing when someone as old as Mr Harrison got smutty. "Will you be wanting a wake-up call, Mr Harrison?" he asked quickly.

Harrison shook his head, warming to his theme. "Then there's the arrow. Think about it, Darrell. There it goes all of a quiver right into the heart that isn't really a heart. God! When I was your age I was like a walking advert for the rampant sexual orgies of Sodom and Gomorrah. Well, p'raps, not so much of the Sodom," he corrected himself. "That was more down Brighton way . . ." He laughed at that, then continued, "But girls? I couldn't get enough. And nor could they."

Darrell had heard enough. "Well, if you don't mind, I'm not exactly looking for rampant sex orgies at the moment," he said, and went back into the hotel lobby.

From her ladder Shona watched him, quiet now. He knew she'd been listening.

The older man followed. "Sorry if I've upset you," he pretended, a bit drunk, mock contrite. "Just a little joke . . ."

Darrell concentrated on sorting out the hearts and Valentine banners, wishing that Harrison would go back into the bar or to bed and leave him alone with Shona. Heaven alone knew what he'd say next.

But at that moment the front door opened with a slap of cold air, and the pianist and young woman from London hurried in out of the rain, laughing, their faces and shoulders soaked.

"I wonder, can you do me a very great favour?" The woman approached Darrell. "Could you open the hotel shop and sell me a decent umbrella and cagoule?" She was in much brighter spirits than she'd been a couple of hours earlier.

122

"Of course." Darrell was already halfway across the lobby to the little shop, noticing that she was deliberately ignoring Harrison's presence, while Harrison was taking a great interest in a painting of a stag in a mist, which hung on a wall over a radiator.

There actually wasn't much choice in the shop, burgundy or blue in cagoules and just one umbrella, which had *North Devon Riviera* in script down one side. The guest wasn't the fussy type. She chose the blue cagoule.

"Can I put it on my bill?" she asked.

"Actually, I'm afraid head office in Bristol say we have to take payment for the shop separately," Darrell said. "It's a different account."

She pulled out a credit card. "That's fine."

Darrell swiped the card, and, as she signed, packed the cagoule into a bag. He was aware now that Mr Harrison was watching the couple through a mirror next to the fireplace, while Shona was observing everything from her stepladder. Both seemed to be caught in suspended animation.

Then, wishing everyone goodnight, even Harrison, who pretended not to hear, the guests went up the wide staircase together.

As soon as they were out of earshot, Harrison sprang to life, his face a contorted freckle of exasperation. "Did you see that?" he snorted, staring up the stairs. "I pump up the tyres. He rides the bloody bike."

On her stepladder, Shona giggled.

They reached Tim's door first. Amy stopped. "Well, thank you for the drink. I really enjoyed it."

"Thanks for being an audience," Tim returned. He pulled out his key.

She moved along the landing a little and then stopped, with a sudden thought. "Will you be calling Amanda tonight?"

"I'll probably email her. It's easier." He hesitated. "What about you?"

"Me?" She was surprised.

"Don't you have someone to call?"

For a second, Amy wondered if she'd accidentally admitted to something. "Did I say I had?"

Tim shrugged. "No. But if you have, and you believed in surprises, there might be something good waiting for you on your voicemail if you call home. Goodnight." And with a grin he opened his door and went into his room.

Amy was already pulling her mobile phone from her pocket as she reached her door. She'd turned it off hours ago. How could she have forgotten? What had she been thinking of? Teddy could have been trying to reach her all evening. Closing the door behind her she tapped into her voicemail.

You have no messages, came the reply.

Tim stared at his laptop screen. *You have no email,* it read.

He threw his coat on to the bed and sat down at his keyboard amid the litter of discarded manuscript. What had she said? "Why do you do it?"

Why did he do it?

Eleanor listened to the regular breathing from the darkness across the bed. Neither of them had slept much the previous night, but this evening, a little light-headed from dinner when, in nervousness, he'd had more red wine than he was used to, Michael had dropped off quickly. She was relieved. He'd spent the day trying to convince them both that they were happy. It hadn't worked. Before they'd married they'd been unembarrassed to fall silent in each other's company, the sort of silence that comes from a mutual confidence. But now they were inventing conversations, commenting, in little blind alleys, on the ever more mundane. Only now, with Michael no longer awake and worried, could she recognize him again, the quiet man who liked his country walks and detective novels, his historical biographies and television football, the man with whom she'd fallen in love.

She peered through the blackness of the bed trying to make out his features. How easy it would have been for her to move across to him. But she couldn't. She thought about the nurses in the hospital and how she'd been shocked by the things she'd overheard them laughing about, telling each other what they'd done or would like to do. Now she envied them their honesty.

She'd never been honest about her desires, but for so long her life had been lived more in her imagination than in reality. She'd liked her daydreams, reliving her childhood while she did her convent chores, remembering herself as a quiet, unremarkable girl from a village in Norfolk, and trying to remember the moment that had led her to believe she might have a vocation. Her mother and sisters had been confused when she'd told them. Her father had wept. What she hadn't known in the convent was whether she was really happy. It wasn't a prison. She wasn't in an enclosed order. This wasn't the Middle Ages. She went out and saw the world. She could have left at any time. But for some reason she'd chosen not to. Occasionally, the spectre of an alternative life had occurred, and she'd wondered how things might have been if perhaps just one tiny circumstance in her history had been different. But she hadn't reflected too much on that because it suggested ingratitude for all the good things that had happened and the good fortune she'd had.

And then she'd met Michael, and, with her life consumed with thoughts of him, had found herself longing for the road not taken.

CHAPTER
THIRTEEN

Jane ran her hands like smoothing irons down her dark brown skirt, first across her stomach then her hips and thighs. She did it every morning, each day with the same mantra: "No, no, no." But already it was too late for the Valentine's Ball and for the new dress she'd bought specially for it at Monsoon in Exeter. She would be slimmer by the summer, she reassured herself. She would wear it then, at the Midsummer's Eve dinner dance. With those short sleeves it would look better in the summer anyway, the blue nicely offset by tanned arms, even if her tan rarely amounted to more than the colour of marinated salmon. An unwelcome thought hovered as she chose her shoes for the day. Would she still be here in the summer? Would head office keep her on if this spring's figures didn't improve? She couldn't be certain. "Special events," had been the cry twenty months ago when she'd been sent to North Devon, leap-frogging others more qualified in the chain. But with a tiny budget and a wet summer in the South West it had been impossible to transubstantiate events into profits. And all the time self-doubt grew. Personalities made successful managers. Was she just not up to the job?

Turning away from the mirror, satisfied that she looked sufficiently officer class, she pulled on her jacket, left her flat and went downstairs into the main part of the hotel to let the dog out. At the back of her mind the lyrics to "Smoke Gets In Your Eyes" circulated as she watched him tear around the small closed garden in between the hotel and the now, largely empty, staff wing. The humiliation of the previous evening still stung. She'd made a mistake with the pianist. He hadn't wanted to play, but she'd demanded an "event", something special to put in her report to Bristol. She was embarrassed now, as she'd been jealous when it had been the pretty guest, and not her, who'd gone off for a drink with him. In a life of hotels, of watching and waiting, she hadn't often been the one chosen.

She let the dog in again and filled his bowl with water. There were two days to go before the Valentine's Ball, she mused as she watched him lapping thirstily. It would have to be the best ever or she might as well start looking for another job.

Tim was sitting alone by the window, deep in thought, when Amy reached the breakfast buffet. Beyond him, most of the rest of the dining-room had been roped off, while at the far end Darrell and Shona were on a low stage preparing to hang a long banner across one wall.

Collecting her coffee, melon, fruit juice and toast she hesitated for a moment, considered an empty table, then, making a decision, approached him. "Is it all right if I join you?" she asked. It might have seemed rude to have sat elsewhere; on the other hand, was it presumptuous to assume he'd want to share a table?

Tim looked up. "Oh, yes! Of course! Please!" he said, quickly clearing a space for her. His smile told her she'd made the right decision. "No room service for us today, eh!" A note had been slipped under the guests' doors the previous night explaining that as the staff were busy with preparations for the Valentine's Ball it wouldn't be possible for breakfast to be served in the rooms for the rest of the week.

"I would have come down, anyway," Amy said, sitting down and arranging her place. This was the one day of the mid-week when there was no *Teddy Farrow Show*. "How's the head this morning?"

Tim tapped his bandage gently with a finger. "Thick and empty."

"But with new encouragement?"

He didn't follow. "Sorry?"

"From Amanda," she reminded.

"Oh, yes, right!" he said vaguely. "Yes! Lots of encouragement. And you? A nice surprise?"

He's fibbing, she thought, and she wondered why. But now it was her turn. "Oh . . . yes!" And she wondered if she was as obvious in her lie as he'd been in his.

They went silent for a moment as though each wished they could restart the conversation. Amy sipped her coffee and Tim watched Shona and Darrell unroll the banner. "So, it's official then," he said as Darrell tacked it into place.

"What's official?"

He indicated the banner with his eyes.

Amy swivelled in her chair. "Love makes the world go round," she read aloud, then, turning back to her breakfast, thoughtfully cut into her melon. "Maybe. But I'm not sure it's necessarily true down here." She hadn't heard from Teddy since she'd arrived.

"No?"

She smiled, playfully. "You mean you haven't noticed?"

He shook his head. "They tell me my nickname at school is Dopey Plonker, and I don't think it's because the kids think I'm a musical crack fiend, but no, I haven't noticed."

She took a long look around the dining-room and its scattering of guests. "Well, basically, it seems to me, this hotel has all the symptoms of a designated romance-free zone," she said. "Those two, for instance . . ." She indicated Darrell and Shona. "He's infatuated."

Tim nodded. "I think so. And she doesn't realize?"

"Oh, she realizes all right. She just doesn't know what to do about it."

"Well, she's a strange girl."

"Then there's . . ." Amy's eyes now flicked to Michael and Eleanor, who, having just arrived, were standing at the breakfast buffet nervously making their choices.

"Don't tell me. Honeymoon hell?" Tim said softly.

"Purgatory at the very least."

Now it was Tim's turn to look around, his eyes quickly passing the dancing crooner in the brown suit

130

who was sulking over his fried eggs, sausages and bacon, and Jane, the manager, who was pointedly ignoring him. Finally, he reached the elderly couple. "They seem happy enough," he offered as he watched the old lady buttering her husband's toast.

Amy examined them. It was true. This woman was contented. She had a grace in jolliness. "They must know the secret," she said at last.

"Ah, there's a secret?" He was playful now.

"I think there has to be, don't you?" she answered, wondering whether she would ever know such selfless devotion herself.

Tim smiled. His breakfast was finished. "Well, if you find out what it is . . ."

"I'll let you know."

He put his napkin on the table. "So, what are your plans for today?"

Amy reached for the brochures in her bag. "I was thinking of taking a look around when the rain stops," she said. "The forecast is better for this afternoon. Only occasional gales. What about you?"

"Oh . . . I . . ."

"You can come along, if you like." The invitation just slipped out.

She could see that Tim was surprised. So was she. For a moment he looked uncertain. "Well, I'd like to, but . . ."

She nodded, embarrassed now, backing off, wishing she hadn't made the suggestion. "I know," she said. "Your music won't write itself."

"I'm afraid not!" he laughed, getting up. "Enjoy your day. I hope it stays fine." And he loped off back to his room.

She got on with her breakfast, opened a tourist pamphlet on local sea birds, then closed it, and wondered why she felt disappointed.

At the end of the room Darrell and Shona admired their banner. It had obviously been used several times before, but now in one corner it bore Shona's embellishments — a cartoon of a naked Eve standing half behind a tree, holding out an apple to a bearded little Adam who was scratching his bare bottom in a quandary.

"I hope Jane doesn't notice," Darrell worried, though actually he was filled with admiration for Shona's skill with a felt-tip pen.

"We'll tell her it was on when we opened the box. That some rude, horrible person must have done it last year," Shona scoffed.

"You're a good drawer," Darrell said. She was, too, though he half expected to be hurt again with some sharp riposte.

He wasn't. For the first time since she'd arrived at the hotel, Shona looked genuinely pleased. "D'you think so? Thank you."

At that second, time stopped for Darrell. Shona was really pretty when she smiled. Then, awkward again, he began searching for stick-on hearts for the hotel windows. "Well, better be getting on . . ." he murmured.

132

"Darrell," Shona was loitering, "will you be sending any Valentines this year?"

Darrell didn't look up from his quest. "I dunno. I haven't given it much thought," he muttered. He'd never sent a Valentine card in his life.

"No?" Shona looked surprised. "Well, you should. Girls like to get Valentine cards. It makes them feel . . . you know . . ." And she opened wide her big pale eyes.

Darrell looked at her. He thought he knew what she meant, but if he was right, he wasn't sure his mother would approve.

"Anyway, I'll see you later," Shona said, and going across to the buffet she picked out a large piece of crispy bacon. Then, seeming to spill out of her maid's uniform at almost every step, she sauntered casually away towards the back stairs.

Darrell watched her go. She just doesn't care, he thought, imagining her eating the bacon on the stairs, and he hoped Jane didn't catch her. And then he calculated whether he would have time to go down to the card shop in town during his afternoon break.

Still at her table, Amy considered the electric-green screen of her new camera phone, and for a zany moment imagined turning it on herself and sending Teddy a photograph showing her new look. She didn't, of course. Instead, she waited until the dining-room was almost empty, certainly until everyone else was out of earshot, and then made her call.

The message service answered yet again. This wasn't usual. Was it the Press that Teddy was trying to avoid, or her? No, she refused to believe that.

She whispered a message. "Hello, it's me, just to say . . . 'hello', wondering if you got my call about my new phone, and the number. The phone's one of those fancy ones that does everything . . . Anyway that's all. Er . . . bye." Then, as an afterthought, she repeated the number.

She felt wretched. Why ask, when you can beg?

CHAPTER
FOURTEEN

Will Abbott scribbled rapidly on an envelope. "Great! Terrific. Well done, Jerry. I'll make sure the cheque's a big one. Thanks." He put down the phone. "Yes!" he exulted to himself, football style.

On his way to the morning conference across the floor, assistant editor McKenzie noticed. He changed direction. "So?"

"We've found her. Amy Miller used a credit card to buy a mobile phone yesterday and again last night at a hotel, in Devon . . . under her full name Amelia Ann Millerton."

McKenzie nodded without expression. It wasn't like him, or any of the back-bench executives, to show enthusiasm. Highly paid tabloid reporters like Abbott were expected to find whoever they were looking for. "So, let's not frighten her off this time, all right!" he said brusquely, and strode on.

Abbott watched him go, murmured "Prat!" to himself, and cast a brief but grateful thought towards Polly the snitch and her *Silas Marner* inspiration. Then, looking across the editorial floor towards the picture desk, he considered Suzy. Sitting on an empty desk, she was leafing through a large book and amusing a couple of other photographers who were awaiting assignments.

Casually he made his way over to her. "What's that?" he asked, indicating the book. The photographers turned away, sensing this might not be a conversation they were expected to contribute to.

"Oh, just some freebie the miseries on the women's page gave me." She smelled good.

He took the book from her and read the jacket notes. *The Ladder of Sex. Climb the ladder of sexual fulfilment. Chapter by chapter, you, too, can learn the mysteries of perfect physical love.*

"It's a guide book," she said, her eyes never leaving his.

"So I see. Fancy a few days in Devon?"

She didn't answer for a moment, holding her head slightly back and to one side: a confident look. "Work?"

"What else?"

She shrugged. "OK."

Abbott passed *The Ladder of Sex* back to her. "You should bring this with you. It might be useful."

She didn't even raise an eyebrow.

CHAPTER
FIFTEEN

He tried working at first, a couple of hours at his keyboard, but nothing he wrote satisfied him. It wasn't bad, he didn't think, but it wasn't good either. He didn't know what it was. Getting up, he opened the book on film scores he'd bought in the town. Writing film music had been his dream when he'd been younger, using a theme in different ways to mirror and highlight different actions and emotions on the screen. What a life that would be, he used to think. But it hadn't happened. Not yet, anyway. A section on how Francis Lai wrote the theme music for the film *A Man and a Woman* caught his attention. Amanda thought it was sentimental and silly. He liked it because it was sentimental and silly. He liked the movie, too.

He turned back to his keyboard. But once again he couldn't concentrate.

The closing and locking of a door further down the corridor distracted him. He knew it wouldn't be Michael and Eleanor. They'd gone out already. Light footsteps passed in the corridor outside.

He stared at his keyboard.

"Is it too late to have second thoughts?" he called as she climbed the path away from the hotel towards the cliffs.

She turned, surprised. "What changed your mind?"

"Edward Elgar, probably," he answered, catching up, thinking quickly.

"Elgar?"

"Well, there he was writing all that wonderful music that we always associate with the beauty of England, and there I was cooped up inside when it was all around me waiting to be discovered."

"And your own music?"

"For the time being . . . unfinished."

"An unfinished symphony, you might say."

Tim pulled a face. "You might, I wouldn't. Unplugged at best."

She laughed. Then threading their way through the pine grove around the hotel, they set off through the gorse bushes along a muddy path, the beach of wet shingle and pebbles far below, above them the winter brown of the moors. Soon the sun grew clearer as they climbed, lighting up their faces if not exactly warming them, and it occurred to Tim that he felt comfortable. More than that, he felt happy. It puzzled him.

"Aren't you glad that I tempted you away from your work?" Amy asked. They'd been walking in single file for a little way along the cliff path and now that it had widened, they'd stopped to enjoy the curving scallop cut of the bay below. With the light blinking off the sea, and the line of the South Wales hills clear across the

Bristol Channel, the entire world seemed in sharper focus today.

Tim nodded. "Actually, it wasn't very difficult to drag me away," he owned up as they walked on. "I was having trouble concentrating."

"Ah . . ."

"When it's going well . . ."

"Nothing can drag you away, right?"

"Something like that. You know what it's like?"

She hesitated, and then said, "I have friends who write." She did, too. But she quickly changed the subject as a very woolly sheep suddenly appeared, seemed about to challenge them for the right to the path and then, thinking better of it, scrambled nervously off into the heather. "This competition you've entered . . . what is it exactly?"

Tim flicked a stone out of his way with his shoe. "God knows."

"Shouldn't you?" She sounded surprised.

"Yes, well, I suppose I should try to pay more attention. It was Amanda's idea. It's for what they call 'new composers'."

"And is that good?"

He touched his bandage unhappily. It was, Amy noticed, beginning to become slack and slightly grubby. "To be honest, I don't know. It's a sort of post-modern thing."

"I see." For Amy anything with the words "post modern" attached signalled time to talk about something else.

But Tim hadn't finished. "Post structural, too," he suddenly added.

"Yes?"

"Post harmonic, even . . ." he conceded next and smiled to himself.

"Ah." She was amused, too, as he played with the thought.

"Post rhythmic, as well, come to think of it." The litany was turning into a chant. "Post tone . . . post cadence . . . post melody, post . . ." He ran out of ideas.

"Early for Christmas?" she offered.

She was expecting him to laugh, but he didn't. "Without the 'Jingle Bells' bit. That would be too much like a tune for them," he reflected quietly. And as they stopped walking again he stared unhappily at the flashing light on a buoy that marked some submerged rocks beyond the next headland. "Sorry," he said quietly.

"There's nothing to be sorry for." She changed the subject. "Amanda sounds very . . . forward looking."

"She has ambitions for me."

"That's good — to have someone who believes in you — right?" She meant that. For all his declarations of love, and all his passion in the making of that love, Teddy rarely talked about her books. In moments of debasement she wasn't sure that he'd ever read one, not cover to cover. She'd never made an issue of it. The novels she wrote didn't have middle-aged professional male television stars among their target readership. But it still hurt.

Tim didn't reply because as they rounded a large overhanging rock a painted sign came into view. "Here you go! *Lovers' Leap*," he read as they approached it. "Isn't this where you get off?"

She was surprised. Holding on to the post she leaned forward and, looking over the side of the cliff, watched the seagulls riding the convection currents. "You think so?" she said carefully. "I'm not a broken-hearted lover. Do I look like one?" Perhaps she did.

"No, but after hearing your breakdown on the nuclear freeze in the romantic life of the hotel this morning, I don't think you're in the paper business either."

What was he saying? "No?"

"No way. You're running a lonely hearts club, setting up a dating agency at the very least. Or you should be. You're a born romantic."

She was relieved. "All right! If wanting people not to be lonely or unhappy makes me a romantic, I'm a romantic. Isn't everyone? I bet Amanda is."

Did he frown slightly then or did she imagine it? "Actually, Amanda's a flirt more than a romantic," he said.

"Men like that in a girl, don't they? Being flirty, I mean."

"When she's someone else's girl they love it," he said quickly, and set off down the path again.

She didn't mention Amanda for the rest of their walk. She'd touched a nerve. Instead, though she was usually disinclined to talk much about herself, she told him about her mother, whom she saw rarely, but who

141

now lived virtually on a golf course in Connecticut. While for his part, Tim told her funny stories of playing in the bars, the observer who watched the nightly rituals of human mating, slyly adding an appropriate tune to his medley whenever he could think of one that might fit. "You'd be surprised how many feet unconsciously start tapping to 'White Flag' when you get a girls' night out."

"And what do the boys respond to?"

"They don't. Boys like records, not tunes played on a piano. In the bars they're either too busy drinking or too busy pulling. They aren't easily distracted."

It was the prettiest of walks, but still very wet in places, especially when they dropped down from the moors, and returned towards the hotel through the grey haze of a leafless birch forest in the fold of a gorge.

They were in sight of the roofs of the town when Amy's new mobile finally rang. She jumped, she was so surprised. "I'm sorry, I'll just . . ." Already her hand was in her pocket.

"That's OK," Tim said and walked on a little way to the edge of a waterfall.

She'd already checked the caller's number on her screen. "Hello? Hello, how are you?"

"Hi, Amy . . ." Teddy's voice was back to its usual nonchalant confidence.

"How are *you*? I wasn't sure you'd got my messages."

"I'm sorry. I just never got a moment alone to call, but I . . ."

She didn't need explanations. "Teddy, d'you think if I came back now they'd still be on my doorstep?"

There was an intake of breath down the line. "Well . . . I don't know. Yes, probably. You know how the Press are. You're not enjoying it down there, right?"

He sounded so casual she was almost angry. "Well, hiding from the tabloids wasn't exactly how I planned to spend my thirties."

"Yes, I know . . . it must be a drag, but maybe in a couple of days . . . after the weekend —" He stopped abruptly. "Oh, Christ!"

She could sense that someone had entered the room he was in. She wept inwardly. "Teddy . . ."

His voice was now very low. "Look, I've got to go." He stopped again. Then: "I'll call you later, OK. Bye." And he was gone without giving her time to reply.

"Goodbye," she said to no one.

She needed a moment to collect herself. She could feel her eyes brimming, and wiped them on her sleeve. Ahead of her, Tim still waited by the waterfall.

"All right?" he asked kindly when at last she rejoined him.

She sniffed and tried a smile. "He had to go."

"Ah!"

They began to meander on.

"He usually does," she explained after a moment.

"Busy chap."

She nodded. And then, angry that she had to blink back tears, she added, "I'm sorry."

"Don't be."

"It's just the Lovers' Law of the Eternal See-Saw."

143

He didn't get that.

"You know. Me on the ground . . ."

Now he did. "Him in mid-air. Stephen Sondheim, 'Send In The Clowns'?"

"Right. The see-saw's never in perfect equilibrium. Not when it comes to relationships. Not when it comes to love. Do you know what I mean?"

He thought about that. "Yes, I think I do."

She smiled an acknowledgement of his empathy, and then together they turned to cross a small iron bridge that spanned the gorge, twenty feet or so above the fast-flowing river.

For a few minutes they watched the cascades of water bouncing and leaping off rocks and boulders. "Can I ask a favour?" she said quietly at last.

"Of course."

"Well, you see, I've always wanted to play the piano. You couldn't give me a lesson, when you have a minute, could you?"

CHAPTER
SIXTEEN

It had been an accidental discovery, but Michael felt almost furtive. The dead hour before dinner had driven them from the cherubs and jet bath of the honeymoon suite, and now, while Eleanor searched through the souvenirs at the back of the tiny hotel shop for a present for Sister Catherine, Michael was sifting through the postcards. He'd already chosen a couple showing impossibly sunny beaches and rose-garlanded Devon villages, when he reached the saucy seaside selection. When he'd worn his black suit and clerical collar he'd rarely noticed them and certainly never studied them. They'd been considered rude in his childhood, and he would have been embarrassed to have been seen chuckling over illustrations of red-cheeked women, all bosoms and bottoms, when he became a priest. But he was a married man now.

A cartoon drawing of an unhappy shipwrecked mariner sitting on a desert island beside a beautiful mermaid, her blonde hair falling around D-cup breasts, made him smile. *I don't know what you mean when you say you still miss the better half*, the mermaid was saying, swishing her fish's tail coquettishly.

"What's the joke, Michael?" Eleanor was at his side.

Michael felt himself blushing. "Oh, just a silly thing."

Eleanor looked innocently at the cartoon. For a long moment it seemed that she didn't get the joke. Then she obviously did. Her mouth suddenly sagged as though she'd been insulted. Immediately she tried to hide it. "Yes!" she said, faking amusement. "Yes! Funny!" Then hurriedly she showed him a plate depicting a couple of yearling deer grazing on the moors. "Do you think Catherine would like this? She's very fond of animals."

"It's very nice," Michael said.

"Yes," Eleanor said again. And crossing the hotel lobby she put the plate down on the reception desk and looked in her handbag for her money.

Michael put the mermaid back in her rack.

The scream could have been heard in Taunton.

"What is it?" Shona demanded, rushing into the kitchen, Giles, the dog, bouncing after her.

But before there was any answer, sous-chef Agnieszka had scrambled on to the kitchen stool and was pointing in horror into a corner. Giles didn't need any directions, immediately beginning to play football with something on the red-tiled floor, barking and yelping with excitement.

"What's he got?" Shona asked, as Darrell grabbed at the dog's collar and tried to pull him back. Domingos, the chef, stood watching, a knife in his hand, an expression of deep distaste on his face.

Then Shona saw it. A huge black spider, a truly vast one, was struggling with its five remaining legs to get away from the tormenting dog, limping away across the floor.

"My God! It's bigger than the Gdansk shipyards," Agnieszka gasped, her face screwed in disgust, her hands clutching her skirt at her knees.

"I'll get it!" Shona offered quickly.

"And get that dog out of here. This is a kitchen not a pet shop!" snapped Domingos in defence of his territory.

Struggling with the still straining, snapping dog, Darrell pushed Giles out of the kitchen and closed the door.

Carefully Shona picked up the spider in a sheet of paper towel.

"Ugh!" Agnieszka moaned from the stool.

Domingos looked across at her, amused by her reaction. "They don't have spiders in Poland? Come on! In Amazonia . . ." And he held out the fingers of his hand to their fullest extent and wiggled them at her. "As big as your hand! Furry legs, too."

Agnieszka looked sick and said something to him in Polish. It sounded very rude. Domingos just laughed.

Shona watched them. He enjoyed baiting her, it was obvious. Did she secretly like it? It was hard to tell. Returning to the spider, she folded the paper towel into a little pouch and headed towards the kitchen door. "I'll put it outside," she said, and stepped out into the courtyard. From inside the paper she could feel the spider still wriggling. "Sorry about this, fella, but you should have kept out of sight," she said as she hurried across to the staff accommodation and up the stairs.

"See what I've got for you today," she said out loud as she entered her bedroom. Then kneeling by the bed she pulled out her glass box. "How about this for a treat, then?" And she tipped the spider into the box.

Romance.

Amy stared at the word on her laptop screen. Tim had called her a romantic. Of course she was. But what exactly was romance? She began to write.

Romance. Scientists explain it as a sudden flow of an endorphin called oxytocin to the brain; evolutionists consider it a trick by nature in order to persuade us to perpetuate our genes; teenagers think it's not noticing each other's pimples, and cynics call it sex through rose-tinted condoms.

She hesitated, running the sound of Teddy's voice through her imagination as it had sounded on her mobile that afternoon. Had she dreamed it or had there really been a slight sigh of impatience? Better not to think about it.

Returning to her laptop she read her notes again and then added:

But something that hurts so much can't just be sex, can it?

Then, because she really needed to think, she went to run the water for a very long bath before dinner.

In the Exmoor Suite, Tim was waiting for the hotel operator in Denver.

"I'm sorry, sir. I'm getting no answer. She must have gone out. I'll put you through to her message box."

"Thank you . . ." he said. Then he stopped. "On second thoughts, don't bother. It doesn't matter. Goodbye." And he hung up.

A few minutes later he slipped out of his room and pushed a sheet of the hotel stationery under the next door but one. On it he'd written:

I was wondering if instead of sitting at separate tables we might make it easier for the staff tonight and share one. Just a thought. Tim.

CHAPTER
SEVENTEEN

"Not a bad little hideaway as hideaways go." Will Abbott sat at the wheel of his black, second-hand Porsche at the back of the car park and surveyed the North Devon Riviera Hotel standing white in spotlights against the night sky. Above the car the pine trees swayed in the sea breeze. From the passenger seat Suzy stretched out a hand and ran a finger along the crease in his trousers at the top of his thigh. He felt his eyes flicker slightly at her touch. This was the fifth time she'd done that since they'd left London four hours earlier. He'd never known such a sensuous woman. Well, not recently. He glanced across at her. She was smiling at him. With difficulty now, because the car was small, she began to pull on her denim jacket over her T-shirt. It hardly fitted. Abbott looked back at the hotel. "Not a bad little hideaway at all," he repeated.

From inside the hotel the sound of a gong reverberated across the car park.

"That's for the entire Valentine's weekend, I assume?" the hotel manager asked as an elderly woman wheeled an old man in a chair past them through the lobby towards the dining-room.

Abbott nodded. Suzy tapped one of her expensive boots into which her jeans were tucked. They were hardly walking boots, it occurred to him.

"Jolly good. I'm afraid our porter is helping to serve dinner at the moment, but . . ."

"We can manage quite easily, thank you." Abbott responded, picking up a bag. Apart from Suzy's cameras and modem, hidden inside her case, they were travelling light. They weren't here to enjoy the sights.

"If you're quite sure. Your room is on the first floor, just over the dining-room, up the stairs and to the left . . ." A key slid across the desk. "We take orders for dinner until nine."

"Thank you." Abbott was taking up the key when a peripheral movement on the stairs caught his eye. A man and an attractive woman were coming down. He looked casually away, waited until the couple had passed, and then followed Suzy up the stairs. Her expression had never altered.

Only when they were alone on the landing did he allow himself the smile of the triumphant. "Got her!" he whispered. "She's got new hair, too."

"Who was the guy with her? It certainly wasn't Teddy Farrow."

Abbott shrugged. "Gay cover. That droopy bandanna said it all." Then finding their room he opened the door for her, and followed her in. "We'd better get down quickly for dinner."

Suzy flopped back on the very large bed. "Are you sure?"

"What?"

"Well, if we're going to do this right . . . not rouse suspicions like, shouldn't we take our time?"

Abbott looked at her. "Well . . . I don't know . . ."

But already Suzy was pulling from her bag the book which, with the help of a map-reading torch, she'd been looking at on the drive down to Devon, *The Ladder of Sex*. "It starts getting really interesting in Chapter Nine," she said. "One to Eight aren't bad either, but a bit routine! What d'you think?" And as an invitation she smoothed out a crease on the patchwork counterpane alongside her with the palm of her hand.

Amy looked around the quiet of the dining-room as Darrell reset a table for two. Tonight, the murmur was even more hushed than usual as eyes were on them. By the window the old lady said something to her husband and smiled, while the two elderly women in floral dresses carefully considered the new dining arrangement. "You know, I have a sneaking feeling that we might just have become . . ." she began.

". . . a talking point?" Tim finished. "I hope so. After the music I made them endure they deserve some light entertainment."

"I won't disappoint them, if you don't."

And, as Darrell lit a candle and stepped back from the table, they sat down.

"What did you do with the spider?" Amy heard Darrell whisper as Shona passed with a tray.

"Just don't eat the boeuf bourguignon," Shona hissed back, and, flouncing on, put a plate down with a flourish in front of Barry of the brown suit. "One boeuf

152

bourguignon!" she gushed. "Enjoy!" And she marched back towards the kitchen.

Amy looked up at Darrell. He was staring at Harrison with a mixture of awe and dismay as the guest stuck his fork into a piece of black marinated meat and put it to his mouth. "I'll just get your water," he said, and hurried after Shona.

Putting aside whatever little games might be being played by the staff, she turned to Tim. "You never told me how long you intended staying here."

"I wasn't sure when I came."

"But you'll be here for the Valentine's Ball tomorrow night?"

"It's beginning to look that way."

She nodded to herself. "Well, at least there'll be someone else in the hotel not involved."

Tim smiled, then, in keeping with the other guests in the room, they both fell silent, watching as Michael and Eleanor entered the room and made their way to the next table. Even with an easy-going companion like Tim, Amy thought, dinner at the North Devon Riviera Hotel could still be a serious matter.

A murmur close by soon caught their attention. It was Michael making the sign of the cross. "In the name of the Father and of the Son and of the Holy Ghost," he began.

"Amen," responded Eleanor, her voice just audible, too. The honeymooners were staring at their soup in contemplation.

"Do they say grace at your school?" Amy whispered.

"Actually, they're bigger on the last rites."

Amy giggled.

"Bless us, Oh Lord, for these Thy . . ." Michael began.

Suddenly he stopped as a low, rhythmic, pumping sound interrupted the hush of the dining-room. Eleanor looked up from her folded hands.

At their table Amy looked around. "Can you hear that?" she asked. Tim looked up. The rhythm faded. Amy shrugged.

Alongside, Michael continued his grace. "These Thy gifts which we are about to —"

The thumping sound came again, but now louder and more urgent. Again, Michael stopped.

Oh, no, Amy thought, recognizing the rhythm.

Facing her, Tim put a hand to his bandage, covering his face. When he took it away their eyes met in amused embarrassment.

Michael still hesitated in confusion. The sound faded once more and then returned even louder. At the door to the kitchen, Darrell had stopped with a tray and was looking up. Next to him, Shona was giggling. By the window, the old lady was smiling and nudging the old man in his chair, while Barry in brown had stopped eating in amazement. Only Eleanor looked puzzled.

Michael struggled to finish: ". . . which we are about to receive from Thy bounty —"

But at that moment a woman's distant cry interrupted.

"Was that a seagull, Michael?" Amy heard Eleanor ask.

Tim was now smiling.

Amy bit her lip as the cry grew louder and more desperate. It was like one of those moments at school when she'd got the giggles. The more she tried to hide it the worse it got.

Michael, meanwhile, was still staring at his soup, his face reddening. At last Eleanor seemed to realize what was happening. Her expression was one of confused surprise, as though she was trying to make sense of something foreign.

"Someone got lucky," a woman's voice said behind Amy. It was the Polish sous-chef talking to Shona at the door to the kitchen.

Hearing her, Barry grinned: "That'll give them an appetite." And he guffawed, eyeing Agnieszka.

She ignored him, as across the room the old lady's face twinkled with fun. Even her husband seemed to be smiling about something not quite forgotten.

By now, Amy's face was in her napkin.

"Are you all right?" Tim asked.

She couldn't answer. Tears were rolling down her cheeks which she was desperately trying to hide from Michael and Eleanor.

Michael wasn't giving in. As the final sob of relief broke in the room above he made one last effort: "Through Christ, Our Lord."

"Amen," murmured Eleanor.

At which point, Giles, the dog, began to howl, too.

In their bedroom above the dining-room, Suzy languidly opened her eyes.

Alongside her lay Abbott. He'd been around quite a bit, and seen all those programmes about orgasms on late-night satellite TV. But nothing had quite prepared him for Suzy.

"Not bad, eh?" Suzy said, and stroked his bottom. "D'you think there's time for Chapter Ten before dinner?"

CHAPTER
EIGHTEEN

He was comfortable at a piano, confident. Just sitting at a keyboard made him feel empowered, his fingers finding the notes as though magnetically drawn to them. Here he could do anything, anything he wanted to, anyway. He was in control. As a boy he'd enjoyed his piano lessons, but best of all had been those evenings when, homework finished or skipped, he'd just sat and played, discovering new structures and where the notes might take him, while his parents and older sister had watched television in the next room. When he'd been a little older he'd sometimes played at parties in the houses of friends' parents when they were away. This was usually late at night after most people had gone home. He'd read somewhere that Billy Joel had done that and it had been a good way to get off with girls. It might have worked for Billy Joel, but Tim had never noticed it working for him. By the time he'd got around to playing, the remaining guests had usually been too out of it to notice. He hadn't minded. He'd never minded, not even at college when he'd been keyboard player with a student grunge band and had his contribution completely hidden by howling guitars and drums. He just liked playing. He could imagine the notes even if he couldn't hear them. Sometimes when they'd first got together, Amanda had watched and listened as he played. It was the most flattering thing she could have done. But then, she was a musician, too. She hadn't asked him to play for her for some time now. She'd been very busy.

Sharing the piano stool he could now feel the outline of his new pupil, the girl who liked to weigh everything before she answered, and who was having a tough time with some man she didn't want to talk about. It sounded a familiar story, but he hadn't told her that. She was a mystery to him, and probably he to her, if she thought much about him at all. But they got along in some carefree, indefinable way, both amused at the way the hotel was governed and staffed, and both intrigued by its winter guests and the situation in which they'd found themselves. It was good to have a new, albeit temporary, friend when the foundations of so much else seemed uncertain.

She'd asked for a lesson, so, driven by the giddiness of dinner, they'd soon found themselves at the Korean piano in the sitting room. It hadn't taken Tim long, however, to realize that what his pupil really wanted was to play without learning, certainly without practising. It wasn't an unfamiliar wish. "I think your best bet would be if we doubled up and played a duet," he said after a few minutes' dancing her around middle C and some basic chords.

"Yes. That's what I want," she said with a smile. She was still giggly; a bit drunk. "Like Elton John and Jools Holland do sometimes."

"Exactly like them!" he agreed. "Put your finger here." And taking her forefinger, he placed it on a note. Her hand was cold and he felt a tingle of intimacy as he touched her. Once again his reaction came as a surprise. "Now keep pressing on that note like this . . . like a pulse." With his finger on hers he began a steady rhythm. "And let's see how we get on."

Concentrating hard, she now kept the rhythm going as he began to play around her, building the tune as he went, moving her one finger up and down the keyboard as she, delighted, accompanied him. Occasionally he glanced at her, noticing for the first time the palest of marks on the sides of her nose where her glasses had pinched, and the slight vertical scar to one side of her eye. But when she caught him looking he glanced quickly back at the keyboard. "You've had lessons before, haven't you?" he teased by way of distraction. "See, you can already change key." And again he moved her finger as they wound their way through "Anything Goes".

"Ssh," she scolded. "I'm trying to concentrate."

They played on, songs by Cole Porter, Aimee Mann and Smokey Robinson, until in ones and twos the other guests made their way from the dining-room, and sank into the sofas and the faded cushions of wicker chairs to listen while waiting for their coffee. Apart from watching television there wasn't an awful lot more to do after dinner in mid-February in the North Devon Riviera Hotel.

Eleanor didn't know what to say. Actually, she didn't know what to think. She couldn't really remember what she'd expected marriage to mean just a few days earlier, but now she felt as though she was sailing further away from Michael as each day passed. She'd hardly eaten at dinner, longing for Michael to say something about what they'd both heard, to make a joke perhaps, because it had so evidently amused most of the other guests. But he hadn't been able to find the words.

Now they sat distantly together, aware of the fun being enjoyed at the piano across the room, but hardly listening. After a little while, a still smiling Shona served them coffee and a couple of After Eights. Slipping the dark mint chocolate from its black envelope, Eleanor bit off a corner. Then she put it down again, no appetite for luxuries.

Michael noticed. "Don't worry," he said at last, his voice low, although there was no one close enough to hear above the merry sound of the piano. "It'll get better."

It took her some moments to formulate an answer. "I feel like a relic from another age," she trembled. "Like the Latin mass."

She didn't look at him but she was aware of the line between his eyes deepening. "No," he protested. "Don't say that. That's just silly. Ridiculous."

"Ridiculous?" she repeated softly. "Two late-middle-aged virgins in a honeymoon suite, with a mirror over the bed, naked nymphs on the walls, a whirlpool in the bathroom, and adult videos on Channel Thirteen! *That's* ridiculous, Michael."

This time she saw the pain. Immediately she was sorry she'd spoken. That had been too unkind. He looked so defeated, so completely at a loss to know what to do. And for the first time she found herself hating her religion for misshaping their minds and needs, Michael's as well as hers, and for leaving them out of the real world for so long. But then just as quickly she made a short prayer asking for forgiveness for her momentary loss of faith. "I'm sorry, Michael," she said at last.

Michael watched the piano players.

Will Abbott was watching them, too, his eyes on Amy Miller, but mainly he was wondering where the guy next to her fitted in. He'd been sorry to find him with her. He might be a complication. It would have been easier if she'd been on her own. Mainly, however, at that moment he was telling lies. Standing in the semi-darkness in the doorway that linked the sitting room with the sun lounge, called the loggia in this hotel, his view partially obscured by the fronds of large date palms in pots, he was feigning world-weary boredom into his mobile phone. "No, it's a bit of a dump, really," he was saying. "The back of beyond, only worse." Then to a question: "I can't say really. I could be stuck down here all weekend. Yes, it's a shame, but you know what they're like. They don't care about any home life I might be missing as long as they get their story. Anyway, I'd better go. Kiss the boys for me. I'll call tomorrow. Goodnight, God bless." And hanging up he returned the phone to his jacket pocket.

Seeing that, Suzy moved towards him. She'd changed for dinner, a red shirt in exchange for a blue one, which fell apart at her belly button. She stood close, close enough for him to smell her. She smelled of scent and passion. Sex, actually. "All right?" she said.

He nodded.

She smiled to herself, one of those satisfied little smiles of quiet triumph that some girls wore when they thought they'd won a tiny skirmish over a sexual rival.

He didn't like it and turned away.

She moved closer, the top of her thigh resting against his.

He did like that.

"Then there's Chapter Eleven, 'The Wheelbarrow Position'," she murmured.

Abbott looked back at Amy Miller. He'd wait a while and keep watch on her before he confronted her. There was no hurry. He had all weekend.

They stopped at Tim's door, lingering in the corridor. She was still giggly. "Thank you *so* much. That was fantastic. I'm a pianist. My second greatest ambition fulfilled."

"Only your *second* greatest ambition?"

"Well, yes, I mean, if I could one day play in a band! At school I used to dream about being a member of Fine Young Cannibals. Or The Smiths. That would be the ultimate. Can you imagine!"

Actually, that was something Tim couldn't imagine, but why spoil things? "Well, they say nothing's impossible."

They both hesitated. She looked towards her door.

He took the hint. "Anyway . . ." he began, a stillborn beginning to a sentence.

"Yes . . ." she agreed, but didn't move. Then suddenly she leaned forward and tried to push a loose strand of his bandage, which was hanging down towards his right eye, back into place. It still didn't feel quite right. She tried again, then wagged her head. "No. It won't go. Look, can I return the favour?"

He didn't follow. "I'm sorry?"

"Your bandage. Perhaps I could . . . you know." Vaguely she made a circular movement with her hand. "I was a Girl Guide when I was twelve. For five weeks. We did elementary first aid."

"Oh!" He was surprised. "I mean, yes, please. Actually, I have a new bandage in my room. In my bag. It's been difficult for me to put it on."

She smiled. "I can see."

He was strangely embarrassed. Pulling his room key from his pocket, he opened the door for her to go in, glancing guiltily down the empty corridor before following her, although he had nothing to feel guilty about. Hotels could do that.

"Right," he said, putting on the overhead lights, "I'll just get the stuff they gave me in the hospital." And he went into the bathroom, leaving her to look around the room, which had been so quickly turned into a makeshift music factory.

When he returned she was toying soundlessly at the keyboard, pressing the single notes she'd just learned as

163

though imagining his contribution. He watched her for a couple of seconds.

When she looked up she was wearing an expression that said she felt rather silly. Quickly leaving the keyboard, she switched on a desk lamp, and turning around the chair on which he worked, she patted it. "Sit here," she indicated, taking the bandage from him.

He sat down.

Standing behind him she now very carefully unclipped the safety pin that was holding the bandage. "Tell me if I hurt you!" she said, beginning to unwind the bandage from his head.

"Actually, I think I'm pretty well immune to —" he began. "Ooh!" he gasped. The bandage had pulled the lint from the wound on the back of his skull.

"I'm sorry," she apologized. "There's a lump like Australia, well Tasmania, here. But the cut's healing. It's closed. Well, it was until I just opened it again. They could have killed you."

He laughed at that. "Not really. It was my fault. Playing them 'Romeo and Juliet' without the gang fights and stabbings. They probably thought they had to improvise their version of *West Side Story*." From the corner of his eye he saw the old, dirty bandage and bloodied lint drop into the bin on top of some abandoned pages of music manuscript. Then, as she carefully began to re-dress the wound, he felt strangely contented.

"You must be a good healer," she said as she worked her way through his hair.

"You're a good nurse."

"Not really."

He winced as she pulled the new bandage too tight. "No, well, you might be with practice," he added. The re-bandaging now progressed more slowly. For a few moments they didn't speak as she concentrated. Then: "This afternoon ..." he began. "That chap who phoned you ...?"

"Yes?"

"Is he in love with you?" Where the question came from he would never know.

"Yes."

"Good. That's nice."

He couldn't see her face, but he could feel the hesitation in her hands. "Actually, to be honest, I'm not sure if he is in love with me."

"Oh, I'm sure he is. He's bound to be." He surprised himself with that, too.

Perhaps she didn't notice because she suddenly said, "He's married."

"Yes." He'd assumed that.

"Yes," she repeated, and went back to her task. "And Amanda?"

Her question came when he thought that part of the conversation had ended. He thought about Amanda, pictured her pretty face and dark hair. "She's more than a flirt," he said at last.

There was the slightest movement behind him, as though she was shifting her weight from one foot to the other before she answered. "You don't know that."

Unfortunately he did know that. "She's away a lot. On tour."

"Oh, come on. That doesn't mean anything. Lots of people hardly ever see each other —"

He had to interrupt. In Amanda's case it did mean something. She'd always been careless with the evidence. Perhaps she wanted him to know. "It's someone in the strings," he said. "A cellist."

The bandaging had finished. Now she came to face him, perplexed. "But if you know that . . . I mean, if you're certain . . . I don't understand . . . why do you carry on?"

"Why?" It was a question he couldn't answer. Because he loved Amanda; because he didn't want to admit the failure of their relationship; because, despite everything, he didn't want it to end. People stayed with unfaithful partners all the time. Why? Because they were remembering when things were better, or because they were hoping for things to improve. Was it both or neither?

But then there was the music he was writing. *Why do you do it if it's so difficult?* That had been yesterday's question. He hadn't been able to give an answer then. But he knew now.

The new bandage was in place. His Girl Guide was watching him.

He didn't want this conversation to go any further. "Hey, that's pretty good!" he laughed. "Thank you."

She looked at her watch. "Good. Well, I'd better go." She went to the door. "Thank you for the piano lesson." She stopped as the door swung open. "I'm very glad I met you," she said. And with that she was gone.

Tim stroked his new bandage and stared at the door.

166

It was after midnight. The hotel was silent. Even the Shaggy Wallbangers, as Shona had immediately christened the newly arrived, seemed to have gone quiet for now. Darrell was still thinking about that. He'd never heard such a racket before, not even in the summer when he knew there were all kinds of goings-on. It had both embarrassed and excited him. Shona, of course, had taken it in her stride, which just went to show what kind of world she lived in, but Domingos and Agnieszka in the kitchen had been giggling about it all night. And that was strange, too, because they rarely spoke to each other, not civilly, anyway. What was it he'd read in the *Sun* about football and sex being the only true international languages?

Now the last chairs and tables had been cleared away in the dining-room to turn it into a ballroom, and he and Shona had stuck the last of Jane's red hearts to the last window panes.

"Well, that's about it for tonight, I think," he said, looking around the room with satisfaction, wishing he could think of something else for them to do together to prolong the moment. "We'll have to do the balloons tomorrow when they arrive."

Shona didn't appear to be listening. "You know something, Darrell . . ." She stopped.

"Something what?" he asked warily.

"Well, I was thinking, seeing all those hearts we've stuck up, it makes me feel quite romantic. D'you know what I mean?"

167

Darrell looked at her, expecting some put-down to follow. There wasn't one. She was smiling, more friendly than he'd ever seen her. "Well," he said studiously, "I imagine that's probably just the ozone in the air."

She frowned now, as though that wasn't the answer she'd expected. "What ozone?" she asked.

"Don't you know? It was in the *Reader's Digest*. Sea ozone makes everyone feel a bit, you know, fruity. It's a normal chemical reaction. It's the same with chocolate."

For a moment he thought she was going to laugh at him. But she didn't. "Will you dance with me at the ball tomorrow night, Darrell?" she suddenly blurted.

He couldn't have been more surprised. "Well, I dunno . . ." he began, looking away, awkward, rubbing his nose, although it wasn't really itchy.

She hadn't finished. "The last waltz, perhaps?"

"I've never done a waltz," he said. In truth, he'd never done any sort of dance with a girl. The limit of his experience had been a limp, solo, robotic effort on the periphery of the school disco. "A waltz is old fashioned, isn't it?"

She was having none of it. "A dead camel could manage the last waltz, Darrell. See, I'll show you."

And stepping up to him she put his right hand on her waist and taking the left one began to turn him around slowly on the spot. "I think you're meant to count 'one-two-three, one-two-three' as you go," she said, "but as we're only on the North Devon Riviera we can dispense with the formal niceties."

He didn't answer. He couldn't think what to say. He just grinned like a madman and looked into those bright blue, magnified eyes as she moved him in tiny circles around the dining-room, and felt her soft, round hip pressing into him when he was supposed to change direction.

"Not bad," she said at last as they paused for a second. "But we might have to rehearse a bit more if you're going to get the hang of it in time. Now, let's try again, one-two-three, one-two-three . . ."

CHAPTER
NINETEEN

She couldn't sleep. She was puzzled by a feeling she couldn't quite explain. Putting on the light she felt around for the TV remote, but then changed her mind. She didn't need television. She wanted to write, though she wasn't sure what or why. Reaching for her laptop, she sat up in bed, thinking about her piano lesson and absently tapping the space bar as though it were a note. At last, impatient to see the words, because she knew that with the words would come fresh thoughts, she put down whatever came into her head.

So, love, as we all agree, is an evolutionary mechanism. But it's also the decoration we give to our lives. It's a comedy, a tragedy, a sport and a farce. It's biological, psychological, chemical, olfactory and blind. It can be promiscuous and fleeting, or lifelong and exclusive, as is the case with sea horses and beavers, although not usually the ones illustrated in *Playboy* magazine. (Bad joke!!) There's secret love, and imaginary, illusionary, delusional, selfish, generous, demanding, supplicating, painful or life-enhancing love, sometimes all at the same time. Love can be lonely and crippling, or euphoric and joyful. It can also be erotic or chaste, exotic or quixotic, both faithful and treacherous, platonic, heroic, shared, one-sided, addictive, hallucinatory, a game two can play, a three-in-a-marriage Princess Diana style, or a dream for one more vivid than reality. It can hurt, it can bite, and it can be cosy and warm; a fairy tale or a nightmare, sensible or irrational, idealized and unrealized. It can be all of these things. And none. And sometimes it dare not speak its name. It can, they say, help heal people, and, if deaths from broken hearts are to be believed, kill people, too. It can be lustful or companionable, provide the will to live and the inspiration for great and not so great works of art, and when it really gets going it can instigate murder and suicide, even war — although frankly some of us find the Helen of Troy story a bit hard to believe, especially after seeing the film. All the same, most of the time it can cripple the lovelorn, and everyone has experienced those long, clammy, sleepless nights, with sheets soaked from worry and tears. But on the good days, on the days when it works, when the see-saw is in balance, and adoration and desire are met and returned . . . is there any feeling better in the entire world?

She stopped writing, wondering where she fitted into all this, and if Teddy had a place at all. And lastly she thought again about Tim and her piano lesson.

Laying her laptop down on the carpet beside her bed, she switched off the light. She would make sense of all this tomorrow. Then, lying in the dark, she remembered. Of course she would. Tomorrow was St Valentine's Day.

Only when Tim noticed the light go off the next balcony but one did he realize that his pupil had been awake, too. He stroked his new bandage at the thought of her, and wondered about the married man in her life. Finally, something she'd said came back to him. "I'm very glad I met you," she'd said. Mentally he repeated it. *I'm very glad I met you.*

He returned to his keyboard. The ideas were coming tonight better than they'd ever done. He had to get them down before they dried up.

CHAPTER
TWENTY

Jane watched the red Royal Mail van make its way through the avenue of scraggy, windswept rhododendrons and then cross the wet car park towards the hotel. It would help to get good news, she thought, as the van drew up; thanks from head office, for instance, or a ten-day trade union convention booking for March. Trade union bar bills were always welcome. Failing that, a morning without worry would do.

She'd been awake since before six, making plans. There was still much to do before the ball. The current resident list was light and tickets in town had been slow, the shops were reporting. Not surprisingly, because Darrell could always be counted on to do his best, he seemed to have prevailed upon the dippy work-experience girl to help and they'd made a good job of decorating the ground floor. Jane had even taken a photograph of how they'd turned the dining-room into a ballroom to show Bristol. Not that it would matter how much energy was expended if the takings were disappointing. Valentine balls were major events in a hotel calendar these days, winter cash crops. Head office had high expectations.

At the sound of the outer door opening, Giles, the dog, trotted amicably to welcome the postman as he entered. It was an unreciprocated affection.

"Morning," the postman said, ignoring the dog, and holding out a wedge of envelopes as he considered the parade of red hearts that Shona had stuck around the walls.

"I hope we'll be seeing you tonight, Adrian," Jane bloomed, taking the post. "There's a free welcome glass of sparkling wine to all guests. And we do still have a few tickets."

The postman sniffed a wet nose. "The wife won't let me out," he said.

"It's a *Valentine's* Ball, Adrian. You're supposed to bring her with you."

The postman looked at her with a vaguely mystified contempt. "In that case, I might as well stay at home," he jeered. And off he went to his van.

Resisting further comment, Jane returned to the collection of trade brochures with their introductory offers and giveaway discounts, which made up most of the post. Business was thin right through the hotel trade in the two months after New Year, and all the ancillary trades had offers to make. The rest of the post was made up of invoices, the usual formal letters that looked like bills and legal documents to the guest in Room 24, Barry Harrison, and a large, white, spongy envelope. It bore a local postmark and it was addressed to Shona McWilliams.

"Oh, God! Oh! Oh!" Will Abbott felt as though his head had been punctured as his face collapsed into the pillow.

174

Beneath him, Suzy sighed comfortably and waited for him to recover. "Lovely," she gurgled.

That was more than lovely, Abbott thought. But even as he did, and, still gasping, as his body seemed to shrivel, a sliver of guilt began to unpeel. He should be at home now, with Jenny and the boys. Why did guilt always have to spoil things? Never mind, he'd make it up to them when he got back. Linking Amy Miller and Teddy Farrow would be page one. And Jenny would be very interested in the story. She loved to read about celebrity adultery. She'd be proud of him for getting it.

The bed, an ancient wrought-iron creature with a thick feathery mattress and downy duvet, creaked as Suzy turned to face him, a pretty, broad-breasted younger woman.

"Hello, you," she said, and she put a hand to his face.

He didn't show it, but that bothered him. She sounded almost affectionate. He didn't need affection. That wasn't part of the deal. Taking her hand away, he cocked his head comically, as though suddenly becoming aware of something. "Is that bacon I can smell frying downstairs?" he said. "Just what we need to start the day, a good English hotel breakfast."

Michael had made the tea as quietly as possible, closing the door to the bathroom as he'd filled the kettle with water, then putting the cups and saucers on the tray with a silent delicacy. Lastly he added an envelope. Only as he put the tray down on Eleanor's bedside table did she wake.

She smiled. "Good morning, Michael." Then she saw the envelope. "What's this?"

Michael felt the sudden slam of colour to his cheeks. "Happy Valentine's Day," he said, his voice scarcely above a whisper.

"Oh, Michael." Her eyes filled. Very carefully she opened the envelope.

Already he was apologizing. "It was the best they had in the shop. The others all seemed ... well, inappropriate." Sexy and vulgar would have been more accurate descriptions.

"It's beautiful," she said, gazing at a rustic water colour of a couple of black-and-white goats, one wearing a bonnet, the other standing tall by her side, his horns spiky and proud. "To my darling wife," the billy goat was saying to his partner, "the Valentine of my life."

Now tears were tumbling. Michael reached across and offered a tissue.

"And I'm being so terrible to you . . ." She blew her nose.

"No, no, you aren't. Not at all." Tears led to silences. He thought quickly of a way out. "Did you know there were at least two St Valentines?"

"Two?"

"Or maybe even three. One was a third-century martyr in Rome."

"I didn't know that." She wiped her cheeks.

"Oh, yes, the legend was they cut the poor man's heart out while he was still alive and sent it to the emperor."

"Good heavens. On St Valentine's Day!"

"So it became, I suppose."

A sudden new thought must have occurred because Eleanor's damp eyes brightened mischievously. "I wonder, Michael, when they'd cut it out, his heart, did it fit into the envelope?"

Once more with Eleanor Michael wasn't quite sure that he understood. But then, catching her expression, he began to giggle in relief. You would never have thought it to look at her, but she had a very droll sense of humour.

"I was reading the travel books, Michael," Eleanor said at last in between sips of tea. "There's a ruin of an old church along the coast. If it's all right with you, it might make a nice walk this afternoon."

"I'd like that," Michael said.

He heard the laptop *twing!* of the incoming email as he was shaving. Still holding his razor he went to check his messages. There weren't many. One from Valerie, the school secretary, wondering how he was getting on; another from Razza at the Settle Bar, and a couple of special offers. Only one interested him. Actually, it surprised him.

I'm sorry if I've been difficult to get hold of these last few days. But things have been tricky here. See you soon.
Love you.
Amanda
xxx

He read the message several times, not because he didn't understand it or because he was wondering why Amanda had been impossible to reach for days, or even because he wanted to know why things might have been tricky for her. What puzzled him was that he didn't know what he was supposed to be feeling. And as far as Amanda was concerned, this had never happened before.

He was finishing shaving when his phone rang.

"The bandage wasn't too tight, was it?"

She didn't have to introduce herself. He was already smiling. "It was fine. Still is." And he checked it in the mirror.

"Good. Slightly amazing, but good. Look, it's a sunny morning and I wondered if you were free for breakfast. Somewhere out, I mean . . . if you're not working."

He didn't know what he was supposed to be feeling about this invitation either, but it pleased him. "I'm not working," he said.

And inside he heard himself singing a line from a Johnny Nash hit, which always seemed to be included in the days when newspapers gave oldies-but-goldies away. It was the one with what sounded like a squeeze box accompaniment. "*I can see clearly now the rain has gone,*" he sang as he hurried to dress.

She was waiting for him in the garden, watching the sunshine on a pattern of gold and purple crocuses that stretched across a lawn. This place got prettier all the time, she thought, as together they strolled down the

178

hill to the little town. It was a warm and clear day, and when they passed the empty beach Tim reminded her of how he'd watched her there that first morning, all of two days ago. It pleased her to think he'd noticed her.

This being February there was, of course, nowhere in town for them to buy breakfast, other than another hotel. Instead, they settled for some croissants from a tiny supermarket. And, after picking up a couple of coffees in polystyrene cups from a van by the bus stop, they strolled out along the stone quay, which, built like a battlement, guarded the entrance to the harbour.

She knew Tim wanted to know more about her, but having started out with a lie there was now no way of going back. Besides, his life seemed so much more real than hers, his days fuller than any of the recent phoney, lonely hours she spent at her computer daydreaming imaginary situations for made-up people while waiting for Teddy to call.

When they'd talked in the bookshop she'd seen Tim as a diffident, uncertain man, who made a conversation out of half jokes. She'd misread him. Today he was excited, even though he said he'd been working half the night. "Does that mean the music's going well now?" she asked.

"For me. Yes. I think so. Last night was good. The best it's been. I don't know if it will work out, but *I'm* happy with it."

"So the kids who crowned you did you a favour."

"It didn't feel a lot like it."

"But they made it possible for you to come down here to work without any distractions."

He reflected on that, then he said, "Distractions aren't always bad, you know. The right ones can help. In fact, sometimes, they *do* help. Definitely." He looked at her, then as though realizing how pointed that had sounded turned quickly away again.

It was almost a declaration, and so unexpected she didn't know where that conversation might lead; or even if she wanted to know. So carefully she steered him towards safer ground. "If you could afford to would you give up teaching and write full time?" She'd given up working in the bookshop as soon as she could.

He didn't have to think about it. "No, I'm sure I wouldn't. There are bad days at school, I know, but there are great days, too, like when you see some boy or girl begin to make the musical connections. And you realize that whatever he or she does his or her life will never be quite the same again, that a whole new world is opening up to enjoy. It's a real thrill to see a life change like that." He was smiling as he was talking, as though he was picturing his successes. Amy felt a twinge of envy for his enthusiasm.

They'd now come to the end of the quay, and leaning on the wall they watched a couple of fishermen cleaning their nets in a green boat bobbing near by.

"I wish I'd had a music teacher like you," Amy said. "All I ever learned were scales. I got bored and gave up after three lessons. Big mistake."

"Well, you do have me for this week. Who knows what you'll learn!"

She laughed, and dropping a burnt corner of croissant into the water she watched as a seagull

180

immediately swooped to take it. Across the harbour and up the hill she could make out a yellow van being unloaded at the hotel. Tim watched with her. "Will you be going tonight, to the Valentine's Ball?" she asked at last.

Tim hesitated. "To be honest, I hadn't intended to. But perhaps if I had someone to go with . . ."

She nodded. "Just what I was thinking."

And, not quite embarrassed, but uncertain, they laughed together as they finished their coffees and dropped their cups in a litter bin before making their way back down the quay.

"Yes! Yes! Very nice! That's it! To me now! To me!" Peering into her viewfinder Suzy was willing her subject on, the way photographers do, despite the fact that Amy Miller was fifty yards away. "Will!" she said quickly. "Pass me the other camera!"

Pulling a face because he didn't see himself as a photographer's assistant, Abbott reached for a second camera armed with an even longer lens. From the cover of a windbreak on the miniature golf course, they were watching Amy and her companion as they walked back along the quay towards the town. They'd followed them since they left the hotel.

"Very nice! Yes! That's better!" Suzy's motor shutter ran a procession of snaps.

"Be careful she doesn't spot you." Abbott was nervous, peering through a slat in the windbreak. Suzy's head was slightly above it.

She didn't bother answering and Abbott wished he hadn't spoken. All photographers were famously touchy when working. The second camera whirred again. "You know, Will . . ." still staring into her viewfinder, Suzy was thoughtful, "from where I'm looking, by the expressions on their faces, if that guy with her is gay, like you said he was, I'm Rock Hudson."

"To many people, Valentine's Day is just a joke," Jane began, "a time for silly cards and pages of lovey-dovey advertisements in newspapers. And here at the North Devon Riviera Hotel we like to enjoy Valentine's Day like everybody else. It can be fun. And we hope it is. But for us it isn't a joke."

Shona looked around the kitchen as the hotel staff, including the two women from the town who did the bedrooms and who spoke only to each other, watched without expression while Jane appeared to draw herself up higher on her heels, her breast in her lemon, polka-dot blouse thrust out like that of an imperious thrush.

"Here," Jane confided, "Valentine's Day and with it the success of our Valentine's Ball is pivotal to the survival of this hotel during the off-season. Because if this hotel had to close during the winter, as have some of our competitors, that would inevitably mean jobs would go. Perhaps mine, perhaps some of yours. So, tonight, I know I'm going to get sterling work from everyone." She finished with a school prize day smile. "Now, any questions?"

182

For a moment there was the usual English embarrassed silence whenever questions are demanded. Then: "Darrell said that it's a local custom on Valentine's night to spike the Devon cider with an aphrodisiac . . ." Shona was smiling wickedly.

By the dishwasher Darrell's pleasant features contorted in a spasm of embarrassment. "I never did," he blurted.

"Perhaps you should then," Shona came back.

Jane looked witheringly at the girl. "Not a beverage you'll ever need, I dare say, Shona," she jibed. But then, turning to Domingos and Agnieszka, she added, "That being said, if Chef can manage anything in that line, any little culinary love potions, romantic treats from South America, I'm sure all our guests will be more than grateful . . . not to mention our bean counters in head office. What do you think, Domingos?"

"Aphrodisiacs?" Domingos pulled on his earring thoughtfully.

"They'd be wasted on the English," snapped Agnieszka.

Jane shrugged. "Ah, well, if anything springs to mind I'm sure we'll all be very happy." She looked around at her staff. "But now I think it might be a good idea if we got back to work." And she marched out of the kitchen.

"Love potions," Domingos said again and wandered away down the kitchen.

Darrell made his way across to Shona, who was surreptitiously retrieving a half of sausage from a guest's plate. "I dunno how you can tell such lies," he murmured, still flushed.

But Shona was ready with her biggest smile. "Sorry, Darrell. It was only a joke. And thanks for the Valentine cards. One would have been enough, though."

As soon as she could, Shona hurried up to her room, clutching the pocket of her maid's pinafore dress where she'd hidden her card. It was the first Valentine she'd ever received, and she didn't mind at all that it seemed to be made of Dunlopillo covered in blood-soaked crimson velvet, or that the message wasn't the most imaginative. *If you'll be my funny Valentine, I'll be your bigga, bigga, bigga hunk of love.* Everybody knew it was the thought that counted.

Inside her room, she carefully took the card from its envelope, and re-examined it for any sign of a signature. There wasn't one. Of course not. That was the point of Valentines. The mystery. Anyway, like a detective of romance, she'd already checked the handwriting on the envelope with Darrell's notes at the reception desk. It had matched.

Propping her open card on her dressing table she smiled to herself, a little ripple of triumph. At home she'd sometimes been embarrassed by the absence of male interest in her, her sisters' universal popularity being applauded by everyone. But then, they never disappointed.

Now, though, she had a Valentine card! And it was beautiful.

Feeling in a plastic bag for the piece of sausage she'd purloined, she dropped down to the floor and pulled her glass box out from under the bed. "And a bigga bigga bigga hunk of love to you, too," she said.

But as the cover slipped away from the box her face buckled. The box was empty.

"Oh, crikey," she gasped. Then lying on the floor she scanned the room. "Come out, wherever you are," she demanded. "This isn't funny. Joke over."

Nothing moved. Then she noticed it. A large gap between the skirting board and the floorboards.

She frowned. "Oh, no!"

CHAPTER
TWENTY-ONE

A brand-new and worrying thought. If love is the all-conquering, single-minded obsession that we know it to be, how do we explain the sudden, unexpected, uninvited, totally irrational, romantic yearning for someone other than the object of one's dreams?

Amy didn't write this then, but she thought it and she knew she would write it later, as she watched Tim make his way back up the hill to the hotel, a footloose piece of bandage beginning to flap from his wavy hair. It made him look slightly madcap, she thought. She would repair it for him when she next saw him. In the meantime, she had no answer to the distraction that was puzzling her.

Tim had left her to go back to his work and now she needed to do some shopping. Leaving London the way she had, she hadn't even packed a skirt, let alone a dress. But she was a conformist. If she was going to a Valentine's Ball she should be wearing something feminine. It vaguely occurred to her that she might have more choice if she took the bus to Exeter, but then that might have been making too much of what probably wouldn't be any more than a local hop. There was something else. Stuck like a fugitive down here in Devon, she was beginning to block out the reason she'd come. More than that, she was beginning to enjoy being the person she was pretending to be. To leave the little town, if only for a few hours, would be to risk breaking the spell. There were shops here, too. She'd surely find something she liked.

So she set off into the little town, offering a friendly smile to the randy couple who'd arrived the previous night and caused such a ruckus during dinner, and who, as she changed direction, she suddenly found coming her way. She'd spotted them earlier mucking about on the miniature golf course, which had seemed an optimistic pastime for February. Now when they saw her smiling at them, they looked slightly shamefaced, the man quickly finding something more interesting to watch on the cliffs above the town. That amused her. If they were having a good time on a dirty weekend, good for them.

He kept wondering if he'd dreamed it, this theme that he seemed to know before he played it, before he wrote it. He'd made a joke about not wanting to subconsciously steal from Chopin or Schubert. Was he doing that now as he sat over his keyboard and copied down what he was hearing in his head? And he remembered a television programme in which Billy Joel had said he might accidentally have borrowed the first twelve bars of "Uptown Girl" from a piece by Mozart. Or was it Beethoven? He didn't think he was doing that, although he always said that if you were going to steal you should steal from the best. And, even if he was, it didn't worry him. He was enjoying his work. He was flying. He was happy. And when he imagined the presence of the beautiful, brow-knitted Amanda looking over his shoulder reading the manuscript as it was shaped, always just about to make a suggestion, he quickly replaced her in the orchestra of his mind with a part for a pianist who only played with one finger.

It was one of those churches that looked as though it might have been built in the Middle Ages as a beacon for sailors returning home up the Bristol Channel. High on a tor above a sheer cliff, where the moors met the sea, it was still a landmark, but back then, the stone crucifix it would undoubtedly have had as its highest point would have been visible for miles.

"*Originally Saxon, then with Norman additions, but sacked in 1536 during the Reformation and later abandoned when the population declined . . .*" Eleanor was reading from her Devon guidebook as, resting at a stile on their climb up the hill, they considered the chapel ruins.

"It must have been quite a scramble for people to get to mass," Michael panted. He was fit but the narrow path had been steep and long. "The sermons would have had to be good."

"But, remember, when the congregation got here they'd have been that bit closer to God," Eleanor offered wryly. "A good fifteen hundred feet, anyway."

Michael chuckled. "As in the Tower of Babel." It was good to see Eleanor making her little jokes again. With this pilgrimage, albeit to the now desanctified St Gytha's, they were doing something together they'd done all their separate lives; which had, in fact, *been* their lives.

He looked up at the crumbling arrangement of grey stones that lay between the thickets of gorse above them. There wasn't much left of the chapel, with barely three walls still standing, the fourth being open to the sea and the wind, while the tower and the roof must have gone long ago, the stones and timbers presumably hauled away for more utilitarian purposes. But it was still recognizably a church, a sanctuary where people had come for solace, for baptism, death and marriage.

Then Michael turned and gazed back at the empty moor they'd hiked across. Had any of the parish priests who'd once lived here faced the moral quandaries he and Eleanor had struggled over? Had they ever fallen in love and had to choose? Surely they must have done. Human nature never changes.

A stray black-and-white goat with horns that curved back in a U shape, like the ones in the Valentine card he had bought for Eleanor, had been trailing them across the moor. Now it lifted its head and watched them.

"Well, Michael, are you ready?" Eleanor broke into his musing. She was back on the path, waiting to climb the last few yards. "Last one in the church is a doubting Thomas." And she set off stoutly up the hill.

Hesitating on the stile he watched her as she went, huddled in her anorak, this kind, grey woman whom he'd admired impossibly from afar in the hospital.

Please let it work out soon, he prayed silently. Then he followed her.

The van arrived from the poultry farm just before lunch. Darrell was on reception checking Mr Harrison's bill. It was three weeks in arrears and his Visa payment had just been turned down. Jane would be facing a difficult encounter, though not as difficult as Mr Harrison's.

"Here you go, every quail's egg in Devon and then some," the chicken farmer said beaming, as he put the carton down on the desk.

Darrell looked at the carton suspiciously. The North Devon Riviera Hotel wasn't the sort of hotel where quails' eggs were on the menu.

"For Mr Domingos," the farmer explained, pulling out an invoice.

"Ah, at last! They come!" Domingos was already hurrying fussily from the kitchen to claim his eggs. "It's nearly too late. Love potions, like love itself, take time to prepare." And snatching up the carton, he hurried away with it.

The farmer looked comically at Darrell. "Love potions! Yeah, well, each to his own. We just use scrumpy and soft talk in our village, but if we could have payment within seven days, that'll be fine." And, with much amusement, he returned to his van, muttering to himself: "Quails' eggs as a love potion! If it works I'll be a millionaire."

Leaving Harrison's account, Darrell followed Domingos into the kitchen.

Already Agnieszka was arguing. "Quails' eggs! What are quails? Pigeons? Sparrows? They're no good. Superstition! Give people vodka if you want aphrodisiac. That get anyone started."

"And finished, too . . . too quickly," Domingos said quietly, examining his eggs. "In my country we do things more delicately . . ."

"With voodoo, mumbo-jumbo from Africa."

Darrell smiled. At least Domingos and Agnieszka were arguing in English today, probably for the theatrical benefit of Shona who, drafted into the kitchen to help prepare the buffet for the ball, was laughing happily. She was really beginning to fit in.

Domingos wasn't insulted. He never was. Reaching for a large bowl, he began to break the eggs into it. "Brazil is the world capital of sex and love, as your country, Poland, is the capital of beetroot and cabbages. Tonight you will see. Now we must make enough choux pastries for everyone. We need at least three hundred heart-shaped profiteroles. Believe me. I will make magic. Now, normally for this I need peanuts and catuaba."

"What's catuaba?" Shona enquired.

"He probably just made it up," said Agnieszka.

Domingos was unperturbed. "I don't know the English name, but it doesn't matter. Today we improvise. Crushed walnuts in quails' eggs to make the vanilla custard. But we must be quick. Love can't be kept waiting."

Agnieszka snorted. "Only a man could say that. Some of us wait for years and still don't get it." But she went to get the flour and utensils just the same.

Darrell watched Shona. She was smiling, lop-sided, comically, as she helped, her arched, pencilled eyebrows high on her forehead like those of a clown. She wasn't what his mother would call a "nice Devon girl". In fact, he couldn't imagine how his mother would describe her, but she was the most exciting girl he'd ever met by a country mile.

Then he looked back at Domingos as the chef began to beat the quails' eggs. Did he really know some black-magic recipe for making people fall in love?

Amy wasn't sure. Was powder blue really her colour now that her hair was copper? Did the fitted bodice make her look long-waisted? And, more worryingly, was the dress cut too low at the front? The trouble was there wasn't another dress in Double Entendre that she liked, and there wasn't a better dress shop in the town. There wasn't another dress shop. And it *was* a pretty dress. *She* was the problem.

Staring into the mirror at the back of the shop, she hoisted up the shoulders. That might help. Perhaps a couple of safety pins would fix it. Or, better still, one in the front. She pulled the dress tighter over her modest hint of cleavage. That looked all right. And yet? She pursed her lips thoughtfully as she considered her reflection.

"It looks lovely, dear."

She swung away from the mirror. The elderly lady from the hotel was standing watching her, smiling, as though enjoying this moment of indecision. Her husband was sitting in his wheelchair by the door, not asleep, but, Amy suspected, not exactly awake either. "Oh, hello. Thank you. I didn't see you come in. Do you really think it suits me?"

"Absolutely. And I'm sure your young man will think so, too."

"Er, young man . . .?"

"Well . . . the young man at the hotel . . ."

"Ah!" Amy was suddenly embarrassed. "Actually, he's just a friend." Then, though she would have denied it, she was aware of a small glow of pleasure at the misunderstanding.

"I see." And the elderly woman gave her one of those knowing smiles that older people wear when they suspect they're being fibbed to. "He seems a very nice friend, anyway." Now Amy noticed that the old lady had the slightest touch of a strawberry-blonde rinse in her white hair.

"Yes. Yes, he is." She looked again at the dress. "You don't think it's too low, do you?"

"For a girl of your age, never! You've got the rest of your life to cover up. When you get to my age they'll be *demanding* you cover up."

Amy laughed. "That's good enough for me. I'll buy it." And she turned to catch the attention of the young sales assistant who was sniggering near by as she showed her equally young, but rather more homely, colleague a rude Valentine she'd just received on her mobile phone.

"Of course you will," said the old lady. "Now, where do you think I might find some North Devon razzle-dazzle for the rock-up tonight? I don't want to be underdressed."

There were probably fifty years separating the two women, but there was something defiantly jolly about the old lady, and she and Amy got on perfectly as, companions in fashion, they now helped each other shop. Firstly, Double Entendre provided a turquoise trouser suit for the old lady, complete with a silver stole, as well as new tights for Amy. Then it was off down the street for shoes with just a hint of dancing glitter, while in a Devon handicrafts shop they went silly and emerged with all kinds of beads and bangles set with local stones from the seashore.

As they shopped, gradually the old lady's situation unpeeled. Her name was Grace and her husband was George. George had had a bad stroke three years earlier. Until then they'd been one of those active old couples who were spending a very long, well-off retirement seeing the world. It was trickier now, Grace said. But although George couldn't walk or talk properly any more, and needed help eating, "and et cetera, et cetera", as she put it, he didn't want to be left out of anything. "He might not be able to do it all himself any more, not physically, anyway, but in his mind he's as young as you are," she explained as Amy took a turn in pushing George. "Probably even

194

younger, because he has a very dirty mind for someone so old and respectable. I sometimes tell him I think he's regressed to his teenage years, which amuses him. One thing's for sure, it's certainly fun living with a teenager again. Isn't that right, George?"

Positioned behind the wheelchair, Amy couldn't see whether George reacted or not. She liked to think he smiled.

Engrossed in their shopping they'd missed lunch at the hotel, so instead they settled for a salad in a pub next to the maritime museum. Watching them together as they waited to be served, Grace the ever attentive carer, George not obviously grateful, Amy was intrigued.

"Do you mind if I ask you something?" she said at last.

"So long as you don't want to know what I was doing on the day Queen Victoria was crowned."

"It's just that . . . well, I couldn't help noticing you both this week . . ."

Grace laughed. "Haven't we all been watching each other? What else would we find to do in a place like this in February when if you aren't careful the wind can bite your face off? We've had our eyes on you, too."

"Well, yes. And it seems to me that you and George are more happy together than almost any couple I know. Certainly more than my parents were before they divorced." She was surprising herself to be even mentioning that. The years before their divorce, when she'd been at school, life at home had been fraught. Then when her father had later died her mother had shown little grief, which had been almost more upsetting than the divorce.

"Yes, you could say we're happy," Grace was saying.

"What I mean is . . ." Amy pursued, perhaps now a little too much the writer in search of a new chapter. "You seem to know the . . . secret."

"There's a secret? We know a secret? Well, aren't we clever!" Grace gave her a sidelong doubtful look, only slightly more polite than a scoff.

"Well . . . you know, the secret to the stuff the Valentine cards tell us to dream about: lifelong love, romance, devotion, fidelity . . . all those things."

Grace's smile faded into a deep crease between her eyes at this point. "Don't you think you're being perhaps a little presumptuous there?" she said.

Amy was instantly apologetic. "I'm sorry, I didn't mean to pry. I just . . ."

Grace was wagging her head, shushing her. She looked at George for a moment, hesitating. He'd now fallen asleep in the warmth of the pub. "How do you know we've always been loving and faithful? Yes, we've loved each other all our lives, well, since we met, I'm sure of that. But things happen in a long life. People have opportunities they didn't anticipate. I wasn't always eighty. And I imagine George had his moments, too. Well, I know he did, though he thought he'd made sure I'd never find out. He's always been very kind like that."

Amy was ashamed, embarrassed. "I'm really sorry . . ." She hadn't been looking for a confession.

196

With a wave of her hand, Grace dismissed her worries. "Don't be. Just don't run off with the rose-tinted idea that just because you see us happy together now, the path was always straight. I don't think it's ever completely straight. Not for anyone. We're just lucky that we always seemed to find our way back on to it."

"Promise." Amy felt chastened. "There goes the last of my romantic illusions. There's no great secret," she said, and watched George's eyes open as Grace arranged a cover of paper napkins under his chin.

"No, I don't think so. To be honest, I've always thought that St Valentine is a bit like Father Christmas. He only works if you believe in him. Like fairies, the old-fashioned Tinkerbell sort, I mean. I think that's a big part of it."

"Believing in the idea of love, you mean?"

"Or perhaps making a decision to work for it, to believe in it, even when things go wrong. That's it. Making a decision. But, then, what do I know?"

"And the other half?"

George's soup had now arrived.

Grace had had enough. "I don't know, ask me another time. Can't you see the poor man's starving?" And putting a spoon to the soup, she tasted it to make sure it wasn't too hot, and then held it to George's lips.

Tim would never know where the day went. The music stole the hours as he stayed at his keyboard. The competition that Amanda had insisted he enter, with its rules and expectations of content and form, was forgotten. He was writing for himself.

In mid-afternoon, having taken off his headphones for a break, he heard footsteps in the corridor outside, then the sound of the door next but one to his being unlocked, opened and closed. And for a moment he allowed his forefinger to play a solitary, rhythmic, silent note, over and over as a welcome ghost sat beside him.

Then he returned to his work, composing for the joy of it.

CHAPTER
TWENTY-TWO

Inside the three standing walls the church was even more reduced than it had appeared as they'd pushed their way up the hill and across the little plateau of grass outside. Only one wall was still high enough to show the gaps where a couple of small stained-glass windows would once have stood, while at the far end, where they imagined there might have been a little altar, all that was left was a pile of lichen-covered stones.

Yet to Michael and Eleanor, everything was of interest as they picked their way through the centuries of weed-covered rubble, oblivious to the graffiti smeared and chiselled, like lewd testaments, wherever space permitted.

"I wonder would these be the remains of a primitive baptismal font?" Michael said, pulling back a stone to reveal a smoother, rounder one beneath. "Or perhaps it was for holy water."

It was possible, Eleanor agreed without much conviction. More certain was the outline of the ancient square cross roughly carved into one of the large stones close to where they decided the main door would once have stood.

At first they were busy pointing out various features to each other, surmising where, had there been one, the pulpit might have been, and where a simple confessional box, but there wasn't much to work on and after a while they went quiet. Then, stepping outside and standing by the remains of the lowest wall, they gazed across the sheer line of cliffs and down to the pebbled beaches and shining sea below.

It was already nearly four and, because it was a long walk back to the hotel, Michael knew they couldn't stay long. But there was a restful solitude here and with the afternoon sun coming from somewhere way out to sea towards Ireland, it was casting a rosy glow on Eleanor's pallid winter complexion. Michael smiled as he looked at her.

"What is it, Michael?"

"I was thinking how pretty you looked."

"Don't be silly." She was embarrassed, yet obviously pleased. Then, probably because she didn't know what else to do, and because he kept looking at her, she turned away and went back inside the little church.

He watched her go, seeing her foot just miss crushing a tiny patch of white crocuses flecked with a suitably ecclesiastical purple, which were growing in the damp shelter of a stump of gravestone.

By the time he joined her, holding a posy of those crocuses, she was standing in front of the rubble that might have been an altar. He passed the flowers to her.

"I missed the mass, Michael," she whispered sadly as she took them. "The nuptial mass."

200

He understood. The Church had never acknowledged that a priest could abandon his order and marry, so a church wedding for them had always been out of the question. That Father Dermot had attended their ceremony in a register office must have been tantamount to condoning heresy in Dermot's eyes. So, yes, Michael understood.

"It was a lovely day and I love you, but . . ." She searched for her meaning. "God makes marriages, not a civil servant from the town hall in a navy blue suit and brown shoes."

"God and two people," Michael corrected quietly.

"Yes, God and two people."

They were silent for a little while, alone with their separate thoughts. For a second, Michael wondered if Eleanor was about to tell him their life together would never work. But she was too still for that. After a while he said, "You know, in America it's becoming fashionable for couples to sometimes reaffirm their vows, get married again, as it were . . . to go to a chapel and tell God and each other how much they still love each other."

"So I've read," Eleanor murmured.

He left the thought with her.

Then slowly she turned to him with a smile of pure hope. "Will you marry us, Michael? Marry us properly."

For a moment he didn't follow.

Eleanor touched his arm. "You could, Michael. Here. Now. In a church, as it should have been before. You're a priest. A priest is a priest for life. Yes? I know you know the words."

He was so surprised he didn't answer for a moment. Then he said, "I don't think Canon Law has made provision for this sort of situation." But he was suddenly smiling. "It's a very unusual request. In fact, it might be considered sacrilegious. I might have to ask a higher authority."

Eleanor looked up at the gaping open sky above them. "I'm sure He's listening. We're here in a church, at the altar. I think He'd understand, don't you?"

How could a merciful God who saw, understood and forgave every one of our foolish ways not understand? "I think He might," Michael agreed. "But if we're going to do this properly, perhaps we should kneel down."

"That would only be right."

Taking great care, they found a patch of soft soil among the broken stones. Then, kneeling down together, they bent forward to consecrate their lives to each other, but this time in the certain knowledge of God's presence and understanding.

"Do you take this woman to be your lawful wedded wife from this day forward until death do you part?" asked Michael the priest.

"I do," replied Michael the groom.

"I do," repeated Eleanor when the time for her response came. In the register office her expression had rarely been less than worried. Now her soft eyes brimmed with happiness.

It wasn't entirely a lonely wedding. There was one witness, the black-and-white goat who'd followed them up the hill and who poked his head through first one then another of the gaps in the walls; and who, on St Valentine's Day, watched and grazed as they prayed for a happy life together.

For a couple of hours, something had been irritating him, trying to distract him from his work, and by late afternoon he had to confront it. Ever since Tim had arrived he'd regretted not having the legs for his keyboard, the table he'd requisitioned never being completely satisfactory. Now, after hours of work, it was wobbling more than ever as he played. He couldn't ignore it any more.

Reaching across to the chest of drawers by the bed he pulled out a couple of telephone directories. They might help, he thought, and lifting the keyboard up he prepared to push them underneath. Then another idea. Would it work better without the newspaper he'd stuffed there on his first morning in the hotel? Propping up the keyboard one-handed he began to withdraw the newspaper with the other hand.

It was her chin and mouth he saw first. Then the tiny nose. He stopped. Then, more slowly, he pulled again to reveal the eyes.

For a moment he thought he might be imagining the likeness, that it was just a face he wanted to see, and quickly pulling out the rest of the paper he held it up to the bedside light. He wasn't imagining anything. The hair was different. It was long and fair in the photograph, now shorter and darker. But it was her all right. The girl who'd told him her name was Millie.

WHERE IS AMY? read the headline above a caption.

Amy?

Amy Miller, best selling romance author, was last night said to be in hiding after rumours about a mystery man in her life . . . Then came an instruction to turn to page 5.

He turned on. Here there was a different, bigger photograph. And now there could be no doubt. There was also a short piece about Amy Miller's writing success. *So who's the big secret, Amy?* it finished.

Amy? Millie? Amy? A famous author?

For some minutes he stood confused, rereading the article, looking again and again at the photographs. Millie or Amy? Did it really matter? Someone who worked in the paper distribution business or a best-selling novelist? It was hardly even a white lie when you thought about it.

At one moment he stopped and listened, imagining he could hear her on her balcony. But it was only the sounds of activity by the hotel staff outside.

The newspaper referred to some unnamed lover as "mystery man". The previous day when he'd waited by the waterfall as she'd taken a call, he'd imagined a stolid, rich, married businessman, possibly someone in paper production. But the famous Amy Miller would surely have someone more glamorous.

Second by second, his mind was retracing their moments together, every word she'd said. The collision in the hotel lobby when they'd arrived, the fit of giggles over dinner and the way she'd re-bandaged his broken head. "I'm very glad I met you," she'd said as they said goodnight.

I'm very glad I met you.

But mostly he was thinking about the exchange in the bookshop, the display of Amy Miller books and the life-sized, cut-out photograph of the author. She'd stood in front of it, and still he hadn't noticed. He must have been blind. And what had he said? *I can't imagine anyone wanting to steal Amy Miller books, can you?*

Probably not! she'd said and smiled. Of course she'd smiled. She'd been laughing at his ignorance, prejudice and arrogance. He knew nothing about Amy Miller books. He'd never even opened one. She'd guessed that.

He looked again at the newspaper. Then, checking his watch, he got up and reached for his coat.

Mobile phone in hand, Will Abbott, wearing his shirt but no underpants yet, watched from his window as the tall guy with the hair and the bandanna left the hotel, and set off towards the town. Abbott's room didn't have a sea view, but it was excellent for watching the comings and goings of the guests. A couple of hours earlier he'd seen Amy Miller return from shopping with the elderly couple. He'd been pleased about that. It was good to know that she was here in the hotel.

He'd then had a rest, in a manner of speaking. At least, he and Suzy had got undressed and gone to bed. What else were they supposed to do in the afternoon in a crummy hotel in God-knows-where, but put a "Do Not Disturb" sign on the door and enjoy themselves?

Suzy knew more about enjoying herself than any woman he knew. And he'd known a few. It went with the job.

Now, wearing just her knickers, Suzy was bending over her laptop, sending her selection of pictures back to the office. They were good. She was a good photographer: Amy Miller in the hotel grounds with a new hair colour and style, Amy Miller by the sea, and Amy Miller shopping in town as she went unnoticed.

But as the photographs raced down the wire there was a tension at the other end of Abbott's phone that he recognized and didn't like. Why was it that every time he went away those bastards in the office started being difficult?

"So what's she doing down there then?" McKenzie was demanding.

"'What's she doing?' Nothing much. Hanging out with some humpty-dumpty of a pianist." Abbott noticed Suzy smile at that as she logged off and flopped back on the bed.

"Who's he?" McKenzie asked.

"God knows. Some hotel guest she's got pally with, I think. This could take a while."

Suzy, propped up on a pillow, smiled again. She was some girl.

"Unfortunately, we don't have a while, Will," McKenzie suddenly said in a seen-it-all-before voice. "You'd better get on with it."

"What d'you think I'm doing?" Abbott was puzzled.

"I mean you'd better front her up."

"Yes. Obviously, but not yet." He was watching Suzy again as she recovered her *Ladder of Sex* book from her bag. She'd hidden it there when they went out in case the room maid saw it. It was a stupid book, they'd both agreed, but in the right circumstances, such as these, not without its entertainment and instructional value.

"We want it for tonight, Will."

"*Tonight?*" Abbott scoffed. "It's too soon."

"Very possibly. But the word is the *Sunday Times Magazine* has a cover story on 'Teddy Farrow the devoted family man' going in this weekend and we want to spoil their day. So we need the Amy Miller tale tonight."

"Jesus!" Abbott swore. "There's a way of getting these things, you know."

"Yes. I do know. That's why *you're* there." McKenzie's voice suddenly lightened. "Nice pictures, by the way. Very nice. You've got Suzy Tallis down there with you, I see."

"Yes. She does a great job."

From the bed Suzy beamed.

"So Ed Halliwell said when he worked with her in Spain," came back McKenzie. Then very quickly he finished: "Anyway, speak to you later." And he rang off.

The phone was still at Abbott's ear.

"They want you to file tonight?" Suzy enquired. "It's too soon."

Abbott didn't answer.

"Why?"

Still no reply.

"Will?"

"You didn't tell me you'd been to Spain with Ed Halliwell," he said at last.

"You didn't ask me. They liked the pictures, yes?"

"So you did?"

"Did what?"

"Go to Spain with Ed Halliwell."

"Mmm," she said casually, making herself comfortable on the bed, although it occurred to Abbott that she was one of those women who would always look comfortable on a bed. Her body just seemed to unfold that way. "It was a footballers' wives story. A wild goose chase. It never got in." Now she picked up her book, with that naughty chipmunk grin she liked to wear when they were alone. "What do you think, Chapter Thirteen or shall we skip one and go on to Fourteen? That looks really filthy."

" 'It never got in!' " repeated Abbott.

"No."

"And what about Ed Halliwell?"

"What?"

Abbott was now standing over the bed. "Well, he's hardly known for living by a strict monastic code, is he?"

"Oh, right. No, probably not."

"So what happened?"

"When?"

"You *know* when. In Spain. You and Ed Halliwell."

Suzy peered up at him as though surprised she was having this conversation. "What does it matter what happened?"

"It doesn't matter. I just don't know why you didn't tell me."

She shrugged. "It didn't seem important."

"It isn't important."

"No. Well, then . . ."

There was a pause now as Abbott looked away from her. Ed Halliwell, for Christ's sake! He turned back. "How long were you there?"

Suzy shrugged. "About three days. Four, I think."

"And, you didn't say, what happened?"

"What d'you think? We staked the wives out. They went shopping, got drunk. Nothing exciting. I took some pictures. We came back. End of story."

"You know what I mean. You and Halliwell. What happened?"

"Nothing happened." There was now a sullen defensiveness.

Abbott just about smirked. "*Nothing*? With Ed Halliwell? In Spain? For three, four nights? Come on!"

"Well, nothing much."

"And what does 'nothing much' mean?"

"Oh come on, who cares!" Exasperation was turning to anger.

"No one cares. You're a grown girl. You can do whatever you want."

"Thank you. I did." Suzy was now off the bed and examining a camera.

"Fair enough."

"Right!"

From the window Abbott looked down at his Porsche. He'd parked it at the far side of the hotel car park, under the trees. It really was a car for a single man. He'd get rid of it soon. Behind him he could sense Suzy wondering if the interrogation was over. But, God, Ed Halliwell! "What do you mean, you did?" he asked at last. "Did what?"

"I thought you didn't care," Suzy retorted. "When are you going to front her up?"

"Soon. Soon. And I *don't* care."

"That's all right then." She pretended to smile, cheeky, like a young girl.

"Yes." He hesitated. Then: "What did you do?"

"I don't remember."

"You *do* remember."

Suzy shook her head. "I dunno."

"You *do* know."

"Well, the usual, I imagine."

Abbott's brow knitted. "The usual?"

"Yes. Probably."

"What do you mean 'the usual'? What's usual?"

"What's *usual!*" Suzy looked around her in despair. Her eyes fell on *The Ladder of Sex*. "Well, Chapter Ten, I suppose."

Abbott stared in astonishment. "Chapter Ten is *usual?*"

One by one, the bookshop sales assistant ran the bar code of every book against the scanner on the cash register. "That's nearly a complete set. You're an Amy

210

Miller fan, too, are you?" she said, and began putting the books into a bag.

Tim looked at the life-sized photograph of Amy across the shop. "Her biggest," he said.

CHAPTER
TWENTY-THREE

Nursing her laptop at a chair by the window, Amy was fighting to concentrate, as the growing reverberations of expectation echoed throughout the hotel. Usually dismally quiet in the afternoons, the place now sang with shouts and instructions as last-minute preparations for the ball were demanded.

So, what is it? What *is* love?

She wrote against the growing, noisy anticipation.

Is it spiritual, psychological or biological? Too many pheromones up your nose, a chemical screw come loose on the Eternal See-Saw, or just some celestial marketing spin on the sexual necessity for reproduction? And if there's no secret, what's left? Love, believe and don't look in the rear-view mirror? Surely not. There must be more to it than that.

Putting cotton wool in her ears, she tried hard to concentrate further, wondering about the fabled sense of smell, well-balanced features, wide hips, lustrous hair and the effect of the time of the month in choosing a sexual partner. But when the band arrived, and began setting up downstairs, with fragments of electronic music rolling up the staircase and along the landing, capitulation was close.

Again and again she cast glances at her new dress, hanging in the doorway to the bathroom, liking it more all the time, though it had hardly been expensive. Then the matter of deciding which of her new earrings to wear became a further distraction, until at six she closed her laptop and ran her bath. It was all very silly, just a Valentine's Ball in an out-of-the-way, unfashionable, out-of-season place, yet she was as excited as a teenager.

Back in his hotel room, at first Tim just turned the books over and over, feeling the smoothness of their covers, studying their uniformly similar jackets and spines, examining the identical photograph of Amy Miller on the backs of all of them. It made her look slightly misty, more whimsical than the woman he knew. Inside each book was a curt, italicized paragraph of biographical information about the author.

> *Amy Miller was born and lives in London. Educated in England and Scotland, she is the winner of several international awards for romantic fiction.*

That was it. She was as secret to her readers as she nearly was to him. And although when he looked her up on Google he found thousands of reviews, blogs and comments about her, and inducements to buy her books through eBay and Amazon, in French, German, Russian and numerous other languages, she remained an enigma.

He chose a recent book called *Drifting Without Guilt* to read. It was the story of a single woman in her thirties who couldn't settle down to a profession, a home or a regular partner. But, while neither sad nor happy, the character was aware of a general ennui in her life. Whether the book was good or not, he had no way of knowing. It hadn't been written for someone like him. But he read on, laughing at the good jokes as the main character's life unravelled, while all the time seeking cryptic little clues to the personality of the author, though never knowing if he'd found any. Not that it mattered. True or otherwise, he could hear Amy talking on every page. And mainly, it seemed, she was talking to him. And when he took a break from reading it was only to go to his keyboard and remind himself of what he'd been composing, to listen to the music he'd written again, and to imagine her face.

Shona took one last look under her bed, taking great care not to get any dust or cobwebs on her white tights or the apple-green velvet mini-dress she'd bought for eight pounds at the charity shop in Midhurst for occasions such as this. A larger size might have been preferable but the colour was deliciously vivid, especially when worn with the bright crimson sash she'd rescued from the bottom of her eldest sister's cupboard. Natasha had worn it when she'd played

Napoleon's beautiful, sexy first wife Josephine — very successfully, as usual — in her second year at Oxford.

Finally giving up the search, she stood up. "OK, suit yourself," she said out loud. "You can play hide-and-seek for ever if that's what you want. But I've got stuff to do. Tonight's the night on the North Devon Riviera and you're going to miss it."

Then she turned to the round, yellowing, plastic-framed mirror by her bedroom door and, for luck, applied a final lacquering of guillotine-red lipstick to a mouth that was already as shiny and swollen as a painted plum.

Satisfied that she was at least kissable, she considered her reflection for a moment. Somehow the Bo-Peep ribbon, the dangling Somali earrings from Camden Market and the liberally applied mousse that had made her hair fizz out like a dead dandelion hadn't quite produced the effect she'd hoped for. Did she look interesting though? she wondered. Interesting enough? She wrinkled up her nose. She would never be as glamorous, clever or as beautiful as her sisters, no matter how much she tried. But "interesting" might be in with a chance.

Last of all, she fiddled fretfully with her hair. She'd really needed more time to get ready. It wasn't fair that Jane had cut short the staff's afternoon break to just a single hour, and that she'd had to wait as Agnieszka had taken forever in the girls' bathroom. Still, at least she wasn't being forced to wear that hideous French maid's uniform to the ball. "A North Devon Riviera Hotel name tag will be quite sufficient to let non-residents know who you are, should they be in need of assistance," Jane had said as she'd passed the plastic tags around. Perhaps no one will notice it, Shona, who'd never even worn a school prefect's badge, had thought. (Actually, she'd never been made a prefect.) And even if they did, with the psychedelic-coloured bubbles she'd added to hers, it almost matched her dress.

There was still an hour before the guests would begin to arrive, but she could hear the band testing their equipment. It was time to go and meet them. Goody-Goody-Darrell would already be down there. And she smiled fondly as she pictured him waiting anxiously at the hotel door.

Before she went, though, there was one further thing to do. Wrapping her right hand in a pair of knickers, she pulled a chair to the middle of the room, climbed on to it and carefully removed the light bulb.

It had been such a fine anticyclone of an almost spring day that they'd scarcely noticed the bank of mist lolling off the coast. It was their wedding day, their real wedding day, why would they notice it? But now, as, arm in arm, they made their wedding march back along the cliffs and across the edge of the moor, no longer followed by that chewing page boy of a goat, the mist was creeping off the sea and joining them in the heather. Now, though, they called it fog.

Perhaps Eleanor should have been afraid as, eyes focused on the path, they followed the coastal route home, but there was no fear in her. For the first time

216

she felt like a proper married woman, and the grey clouds swirling around her were just the clouds of the new heaven she'd entered that afternoon in the ruins of St Gytha's. To one side there was a drop down to the sea, hundreds of feet, she imagined, while to the other was the danger of being lost on the moors and of wandering into a bog, as travellers so often did in Victorian books. But Michael was with her, his arm warm, pressing hers tightly against his body. No bride ever felt more protected.

They didn't say much, other than to agree on the route they were taking, or to periodically, optimistically observe that they thought the fog was lifting as the night drew in, and to reassure each other that they would surely soon see the lights of the little town. And after a while they found themselves singing, not to keep their spirits up, because they were not at all afraid, but out of pure happiness. Michael began it, humming quietly, before Eleanor joined in with the words to tunes they both knew, hymns like "Faith of Our Fathers" and a few verses of "Immaculate Mary Our Hearts are on Fire", which, Michael said, reminded him of a pilgrimage he'd once made to Lourdes.

But today they'd made a pilgrimage back into history and forward into married love. And Michael knew another song, one based on an Elizabeth Barrett Browning poem he'd read at school, which someone, he didn't know who, had put to music. He sang that, too, in his croaky, middle-aged murmur.

Grow old along with me
The best is yet to be
When our time has come
We will be as one
God bless our love
God bless our love.

"God bless our love," murmured Eleanor, too, as they walked on through the fog and the night. "God bless our love."

CHAPTER
TWENTY-FOUR

They'd come from much further afield than Taunton. There must have been people from Minehead and Tiverton, from Bridgewater and Bampton. There was even a coach party from Wiveliscombe. Darrell had never seen so many cars in front of the hotel, never known a jam like it. He was almost sorry he'd advised his mother not to come, but she wasn't really one for dances. It was at a dance that she'd met his father, she'd always complained, before adding darkly that he knew where that had led, which always made him feel uncomfortable. Besides, by all accounts Valentine balls could get a bit lewd later on when the drink started working and the music got slower. His mum didn't like anything like that.

Unlike Shona, he was proud to wear his name badge and had pinned it to the lapel of his Gap sports jacket. There would be people coming tonight who'd been at school with him. A name tag made him look more like an assistant manager than a porter, and to give Jane her due, she did give him all kinds of responsibilities above his station. Some people had suggested he was being exploited: he liked to think he was being trained up. But it was sometimes hard to tell.

Anyway, stationed tonight in the lobby it was his main job early on to greet the guests with a glass of sparkling wine and direct them to the bar, where Ernie Loxton with the one arm, and his son Gary from Shillingford, had been specially employed for the night to deal with the optimistically hoped-for crush. And as they wouldn't be having any heavies on the door, Jane had also stressed that he keep his eyes skinned for any undesirables. Frankly, Darrell thought the most undesirable elements likely tonight were the band, Lorna and the Doones, especially Lorna, but as they were to be the centrepiece of the evening it seemed unwise to express that opinion too loudly.

Not that anything he said could be too loud when the Doones were playing. They weren't a bad band, especially when they put on their sunglasses and did a little Blues Brothers section, which, to be honest, with a lot of old Sixties stuff, was what most people in these parts wanted to hear. But they were very loud, especially when they went off on an AC/DC trip. They loved AC/DC, which just showed how narrow a mindset you could get if you grew up in North Devon. Darrell liked to think of himself as more of a romantic Coldplay man, although he knew they were considered very wet and old fashioned these days. Hopefully Shona might be a Coldplay fan, too, he thought, but he hadn't dared confess his admiration for them yet, because people could go right off you if you followed a band they hated. And with Shona you could never tell in which direction she was going to go with anything.

"Hello, Darrell. I hope you're suitably armed tonight," Barry Harrison, the floor coverings man, was standing behind him in the lobby, smirking.

"Armed?" Darrell was puzzled. "I don't think we'll be having any trouble!"

Harrison smirked. "Armed in case you get lucky." And taking a glass from the tray Darrell was holding, he indicated a troupe of young girls from the town arriving, all hens' legs, bare midriffs, a pierced navel or two and very high giggles.

Oh, God! thought Darrell, hoping none of them had heard him.

"They say they like the taste of the vanilla-flavoured ones best," Harrison continued. "Followed by the chocolate banana, if you get my meaning." And he guffawed.

Darrell felt the beginning of a blush.

Harrison hadn't finished. "Did I ever tell you about that dance I went to in Swindon? I'd be about your age, maybe a bit younger. Anyway, I picked up some girl and when the interval came I took her outside and round the back for . . . you know . . . So, there we were going at it in a stand-up against the wall. Very nice. When suddenly she says, 'Eh, can you hurry up? I think the band's coming back on'." And again Harrison rocked with laughter.

Darrell stared at the tray he was holding. "I think the manager was looking for you, Mr Harrison," he said quietly. "She asked me to tell you."

Harrison's dirty smile crumpled. "Oh, right, thank you," he said. "I wonder what that's about." And then he hesitated, as though not knowing exactly what to do next.

Darrell felt bad. Both he and Harrison knew very well why Jane wanted to see him.

"Well, perhaps I'll run into her later," Harrison said at last, and pushing through the excited, shrieking girls, whom he seemed no longer to notice, he made his way towards the bar.

Darrell crossed his fingers for him. Ernie Loxton was under instructions to only accept cash tonight. He hoped Harrison would have enough money in his pocket to at least buy himself a drink, otherwise he might have to make that free sparkling wine last all night.

Crrrrrannnnnng!! The violent storm of an electric chord reverberated into the lobby. Then another and another.

"Crikey, are they starting so soon?" It was Shona running up behind him. He'd heard she'd been helping Domingos and Agnieszka out with the experimental profiteroles in the kitchen but now here she was looking as he'd never seen her before. Part Sugar Plum Fairy, part vamp and wholly zany. His heart flipped. It did. He felt it. He really felt something happen inside him. And it was wonderful.

Together they peered past the crowd and through the doorway into the dining-room, now festooned as the ballroom. With the lights turned low and reflected through pink filters it looked more romantic than should have been possible at the North Devon Riviera Hotel.

222

Darrell stole a glance at Shona. For once she wasn't smirking, but laughing at the joy of it all, with her eyes drawn inevitably to the collection of six cadavers in black T-shirts on the low stage under the big red heart that she and Darrell had hung there — *Love Makes The World Go Round*.

"*They're* the Doones?" she asked.

Darrell nodded. "Not bad, eh? I mean, for those that like this sort of thing," he quickly added. You could never be too careful.

"Not bad!" Shona repeated. "Where's the girl?"

"What girl?" asked Darrell.

"You know, Lorna. The lead singer."

For a second Darrell wanted to laugh. Was she being funny, or did she really not know? "Lorna's a boy," he said.

Shona's face puckered. "Lorna of the Doones is a boy? He wasn't in the version I saw on the telly."

"No, well, that's the joke, you see. Lorna's that one at the front with the long hair? His real name's Craig. He'll start singing soon."

Shona edged closer to the door to get a better view of the band. "You mean Lorna's the one who looks a bit like a young George Clooney? Wow!"

Now Darrell felt another lurch to his heart. But this one was quite different from the first, more of a sag into his stomach.

Shona was gazing, amused, at Lorna and his tumbling, black, shoulder-length hair and sleeveless black vest. "*He's* Lorna," she repeated. "It never occurred to me."

"Yes, well, he . . . he was at my school," Darrell stammered. "His real job is working for the council. He drives one of those motorized hedge cutters in the summer. Actually, he's useless at it. The farmers all complain when he's been round, but he don't care."

But Shona didn't appear to be listening. Following the crowd, she stood just inside the ballroom, carefully watching Lorna as he began to wrestle the microphone and strut the tiny stage in the way they always did on television.

Darrell felt his mouth drying. If Shona fancied Lorna, what chance had he got against a star?

She had to admit it, she loved the dress. It was loose and flowing and girly. Altogether she liked the way she looked. Surprisingly, blue did work with her new brown hair. Actually, it was golden, not khaki. The girl in Economy Cutz hadn't done too bad a job after all. It already seemed like weeks since she'd looked like Amy Miller, not just four days. She stared at herself in the long mirror. She liked her new shoes, too, dainty little dazzly things. She would never have worn them in London, but then she didn't go to Valentine balls in London. In London she was more the bookish sophisticate; more sensible; earnest and snooty. Christ, she thought. A bit of a bore, really.

The music was roaring from downstairs now. She checked her watch. It was 8.30. That was the time she'd agreed to meet Tim. She was surprised she hadn't heard from him since the morning. He must have become engrossed in his work and lost track of the time. She'd probably have to drag his headphones from his ears. And yet she waited.

Twenty-five to nine. She was nervous. She looked again at herself in the mirror, then added a touch more scent to her wrists. At twenty to nine she opened the door.

At that moment her laptop pinged. She'd forgotten she'd left it on. *You have email*, said the AOL voice.

For a moment she considered ignoring it. Of course, she didn't. Leaving the door ajar she crossed to the computer and opened the file. She was surprised. The message was an electronic Valentine's card, a simple screen showing just a bright pink heart and the lines:

Come live with me and be my love,
   And we will some new pleasures prove . . .

John Donne, she said to herself. Teddy liked to quote John Donne. He thought Donne was sexy and that she would be impressed by his literary knowledge. Actually, she'd quickly discovered that Donne was the only poet he could quote. She scrolled down the page.

Happy Valentine, Amy.
   I've managed to sneak a break. Will be driving down first thing tomorrow morning. I'm borrowing a pal's cottage near Honiton so we can have a couple of days together. Pick you up around ten.
   Longing to see you. Love you,
   Teddy

PS Better be ready on the hotel steps so that we can be off before anyone spots me.

She reread the message. And then, sitting down on her bed, she read it again.

Her door was ajar. Tim knocked lightly.

"Yes? Oh, sorry. I'm coming," she called as the door swung slightly open to his touch. She was sitting with her laptop, looking serious, but she smiled as she saw him. Then quickly closing the computer, she hurried towards him. "So, did you have a productive day?" she asked.

"A *great* day!" He was waiting on the landing, wearing the black velvet jacket that Amanda had insisted he buy and a clean pair of jeans. He'd just washed his hair, and his bandage had become soggy, and he could feel a drip of water working its way down the back of his neck and into his open shirt. "Wow!" he said, as she locked her door and turned to face him.

"*Wow?*" She looked puzzled.

"As in '*wow*, you-look-sort-of-wonderful-wow'!"

She laughed. "Well, it *is* a ball!" She was trying to be casual. "You're supposed to make a little effort. And you look very smart, too. I didn't know you owned a jacket."

He was still staring at her. He couldn't stop.

"What is it?" she asked. "You're looking at me differently all of a sudden."

"I am?" Tim shrugged. "That's probably because you're looking different all of a sudden." That was true, of course. But it wasn't the truth. She didn't just *look* different to him, she *was* different. Millie the anonymous girl in the paper distribution business was now Amy a famous writer, someone the newspapers speculated about.

"I look different. Good. I'm glad you noticed. Now, it's party time. Shall we go?"

Abbott and Suzy watched through their partly open door as they passed their room.

"Right!" Abbott said, getting up from a chair. It was the first word he'd spoken in two hours. He'd been thinking about Jenny and the boys, imagining her picking them up from school in the Mondeo, wondering what he was doing down here in Devon on a Friday night. And pondering why, whenever he got the opportunity, he just couldn't resist it.

Carefully, he patted the breast pocket of his jacket and felt the outline of his tiny microphone. He wished Amy Miller had left her room earlier. It was getting bloody late if he was to catch even the London edition. But if he'd just knocked on her door and announced who he was she'd have slammed it in his face and that would have been the end of the interview. Far better to catch her off guard in a public place when there was nowhere to run. At least she'd have to say something. The office had no idea how difficult these things could be.

Suzy was already waiting, leaning against the wall, a bag over her shoulder where she kept a lightweight camera. She'd liked him, he realized now. Quite a lot.

But he hadn't asked her to like him a lot, just enough to go to bed with him. She looked hurt, as though he'd had no right to interrogate her about her sex life, especially as he was the one who was married and she was a single, unattached girl. She was right, he hadn't the right. But *Ed Halliwell*! That bastard McKenzie would have made sure he was already the office joke.

"Ready?" he asked. She nodded. "Just take your lead from me. No snaps until I give you the nod."

She made no response.

Together they left the room.

CHAPTER
TWENTY-FIVE

It was a better turn-out than Jane could have dreamed. If the bar could keep up with demand, and this was an occasion when, prejudice against the handicapped aside, she rather wished there were four hands there instead of three, Bristol would have little to complain about this week.

What surprised her most, what *always* surprised her at hotel functions, was how well the local women turned out, how pretty and glamorous and instant-tanned the most dowdy, ordinary girls suddenly looked, how much they enjoyed going out and making the best of what they were. Not many of the men seemed to try very hard, certainly they made less effort to disguise their most unflattering middle parts, but the women were butterflies, almost every one. And, though, yes, she was jealous of the prettiest and the shapeliest and those accompanied by the most attractive and attentive men, she was also pleased with herself that she and her staff had made this night special, not just for the accounts people in Bristol, but for the guests and the people of the town. She hadn't inaugurated the ball, but she was trying to make it better than ever this year. And as she stood on the stairs, hoping she looked reasonably attractive, or at least magisterial, wincing at the music, and making a mental note to do something about that very soon, she felt proud, really proud of her hotel.

"I understand you need a word with me." Barry Harrison was at her side. He sounded awkward. "I know what it's about."

Jane held her smile firm as she gazed down at the assistant manager of Blooming Flowers Nurseries who had provided the floral decorations at a very reasonable price and who was now passing with the new young stem of a wife who had so recently been his secretary. Then she turned and considered Harrison. His eyes were watery.

When he'd first arrived some weeks earlier he'd been full of himself, buying guests drinks, boasting of the new floor coverings company he'd started with what he'd described as solid City backing, thrilled to be finally divorced and "free to roll", as he put it. But week by week she'd watched the cracks in his bluster spread from hairline cracks to deep fissures. The investment he'd been promised hadn't materialized. She realized that when he asked for a deal on his room. And she could tell by his demeanour when he returned to the hotel in the evening after a day on the road that orders had been slow, if any. She'd known for weeks he was existing on a wing and a prayer, but mainly a wallet full of credit cards. One day while he'd been out touring the north Cornish coast she'd taken a look in his room, not prying, just making sure the bedroom staff were doing their jobs. It seemed he'd brought just about everything he possessed with him, including a photograph of a hard-faced, silver-blonde woman and two serious-looking children in school uniform. That was when it had hit her. He was there because he had nowhere else to go. When you ran a hotel you got to know more about your guests than they ever realized.

He could, she knew, be crude and vulgar, and he liked to pretend to Darrell that he was a big hit with women. Everyone in the hotel, apart from Darrell, probably, knew that would never have been the case. The hard, scornful look in the eye of the blonde woman in the photograph had confirmed it.

As the manager of the hotel, Jane ought to have demanded Harrison either settle his bill or leave at that moment and expect legal action. She almost did. But it was Valentine's night. Everybody was having a good time. She didn't want a scene. It could wait until tomorrow.

"Why don't we talk about this in the morning!" she said coolly. "In the meantime, they seem a little short staffed in the bar." And with that thought lodged in his mind she replaced her smile and walked down the steps and into the ballroom to get that bloody band to play something the guests could actually dance to.

"Are you sure these things will be safe to eat?" Shona asked as she watched Domingos squirt a thick yellow paste-like substance from a piping bag to form a heart-shaped éclair.

"Of course," said Domingos, mock offended that she should question his professionalism.

Shona glanced around the kitchen. Just about every flat surface was now covered in baking trays covered in hearts. "Well, I hope so, because we had a lecture at college on public health and the serious penalties they hand out these days to kitchen staff involved in widespread food poisoning. I think they said it falls under mass murder. They execute you for that in China. A bullet in the back of the neck. *And* they make you pay for the bullet."

Domingos shrugged his huge shoulders. "You want aphrodisiac? You want love? Maybe you have to be a little adventurous. Different country, different recipe. If we only had catuaba from the rain forests of Amazonia . . . the bark of the tree of love. There they sing songs in its honour. No more frigidity, no more impotence, no more boredom with longtime married love. Just romance. And everybody happy." And he flicked a kiss to his fingertips.

"It's a pity the catuaba tree doesn't grow in North Devon then, isn't it?" Shona said. "Crushed walnut in quail's egg custard sounds more like something your loopy great aunt serves up for Sunday tea."

"Oops!" Distracted by her chattering, Domingos frowned as a heart turned into a question mark of an éclair.

"Pah!" At his side, Agnieszka wagged her head dismissively. She, too, had spent hours making pastry hearts. "He make up as he go along. This phoney love potion never work. We need vodka."

Shona shrugged. "Whatever!" But she hoped it did work. Just a bit.

And collecting a tray of clean wine glasses from the dishwasher she headed back into the ballroom where suddenly Lorna and the Doones were playing the Rolling Stones' "Brown Sugar" as though their lives depended on it, and the entire floor was alive with some very uncool and over-energetic dancing. You didn't get that in Midhurst, not in the places Shona went to, anyway. Everyone there was too self-regarding. But this looked like fun. She'd hated all the crap rap and AC/DC stuff that the Doones had opened with. At least Jane, who was standing on the short steps to the stage like an overseer, knew what the people wanted to hear, as, all around, guests and Devon faces mouthed in unison: "*Brown sugar, how come you taste so good, Brown sugar, just like a young girl should*". Even the middle-aged Scottish couple of hikers she'd served with porridge at breakfast seemed to know the words, and though the two elderly spinsters didn't, they got the message as Lorna shouted from the stage, "*I said, yeah, yeah, yeah, yeah!*" — which didn't take much learning.

"So what do you think of our Valentine Ball now, then?" Darrell asked, relieved from his duty on the door.

Shona smiled, mischievously. Darrell was so easy to tease. "I think the band's great . . ."

"Hello, Darrell, you're looking fit tonight!"

Shona turned. A couple of young girls, bleached, tripey, leggy little dolls really, prettier and sexier than she would ever be, were smiling at Darrell.

Darrell beamed towards them, obviously flattered, distracted for a moment. Then they were gone. He turned back to Shona.

For a moment she didn't speak. Then: "Yes, I think the band's great," she found herself repeating. "Especially Lorna."

"Lorna!"

"Mmm. He's just my type. Those lips. That tongue. I wonder if he'd like to taste my . . ." And she ran the tip of her tongue sexily across the underside of her top lip.

She regretted it instantly as she saw the sudden stab of pain in Darrell's eyes. She'd never done anything so vulgar in her life before. She hadn't meant it. Perhaps the song had suggested it. But, no, she knew it was just more stupid Shona bravado. More showing off. *You've always been a disappointment to us*, her father had said. But he'd only been half right. She was a perpetual disappointment to herself.

For a moment Darrell looked as if he was trying to reconcile two parts of something that were unfathomably opposed. Then he was gone, moving quickly away between the dancing couples, his pudding-basin head down, gathering up paper plates and abandoned glasses.

Shona watched him go in despair. Too late. She'd spoiled everything.

"*I said yeah, yeah, yeah, yeah*," howled Lorna of the Doones.

The dope couldn't even sing.

CHAPTER
TWENTY-SIX

They'd arrived late, for Devon, then sat out most of the rest of the first half of the evening, taking their drinks into the loggia, where Amy told how she'd met Grace when she'd gone shopping and Tim, quieter than usual, admitted how he was pleased with his writing. They hadn't been able to resist "Brown Sugar", though, not even when it was the Doones' version.

A draggy Commodores song followed, a slow, sauntering-on-the-spot sort of dance, which gradually emptied the floor as it was almost the interval anyway. Tim and Amy stayed, however, dancing slowly, but not holding each other. They'd never touched hands since they'd met, apart from at the piano, though Tim constantly imagined he felt Amy's fingers rebinding his bandage.

"Hey, you're staring at me," Amy pretended to chide.

"I know," Tim agreed.

"It's disconcerting."

Tim smiled. "It is?"

"Not really," she admitted.

"Can I tell you a secret?"

"You're a man with a secret? I didn't know."

"We all have secrets."

Amy thought about that. "That's true. What's yours?"

"That I think you're terrific!"

Amy blinked in surprise and what looked like pleasure. Then an embarrassed mock conceit followed. "Is that it? The secret? I thought everyone knew."

"I mean it. I'm not joking."

"You're still concussed. You must have hurt your head more than you thought. You're forgetting someone."

"I don't think so."

"Her name's Amanda."

"I haven't forgotten Amanda. I'm just not thinking about her. I'm thinking about you."

Amy shook her head, and moved in a little side-stepping semi-circle around him, as though ritually keeping him at a distance. "You don't know me, Tim. You don't know anything about me."

"I know some of you, the part you've let me know. And I think that part's terrific. And, though I know it won't happen, because I'll never see you again after this weekend, if I got the chance to know any more of you, I'm sure I'd grow to like those parts just as much." He grinned. "Most of them, anyway."

She looked at him. "You say the most flattering things . . ."

"Easy to say when they're true."

"But . . ."

"Yes, I know. You're in love with some guy. Which is a shame. But I just wanted you to know how I felt about you." He hesitated. "And now you do know."

236

The band had stopped playing, just drizzling away to nothing halfway through the song, as all the other dancers had retaken their seats or made their way to the bar.

Tim and Amy stood looking at each other, as though stranded after the tide of the song had gone out. "Tim . . ." she began, with a tone of voice that suggested she might have something nice but negative to say.

He wasn't ready for this yet. "Actually, after all that I'm so dry. I've just got to get a drink. What would you like?"

Perhaps she wanted to delay the moment of rejection, too, because she said, "Good idea. White wine. I'll be back in the bamboos. Waiting." She indicated the loggia.

There was something about the way she said "waiting" that gave him some small comfort, and he hurried towards the bar, almost stumbling over the couple who'd arrived by Porsche the previous night. He'd spotted them earlier, sitting glumfaced, not speaking, just watching the dancing. Obviously Valentine balls weren't for everyone.

The table they'd been sitting at was now taken, so Amy pushed on to the end of the loggia where on sunny days there would have been a pretty view of the beach. Tonight, though, all she could see was the swirl of mist around the hotel, and for a moment it struck her that she and Tim were in a cocoon, sheltered tonight from their problems. She liked the feeling. She thought about

Teddy, of course. But Teddy was for tomorrow and another world.

"Good to see you again . . . Amy."

The name "Amy" punctured the air. She stopped dead.

"I'm a great fan of yours . . ."

She turned. It was the couple with the Porsche she'd seen in town that morning. Had she ever met them before? She knew she hadn't.

The man stepped closer to her, smiling all the time. "I love the make-over, by the way. I hardly recognized you with the new hair colour. Shorter, too. It suits you. You look quite different from the other night . . . on the roof."

She'd guessed anyway. Casually, the man pulled a business card from his newspaper and pushed it into her hand. "The name's Will Abbott. And we hear you're having an affair with Teddy Farrow." It was said with the subtlety of a thumb under the eye.

"I'm sorry, I . . ." She was trying to turn away, looking for deliverance. There was no way past them.

Abbott pushed his advantage. "We know all about it. Television people love to talk. Those researchers can't help gossiping. The word is Teddy won't leave his wife. And you've given him an ultimatum. That's right, isn't it?"

"I'm sorry. I don't do interviews. Now please . . ." Her instincts were to flee. She tried to get between Abbott and the wall but he remained blocking the way, still smiling.

238

"Or is it perhaps his image as the nation's most popular television performer that's the problem? I can see why he'd be afraid to lose that."

"Would you, *please*, excuse me?" Her voice was rising.

Now her tormentor tried sympathy. "Look, it's nothing to do with me. But we'll be running this story tomorrow whatever you or I think. People at the office have already written it. But I'm with you, I don't want them to get it anything less than a hundred per cent accurate. So why don't we just sit down and have a drink and you can put your side of things before it all comes out wrong?"

By now she was physically pushing him. "I want to get past."

"So, I'd be right in saying you're not denying you're having an affair with Teddy Farrow?"

"*Please!*"

There was a sudden flash, and Amy looked up into the lens of a small camera being held by the reporter's moll. Flash! Flash! Another and another.

Other guests were looking at them.

On his way to the bar he'd run across Darrell carrying a tray of glasses. "You don't need to queue, Mr Fairweather," the boy had assured him quietly, as though preoccupied by something.

And nor had he. Back almost immediately with the wine, he'd seen it all unfold. As the hunters had closed in he'd heard the name, "Teddy Farrow"; and caught the word: "affair".

239

Teddy Farrow was the mystery lover? Of course. It was bound to be someone rich and famous.

By now he'd reached Amy. She wasn't quite cowering but she was cornered. He'd no experience of these things, but suddenly he knew what to do.

"So, what affair's this then?" he laughed, clumsily elbowing the girl photographer to one side and passing Amy her wine.

"Actually, this doesn't concern you," Abbott spat at him.

Rather comically Tim put his head on one side, suggesting there might be a friendly difference of opinion. "Well, I think it might," he replied. Then he smiled at Amy as he tasted his wine. "Sorry, it's a bit warm."

"Tim!" Her expression warned him not to get involved.

He ignored it and turned back to Abbott. "I mean, if you're suggesting that my fiancée is seeing another man I'd say it very much concerns me, wouldn't you?"

He looked back at Amy. Her eyes were bright in astonishment. At last she said, "It's all right, Tim."

"Well, it isn't all right really, is it?" he said. He turned bluntly on Abbott. "I mean, I know fiancée is an old-fashioned word and all that, but that's the way it is, and I think I'd have been aware if she was seeing someone else, don't you? Especially as she spends virtually all her time round at my place writing. Or with me at her place. Isn't that right, Amy?" And he looked back at her. *Amy!* He'd said her real name! Had she noticed?

She blinked. Yes.

Tim smiled. He was almost enjoying this.

Abbott was smirking. "Listen, mate, we checked you out. You met each other here. Arrived separately, signed in separately, separate tables at first . . ."

Tim laughed in his face. "That's right. Absolutely! Well spotted. Separate rooms, separate beds, pretending not to know each other. Then one day . . . bingo! We meet. Perhaps not quite by accident, and it's like love with a stranger. Have you ever tried it? You should. It makes for a *very* sexy weekend." He smiled cheekily at Suzy. "*You'd* love it. I'm Tim Fairweather, by the way." And he put his hand out towards Abbott.

Abbott ignored it. Suzy looked confused. Amy just watched the performance in wonder.

"I don't believe you," Abbott said at last, but now with the demeanour of a man who'd lost his bearings.

"Oh, yes, honestly. I'll show you my passport, if you like." Tim was mocking now. "But later, because now, if you'll excuse us, Amy and I have something rather important we have to do."

And grasping Amy's hand he positioned himself as a wedge between Abbott and the wall and drew her very firmly away from the reporter.

"I told you he wasn't gay," he heard the photographer say as they moved back to the dance floor.

"Just *shut it!*" snapped Abbott.

"How long have you known?" Amy asked as Tim pulled her towards the stage.

241

"That you were Amy Miller in disguise? Long enough to be glad I didn't know sooner. I'd probably have been too shy to talk to you." Then he turned to the Doones' shaven-headed keyboard player who was drinking from a bottle of beer and talking to a couple of local dads. "Any chance of borrowing your keyboard for a couple of minutes?"

"Can you play?"

"A bit."

The player shrugged. "It's yours then." And he moved aside.

Climbing up on to the stage, Tim pulled Amy up after him. "OK, you said you wanted to be in a band. This is your chance. Imagine you're a Fine Young Cannibal. Big finger on that note there and off we go again . . . it's called "Green Onions", by the way, and you have to play it with a lot of Memphis soul."

And, standing together at the keyboard, off they did go, Amy keeping that one finger going as Tim weaved rhythm and tune around her, but at full, spiky organ volume now. At first she was aware that they were a curiosity, as guests on the side of the floor wondered who the interval players might be. But Tim was a professional, and soon some of the Doones came back from their break to support him, first the drummer, then the bass player, then the two guitarists. And once again the dancers took to the floor. If for Amy the previous night at the piano had been a first lesson, tonight was a recital at the Wigmore Hall and a concert at Madison Square Gardens rolled into one. Alongside

242

Tim at the keyboard with the spotlight playing on them, it seemed the most natural thing in the world.

"What d'you mean 'it's a good story'? It's total bollocks. The bastard just made it up. She's screwing Teddy Farrow. We all know that!" Standing in the fog, hunched outside the front door of the hotel, trying to shield his mobile from the sound of "Green Onions", Will Abbott was explaining the failure of his venture.

"Well, she's not screwing him tonight, is she?" McKenzie's voice was indifferent. "You'd better put over what you've got. We'll go on that. It's a thin night. 'Romantic Amy's secret sex games in hideaway love nest with rock-star fiancé'. That sort of thing."

"But he was lying. And he's not a bloody rock star."

"Well, he's playing 'Green Onions', isn't he? I can hear it from here. We'll reveal him as a fraud next week, and Amy Miller as a fickle, two-timing bitch who's been shagging both him and Teddy Farrow. You'll enjoy writing that one. I'm putting you over to copy now."

There was a click on the line, a pause, and then the voice of a copytaker. "This is for the newsdesk, right? Ready when you are, Mr Abbott . . ."

Footsteps suddenly approaching through the fog prompted Abbott to look around.

"Good evening!" Two middle-aged figures, a man and a woman in anoraks, were emerging, arm in arm, out of the grey mist, their faces bright with happiness. "We've been for a walk along the coast and got a bit lost on the moors in the fog," the man said jovially.

"Hope we haven't missed too much." And still smiling the couple walked on past Abbott into the hotel.

"Mr Abbott?" the copytaker reminded as she waited for him to begin his report.

"Jesus Christ!" snarled Abbott.

There was a hesitation down his phone. "Er . . . is this a religious story then, Mr Abbott?"

CHAPTER
TWENTY-SEVEN

Shona couldn't join in. From across the room she watched as Darrell moved around the floor, dutifully clearing up the mess everybody else was leaving. He looked so broken, scrupulously avoiding her eyes, trying to smile as the guests spoke to him, but distracted by hurt. It was all going wrong. While everyone else was enjoying the music, the Doones' regular keyboard player being not at all put out to have been replaced and now beating a tambourine instead, Shona's mind was a tumbril of regret.

Even the oafish Lorna, who actually looked nothing like a young George Clooney when you saw him properly, was getting in on the fun, especially as the guest artists were now playing, and he was singing, the Village People's song "Y.M.C.A.". God! how he loved himself! Up there in front of a posse of local girls, their arms above their heads as they made out the letters Y,M,C and A.

Young man, there's a place you can go
  I said, young man, when you're short on your dough . . .

Shona's sisters had taught her the movements when she was four, and she'd thought it the cleverest thing in the world. She hadn't realized then that *they* were the cleverest thing in her world and she wasn't. She still loved to go through the letters, though, whenever it was played. But not tonight. Biting her lip, she turned away from the stage.

"Are you all right, Shona?" It was Grace, the old lady. She'd been standing by George's wheelchair, like a physiotherapist trying to get him to do the arm movements, as the Red Indian and the cop had done on the video, and getting it hopelessly wrong.

"Yes. I'm fine!" Shona's voice was breaking.

"Y-M-C-A," roared the dancers in front of the stage.

"You don't look very happy," Grace persisted. "I thought you might be crying."

Shona hadn't been crying. Not quite. But she was now. As sympathy was offered she couldn't stop herself. Tears welled, her nose ran. She stood there and sobbed.

"*Y-M-C-A . . . It's fun to stay at the Y-M-C-A.*"

Grace put a hand out, the other still resting on George's wheelchair. "What is it? Can you say? Do you want to talk about it?"

"No." Shona shook her head, her Bo Peep ribbon falling from her hair and forming a loop around her right ear. She wiped away her tears with her sleeve, though not as quickly as new ones arrived.

"Right then." Grace just smiled. And waited.

"*Y-M-C-A . . . You'll find it at the Y-M-C-A.*" Now everyone on the North Devon Riviera seemed to be joining in.

She'd said she didn't want to talk about it, but she did. "It's just me. I spoil everything. I always let everyone down. I'm not clever or pretty like everybody else. I'm just a big, stupid, odd-looking lump who shows off, always saying the wrong thing, and doing the wrong thing, and I never know why. I don't mean to. But I always do. I just disappoint everyone and get everything wrong."

Her tears were now flash floods, her body shaking and gasping. Even George looked up from his wheelchair.

Grace's hand tightened on her. "You're wrong, you know, Shona. People *do* like you. You're not an odd-looking lump and you aren't stupid. You're witty and clever and you make us laugh. And you have eyes to die for. But I'm sure you already know that."

But Shona carried on sobbing, shaking her head, the make-up she'd so carefully applied to give her her sisters' cheek-bones that she'd always wanted, melting into two dirty smears down the sides of her face.

Grace wasn't giving up. "You know, when I was young I always thought I wasn't pretty enough or clever enough. I'm sure I wasn't. But at some point we all realize that there are always going to be more beautiful people in the world than we are, better athletes in the world than us, and certainly there are always going to be more brilliant people. But, Shona, you can be something much better than any of them. You can be the nicest person in the world. That would be easy for you, because you are nice, not in a dull, flat, negative way, but in an extraordinarily exotic and individual way. You're wonderfully different. And, you know, there's nothing as attractive as being nice. In fact, I was just saying to George yesterday how lucky we were to get you serving us this week. 'Watch that girl, George,' I said. 'She'll go places.' They call it charisma nowadays, I think. And God showered you with it. You might not realize it yet, but you're a very lucky girl."

Shona's breathing was beginning to come under control. Fiddling in her pocket, she found a handkerchief. She suddenly felt foolish to have been seen crying in public. She hoped not too many people had noticed.

Grace hadn't finished. "But you don't have to believe me, because, as you know, there's a boy across the room who knows all this better than anyone." She was looking at Darrell. "And I think if you just tried a little harder with him, gave him a chance, because he's young like you and very shy, like you again, I suspect, I think you might both remember this Valentine's Ball for a very long time."

"But I upset him. I was jealous and said something stupid and dirty and suggestive and crude and . . . I really upset him, because he's not like that . . ."

"Which is why he'll be so much happier when he understands that you didn't mean to upset him, and that it was just a mistake. We all say silly things sometimes, you know, even at my age, things we don't mean, things that come out wrong and things that upset people we love. Why don't you wipe your eyes now and then go over and talk to him again? I bet you a million pounds he's wishing you would."

"Now press C to the count of eight, than E for eight more, G . . . and so on to B flat, eight more, that's the black one, and now we have 'Woolly Bully'," Tim was laughing, holding Amy's hand over the notes, but now his hands were resting on hers for longer, more tenderly, no more the fingers of a music teacher.

He looked at her. She was flushed with excitement as all the band now joined in with them and Lorna strode centre stage, throwing his microphone up in the air and catching it, the way real rock stars did. She looked so pretty, Tim thought, and so happy to be silly. He knew she was over thirty and famous, he'd read it on the internet, but tonight she was seventeen again and anonymous. And whatever age she was she was certainly a good generation too young for Teddy Farrow. Tim had seen his show, not often, and, yes, he was a very successful, smooth-talking, clever guy. A real star. But Amy deserved better than that. Much better.

Something she'd told him was nagging at the corner of his mind, something about being on the downside of the see-saw? He tried to remember it as they played. As bright and vivacious as she was, she was certainly on the wrong side of Teddy Farrow's see-saw.

Then almost at his shoulder he felt Amanda's presence. "Presenting Devon's own Lorna and the Doones, featuring brilliant modern composer Tim Fairweather . . . on rock-and-roll keyboard," she was laughing. But she was mocking, too, that touch of spite behind the pretty, over-intelligent smile. "I don't think so, Tim. Do you? Really? Is this what it's come to?" And then she was gone, to the back stalls of his mind, as he helped Amy change key again.

They were both, he and Amy, on the downsides of separate see-saws. He could see it now. Could she? And as her body leaned comfortably, unselfconsciously, into his as she reached for a higher note, and he heard her giggle softly to herself at the sheer nonsense of pretending she could play, he was aware of a stray thought slipping under his guard: This is what it should always be like.

He looked up at that moment and caught sight of Michael and Eleanor, doing their own, polite, respectful approximation of a dance, almost a minuet, smiling at each other as he'd never seen them smile before.

What a night this was. Such a night.

"So, how go our love potions?" Jane looked down the rows of baked, golden-brown éclairs just out of the oven, as Domingos, Agnieszka and the newly recruited Darrell went about splitting each one to let the air escape.

Darrell really didn't mind missing the dance. He felt as though he'd been kicked in the heart. He could actually feel it, the physical pain, like something pressing on a bruise.

"I thought they'd make nice goodnight presents for our guests," Jane said, quickly checking her watch. "They will all be ready? Yes?"

250

Domingos nodded. "And, as you say, the proof will be in the pudding."

Out of their lines of vision Agnieszka shook her head silently.

"So, if we get a surfeit of buns in the oven after tonight and there's a North Devon population explosion at Christmas we'll know who to blame, ha-ha," Jane trilled. She was a little bit drunk after too many glasses of sparkling wine with her guests. But on seeing the blank faces of Domingos and Agnieszka she quickly re-assumed her managerial dignity. "Anyway, jolly good. And especially well done to you, too, Darrell. You'll go far in this business." And she returned to the Ball.

Darrell had barely noticed the compliment. He couldn't get an image of Shona and Lorna out of his mind, Shona and Lorna doing things together in the Doones' black van with the black windows, where all kinds of things were said to go on.

"So, all we need to do now is add the filling, stand well back and . . . population boom!" And Domingos tapped the large pan of cream filling he'd prepared, before peering inside the oven to check the last batch of love éclairs.

"Boom nothing!" Agnieszka muttered to herself, surreptitiously tasting the cream filling she was stirring. "This never work. Quails' eggs! We need vodka."

Now Darrell rather hoped it wouldn't work.

From the oven there was a sudden outburst: "No!" Domingos' head withdrew. "The power's gone. The oven don't bake no more." And muttering in

Portuguese he withdrew the last batch of éclairs and went down the kitchen to the trusty old Aga.

"Can I help?" Darrell asked, following him.

"No, no. I do." Domingos waved him away. "It's nothing. You go back to the dance. No problem."

Then it happened, so quickly that Darrell could hardly believe what he'd seen. But as he turned he saw Agnieszka empty the bottle of vodka she kept in the kitchen for small celebrations into the pan of cream filling that Domingos had so carefully concocted. In a second, the bottle had disappeared and she continued stirring. She didn't even know Darrell had seen her.

For a moment Darrell wondered whether he should say something. But Domingos would find out soon enough, and tonight Darrell really didn't care about anything.

She couldn't keep up her one-finger recital for ever, and, her ambition achieved, after a storming version of Stevie Wonder's "Superstition", in which Tim managed to make the keyboard sound like the quacking of a very tuneful duck, the guest artists left the stage to merry applause, leaving the Doones to play out the rest of the evening.

Now Tim and Amy did touch as they danced, as the Valentine's mood demanded that the music slow and the lights dim further, his hands on her waist, hers at his shoulders. Nor was she embarrassed to be staring so closely at him, seeing the little cut on his cheek from shaving, and how his bandage looked almost overgrown now at the sides of his head by his long wavy hair. And

252

it struck her that although she'd changed the bandage once, standing behind him, she'd never actually seen his face without it. That white band across his forehead was a part of how he looked, like the colour of his eyes or the size of his wide, curly nose.

All around them couples were beginning to smooch, but not them. This wasn't the start of an affair, she told herself, as she spotted a scowling Abbott and his photographer at the back of the crowd still watching them. They were just two friends who'd seen off a dirty newspaper reporter with a small lie. Tomorrow she'd be seeing Teddy again.

Eighteen inches from her eyes Tim was smiling. She smiled back and, after a short moment, rested the side of her face on his shoulder. But only because it had been a busy day and she was tired. Nothing more.

"So you work here, do you?" Lorna was squatting down between songs, leaning from the stage, as Shona, her face washed and make-up re-applied, filled a tray with empty glasses.

She nodded, getting on with her work.

"Bit of a dump, isn't it!"

Shona continued collecting the glasses. "Actually, I like it here," she heard herself say, noticing for the first time that the singer had some side teeth missing.

"Yes, well, maybe, but there's a party in Taunton when we finish. I bet you'd enjoy that more. You could come with us in the van. You'd like that. There's plenty of room. What's your name?"

For the first time, Shona noticed that Darrell was standing close by, overhearing the conversation, though pretending not to. "Shona," she mumbled.

Lorna made an exaggerated sucking sound of approval. "Shona! That's an exciting name. Shona! Very sexy!" And smiling right at her he handed her his empty glass.

Taking it, she was about to turn away, but at the last moment she just couldn't resist it. Looking back up at him she smiled wilfully. "Do you think so? Do you really think so? Thank you. That's nice. But you can call me B, if you like."

Lorna smirked victoriously, *Pulled!* his eyes said. "B? Ah! A second name. Mysterious, eh! Better and better. What's B short for, then?"

Shona smiled sweetly. "Hepatitis. Enjoy your party, dickhead!" And, picking up her tray, she strutted away towards the kitchen.

Thank you, God, Darrell said to himself. Thank you, thank you, thank you!

On the stage, Lorna, seeing him watching, laughed, not at all offended. Then, standing up, he looked around for another girl who might fancy a drive in the Doones' black van. There were always a couple to choose from, even at the North Devon Riviera Hotel.

"And so the reclusive, romantic Amy Miller and her new fiancé, danced the Valentine's night away, lost in each other's arms, here on the North Devon Riviera, secret lovers no longer . . ." Will Abbott, a hand over

254

one ear, his mouth close to his phone, added additional, late detail to the story he'd filed earlier, his eyes never leaving Amy and Tim. "*Ends*," he snapped.

"Is that it?" the copytaker enquired.

"That's it," Abbott said wearily.

"Just putting it through to the newsdesk basket. There you go. Gone. It's lovely, isn't it? Just like one of her books."

"What?"

"A nice happy ending," the copytaker replied.

"I bloody well hope not," Abbott stabbed back, and hung up.

Suzy was waiting for him, watching the dancers, and looking hopefully towards the dance floor. Surely she didn't want to dance! For God's sake!

CHAPTER
TWENTY-EIGHT

So was this it? Amy thought, as the evening slow-danced towards bedtime, and floating ghosts of light from a revolving glitter ball glanced across faces, hair, dresses and shoulders and moved on. Was this the ritual face of romantic love in its various guises? Love the amphetamine, love the addiction, love the physical tyrant, lips on lips, hands on bottoms, and thighs scissoring? Or even love the fairy tale, leaving some couples dreamy and coy, and others caught in the euphoria before the delusion? Perhaps, for some, there would be no delusion. Could love have a happy ending? And she looked across at Grace moving slowly around George's wheelchair, murmuring along to what everyone knew as the Robin Hood song that Bryan Adams had sung, *"Everything I do, I do it for you"*; carer and cared for, lover and loved. Was this what love looked like?

Or was love just the selfish gene in all of us endlessly reinventing ways to continue the species, dressing, embroidering and decorating our human lives with emotion and urges simply for the sake of procreation?

She knew which she preferred. Again she nestled her head into Tim's shoulder. I must remember this moment, she told herself. When I write again tomorrow I must remember what I've been thinking. And she closed her eyes.

Tim felt her breath on his neck. And exulted in the moment.

Embarrassed, and still avoiding each other's eyes, they nearly missed it. Recalled to the kitchen to be ready with the éclairs, the song was halfway through before Shona realized. Dare she? "Darrell, you promised me!"

He hesitated.

"It's the last waltz . . . you did promise me, sort of. Didn't you?"

For a moment, she thought he was going to turn away, not want her and make an excuse about what Jane would say.

Then suddenly he was pulling her through the swing doors into the ballroom, bossing his way to the middle of the floor.

"Thank you," she whispered.

But he just smiled and smiled, as holding each other they made their tiny circles, more shuffle-shuffle than one-two-three, one-two-three, more a clutch than a last waltz. Not even an impassioned Lorna declaring *"everything I do, I do it for you"* to a girl showing rather too much of the catapult of her thong could spoil their moment. And then, best of all, when the song seemed about to end, the Doones played an extra instrumental section to draw it out even further. And still Darrell smiled, though all around them the room was snogging like crazy.

"D'you ever think about leaving here, Darrell?" Shona ventured at last as they danced.

"Where would I go?"

She shrugged. "Anywhere. I thought about going around Hungary after Easter. We could go together. The hotels are really cheap there. I'm sure you'd like it."

Darrell smiled. "Hotels?"

"Mmm. Really cheap, especially in the country areas."

Darrell's round face was dimpling in amusement.

Shona was puzzled. "Did I say something funny?"

"Well, the idea of me in a hotel!"

"What do you mean?"

He was in difficulties. "In a hotel . . . it's hard to imagine."

"But you're *in* a hotel, Darrell."

He nodded, happily. "Oh yes, but this is different."

"Why?"

"Well, hotels are places to work. I've never *stayed* in one. Not as a guest. I wouldn't know what to do."

For a moment, Shona stared at him. Then she hugged him very tightly. "Oh, Darrell, you are lovely."

The balloons had been Jane's idea, so naturally it was she who released them. As the Doones struck their final chord, Barry Harrison handed her the kitchen scissors and she cut the string. Now the nets opened and down and around the balloons floated, each one bearing the

North Devon Hotel Riviera legend. Head office in Bristol had questioned the extravagance, but this was one battle she'd won.

"Very nice," smiled Barry.

"Thank you, Mr Harrison," she replied graciously. Now there was just one more thing to do, and before the final applause had begun to fade, she'd launched herself on to the stage, her steps careful, anxious as she was not to trip over any of the Doones' equipment. Taking the microphone from its stand, she put it to her mouth, although not too close: she'd seen Lorna virtually sucking it earlier, and who knew where those lips had been?

"Well, that's about it for this year," she said, her voice booming nevertheless out of the rock speakers.

The Doones' bass player moved quickly to turn the volume down.

"Yes, sadly, we have to finish now, but we at the North Devon Riviera Hotel would like to thank you all for coming and hope you've all enjoyed a wonderful, romantic evening —"

A startle of applause from the Wiveliscombe coach party momentarily interrupted.

Jane acknowledged their support, then continued a little spicily. "And I imagine that for some of you the romance of Valentine's Day might not be quite over yet —"

The interruption this time came in the form of a beery guffaw from some lads close to the now-closed bar.

She'd intended to finish there, but suddenly her tone changed and the focus in her eyes clouded as new thoughts arose. "And I hope that will apply even to those who are no longer young and beautiful. I hope that the romance of tonight, whether real or illusionary, whether enjoyed this evening or simply remembered, will stay with you . . . because there are left-overs in love too, you know, those who can't find a chair when the music stops and always seem to be left standing."

The guests who'd been thinking about collecting their coats stopped. A murmur of embarrassment moved across the room and fell to silence.

"You see, being unloved doesn't mean that one doesn't yearn for love. In fact, I'm sure the unloved amongst us yearn for it more than anyone else."

Across the room, Amy was concentrating. Michael and Eleanor were holding hands. Barry Harrison looked uncomfortable. Even the Doones were listening.

"So, for all those here tonight who sometimes feel like the forgotten in love, those who no one ever picks for their team, let me just say, never give up hope, because, though you may not know it, somebody always loves you."

From the lobby came the rude bang of a balloon being burst. Some of the younger girls giggled. But the sight of the manager of the North Devon Riviera Hotel swaying on the stage mesmerized most of those watching.

Finally, Jane remembered the purpose of her speech and raised her hand towards the kitchen. "Anyway, to round off the evening we thought we'd present you all with a little going-home love potion that Domingos, our wonderful Brazilian chef, has concocted for us."

And at that moment the kitchen doors opened and Domingos, Agnieszka, Shona and Darrell emerged bearing trays of éclairs above their heads.

"Love potions!" Grace smiled to Amy, wagging her head. "As George always said, it isn't youth that's wasted on the young. It's sex." Then she pushed George forward in his wheelchair. "Come on, George. Better get in the queue. You never know."

CHAPTER
TWENTY-NINE

"You don't taste anything quite like this every day," Tim mused as he savoured his éclair.

Amy was licking the cream, which was escaping from the two halves of her pastry. "It must be eighty per cent proof. Tastes good! I think! Though God knows what's in it. Some kind of nuts, Devon clotted cream, maybe . . . and is it vodka? D'you think we're allowed another?" And without waiting for an answer, she reached out and took two more from Darrell's plate.

Tim looked around the room. He didn't believe in love potions, but perhaps others did, so quickly were the trays being emptied. Everywhere perplexed-looking guests were considering what it was they were eating, because the éclairs really did have a quite peculiar taste. Close by them, Michael and Eleanor were eating theirs delicately, as though trying to guess what ingredients had been used, Grace was feeding George his before eating her own and Jane, the manager, was giggling over a third helping with brown-suited Barry, who seemed to have been recruited as a temporary member of the staff. And finally, having served everyone else, Darrell was cautiously nibbling at his, while Shona gulped hers down in almost one bite. Certainly everyone was smiling about these love potions, with the exception of the reporter who, having refused his, was now sulking at the back of the room, his eyes still on Amy.

But it was late and, quickly, as the éclairs were gone, the room began to empty. Soon, just the stragglers who'd drunk too much were left. From outside came the growing roars of car engines starting. Now Shona and Darrell began again, clearing glasses and plates, while by the kitchen door the chef and his assistant seemed to be having some sort of friendly argument in a mixture of Polish and Portuguese.

"I suppose that's it then . . ." Amy said, almost sadly, as she and Tim left the ballroom and threaded their way through the last of the local guests in the hall who were pulling on their coats.

"Glad you came now?" asked Tim.

Amy looked over her shoulder at the reporter who was still watching her. "Glad I came," she agreed. "And thank you. For everything. You saved my life tonight."

By now they were on the stairs. "You were hardly drowning."

"I was struggling. Out of my depth. Thank you for the white lie."

"Thank *you*," Tim said. They'd reached the landing and begun making their way towards their rooms.

"You know, you've really helped these last few days —" she was continuing.

"Snap!" he interrupted. "You've helped me write. I was stuck, blocked. Going the wrong way. Blind. Not now."

"That's nice," she said. "It's been . . ."

"A special time. For me, anyway."

"More than special," she blurted. Then she stopped talking, looking as though she'd said more than she intended. They'd reached Tim's door. Amy looked towards her own room. "Well, anyway . . ."

"Oh-oh!" Tim was glancing back down the landing.

From the stairs came the sound of Abbott and the photographer. "If bloody Rambo hadn't been stuck to her side like a barnacle on a barge's arse all night . . ." His voice carried up the stairs.

"Sounds like your pals are coming." Tim unlocked his door. "Maybe you'd better come in here or they won't believe we're really engaged."

Amy hesitated. "Er . . . I'm not sure that's a very good idea. I'm being picked up tomorrow morning and —"

"Shh."

Abbott and the Suzy had rounded the corner and were walking towards them.

"Oh, God!" Amy said and walked quickly into Tim's room.

He closed the door after her. "Did you hear that?" he whispered, mock indignant. "Do I look like a barnacle to you?"

She giggled. "Better a barnacle than a barge's arse."

"I promise you, you're nothing like a barge's arse."

"Thank you."

"Well, perhaps a very small one."

They were both smiling, Amy with her back to the door. "I think you ought to know I don't do this sort of thing," she said. "I mean, I don't go into hotel bedrooms with strange men."

"Nor me," Tim said. "But I'm not really that strange, am I?"

"Not strange at all. But I think you know what I mean."

He knew very well what she meant. They stood and looked at each other. Dare I, thought Tim. If I don't, I'll spend the rest of my life regretting it. But what if she looks pained and turns away?

She was still looking at him.

He dared. Leaning forward, he kissed her neck.

She tilted her head sideways and craned her neck slightly. She didn't look pained at all. Or even long suffering. So he kissed her again. Very gently.

She began talking again: "I mean, I know lots of friends might think, 'Oh, what the hell, Teddy's been messing me around. Now it's my turn to have some fun' . . ." Was she trying to pretend he wasn't kissing her? he wondered.

But he was. "I can't believe that," he teased. And he kissed her once again. She didn't resist.

"Oh yes," she went on matter-of-factly. "But not me. I don't think like that. I'm one of those pathetic, clinging, boring, faithful creatures."

"Good." His lips had now found the side of her cheek.

"I mean. I've never had a one night-stand in my life." Now the side of her mouth.

"No?" He didn't mean to, but he must have sounded surprised.

She looked slightly guilty. "Well, almost never. And it didn't really count."

"No? Because you were drunk!"

"Not me. He was. He couldn't remember anything about it the next day."

"Poor guy." He'd reached her lips fully. A small kiss. "Silly me."

"Everybody has some youthful indiscretions."

"But what I'm trying to say is that whatever you're expecting, don't. Because it isn't going to happen."

"I know." Another kiss. Longer.

"You know?" This time she stopped him.

"Of course."

"How do you know?" she demanded.

"I've made my mind up. What kind of pushover do you take me for, anyway?"

"What d'you mean, 'we're going'? It's after midnight." Suzy was sitting on the bed watching as Abbott packed.

"We're going back to London."

"But why? Why now? What's the hurry?"

"Well, there's nothing to stay here for, is there?" He knew that was a brutal thing to say, but he wasn't sorry.

Suzy's eyes creased as she registered the insult. Then she began to pack, too. They'd brought so little it hardly took more than a few moments. The last item to be pushed into her shoulder bag was her book, *The Ladder of Sex*. She didn't bother to close the bag.

Abbott was ready. "OK, let's go!" And picking up his things, he opened the door and walked on ahead of her down the landing, casting a vicious eye at Tim's door as he passed. He was still glaring at it when he walked right into Michael and Eleanor as they came round the corner, laughing together.

A pace behind him Suzy had to stop suddenly, her bag toppling from her shoulder on to the fold of her elbow.

"Oh, excuse me! I'm terribly sorry," Michael apologized earnestly, although his face was pink and amused.

Eleanor was beaming.

Abbott ignored them, and, pushing past, continued angrily on his way. Hitching her bag back up to her shoulder Suzy followed him away down the stairs.

"Oh dear!" Eleanor said, and pulled a funny face. "Perhaps she should have had that éclair after all."

Michael didn't follow.

"The young lady . . . she said she was slimming when they offered her one."

"Ah, well, that's their loss," Michael laughed and feeling in his pocket for their room key continued on his way.

It was at that moment that Eleanor saw the book lying on the floor. She picked it up. *The Ladder of Sex*, she read silently to herself. Then she opened it. A full-page photograph of a very large and rather shiny penis entering a vagina was the first thing she saw. She gazed in astonishment and wonder rather than shock, then turned the page. There was another erotic picture there and then another and another as she skimmed through the book. So much sex. She'd never realized there was so much to it. "Chapter Fourteen, The Goal Mouth Incident," she read. What on earth could that be?

Michael had already opened the door.

Had the young couple dropped their book? she wondered. She should give it back to them. It wasn't hers. She hurried to the top of the stairs. There was no sign of them in the lobby. Then another thought occurred. Might they be embarrassed if she suddenly pursued them with it? And supposing they hadn't been the ones to drop it. It could be very awkward. Perhaps, in this situation, finders keepers might be the most delicate way of resolving the problem.

She looked inside the book again. On the first page was a section entitled "The Missionary Position". She'd once considered becoming a missionary, she remembered. Her father had begged her not to go so far away. She moved on through the book. On the very last page was a photograph of a naked man and woman on a white bed, the man lying back staring peacefully, happily above him, while the woman was curled up comfortably inside the protection of his outstretched arm, her eyes closed.

"Eleanor!" she heard Michael call from their room.

She moved to the door of the Passion of the West Country honeymoon suite clutching the book. There was so much to learn. "Michael!" she said. "Do you still believe in miracles?"

And smiling happily, she went inside, and closed the door.

Amy watched as Tim poured the boiling water on to the instant coffee in the two mugs. She really didn't know what to think. First he kissed her, *then* he made some coffee. Surely that was back to front. Actually, she was embarrassed. "I'm sorry if I misread the situation, but you're putting out some very confusing signals," she said.

Tim opened a carton of milk. "I don't see what's confusing about it. Milk? You don't take sugar, do you!"

"Yes, milk. Thank you." He'd noticed about the sugar. That was nice. Teddy could never remember.

He passed her the coffee. "I hope it isn't too strong."

"I'm sure it's fine. Look, just before, when you said you'd made up your mind, that it wasn't going to happen . . . were you sort of saying that you just don't fancy me?"

He nodded. "That's right. I just don't fancy you."

"Ah! I see. That's all right then. Good." She sipped her coffee, trying not to show her disappointment.

"No. Bad," he said. "I don't just fancy you. I'm in love with you. It isn't the same."

Abbott and Suzy left without paying, the manager being deep in conversation on a sofa in the bar with a guy in a brown suit, while the two young assistants were too busy tidying up to notice. The hotel had his credit card details. They could send the invoice on.

By the time they reached the Porsche, the car park was empty. "We shouldn't be driving in this fog," Suzy fretted. "It isn't safe."

"It's only a local sea mist. We'll be out of it in five minutes," Abbott said, unlocking the car doors and climbing in.

Suzy slid in and slammed her door.

He put the key in the ignition and turned on the engine. The engine was cold. He revved it for a few moments.

"It's a pity we never got this far," Suzy said suddenly as they waited.

"What?"

"In the book. 'Chapter Seventeen. Spice Things Up with a Different Location.' There's a whole section on sex in cars. It looked interesting."

He looked at her. She was a very, very sexy woman. Then he thought about Ed Halliwell. "This car's too small for that."

"I thought the seats went back," she said, "like recliners."

"You know about sex in cars, too, do you?" he snapped unkindly, and put the car into reverse.

"Thank you." Again she looked hurt. Then she bit back. "Doesn't everyone? Don't you?"

It was true, he thought. Nearly everyone had had sex in a car at some time in their life.

He put the gear stick back into neutral. "We couldn't do it here, anyway. Someone might see us."

"In the fog?"

He hesitated. "Did you read it . . . the bit about sex in cars?" With light from the dashboard he could see she was slumped deep in the seat, her thighs raised slightly.

270

"Yes. But it doesn't matter. Let's just go."

He looked around at the fog. It really was quite thick. He could scarcely see the hotel lights just thirty yards away. He turned off the Porsche's engine. "Do you know what it said?" he asked and put a hand on her knee.

"What's to know!" She looked at him.

"Can you remember?"

A shrug. "I might be able to."

He put an arm around her neck and drew her towards him. "Do you want to try?"

"The car's too small. You said it yourself."

"No, it isn't. Not really. I'm sure we could manage."

"It would be very awkward."

"More fun then."

"You're a real bastard, you know," she said. "I really liked you."

"Yes. I am a bastard. I do know," he replied honestly. And putting his hand to her belt he undid the top metal button of her jeans. "So, what do you think? What should we do now?"

She looked at him and it occurred that her pretty pug-like face was smiling as though she'd won a final little victory. She had. "What do *you* want to do?"

"Well . . ." He couldn't resist it.

She leaned across and kissed him with those succulent red lips. "Just unzip and pull."

With the absence of a sofa in the Exmoor Suite, Amy made herself comfortable on the bed, propping her back against the headboard as she drank her coffee. "I think you're just imagining you're in love with me because Amanda's away and you're lonely," she said. "It's a well-known fact. Abstinence makes the fond heart wander."

"Not in my case," Tim said. "I really am in love with you." And he joined her on the bed.

She made space for him, puzzled for a moment, and then said, "Or perhaps it's because it's Valentine's night and you want to feel romantic."

"Wrong again," Tim came back, watching her closely. She sounded sleepy, but was making no attempt to leave.

A sudden look of triumph appeared. "I know. It's the Brazilian love potion they gave us. It must have worked . . . like in *A Midsummer Night's Dream*."

"Meaning that if you'd been an ass, as well as a barge's arse, I'd still have fallen in love with you. I doubt it. That was just a profiterole with a funny taste and soaked in alcohol."

Finally she sighed. "Well, there must be some explanation."

Tim nodded. "Yes. There is. I keep telling you. But you just don't want to hear it."

CHAPTER
THIRTY

The guests were long gone. Only the staff remained, Jane having reopened the bar, sharing a last drink with Barry Harrison, Shona taking down the Valentine decorations, Darrell patrolling the ballroom, filling a series of plastic bags with party refuse, and Domingos and Agnieszka tidying the kitchen and already preparing for breakfast. There'd nearly been a row earlier when Domingos had tasted one of the éclairs, and almost, but not quite, spat it out. Then catching Agnieszka watching him to see his reaction he'd suddenly burst into laughter, and said something in Portuguese that had made her laugh and reply in Polish. How much they each understood of what the other was saying was hard to tell, but probably more than Shona had initially realized. Their relationship was a puzzle, but, in its off-hand, sniping, duo-lingual way, it seemed to work. And she wondered whether she'd been missing some unspoken little attraction, whether behind the banter and insults there was something else lurking, just waiting to be freed.

"Oh dear, are you all still up! I think you can leave the rest until tomorrow, don't you!" Jane was standing in the door to the bar holding a glass. Shona had never seen her so friendly. Behind her Barry Harrison, now in his shirtsleeves, was watching.

"Thank you," Shona said. "Goodnight."

Darrell put down his plastic bag as Jane returned with Harrison to the bar. "Well!" he said, watching them together, and shook his head in astonishment.

Shona didn't care about Jane and Harrison. Grabbing hold of a streamer made of red plastic hearts she put it around Darrell's neck like a Hawaiian garland. "That's my Valentine to you."

Darrell shone. "Thank you," he said and glanced towards the kitchen to see if Domingos and Agnieskza had noticed. They'd already left.

"I suppose we might as well go to bed then," Shona said, and picking up a stray balloon and a bottle of red wine that wasn't quite finished, she led the way across the ballroom.

At the door, Darrell looked back at the rubble of the evening. "We'll have a bit of a job tomorrow tidying this lot up," he worried. But Shona was already heading towards the staff quarters.

Turning out the lights, he followed her out of the back door, across to the old stable building and up the stairs to the bedrooms. She didn't look back, not even when she sensed him hesitate at his door.

Shona was already unlocking hers. "You've never seen my room, have you, Darrell . . ." she said. "It's really nice." And she stepped inside leaving the door ajar.

There was a second hesitation from the corridor. Then Darrell followed her in.

She tried the light switch. As expected, the room remained in darkness. "Oh, no! The bulb seems to have gone," she said, hoping she sounded convincingly surprised.

"Not to worry, I'll just pop down to the storeroom and get another," Darrell offered quickly, ever helpful.

Quickly she leaped between Darrell and the door and closed it. "Oh, no! No! It doesn't matter! Honestly! It will do tomorrow!"

Darrell looked at her. Standing there, her balloon hovering at her shoulder, in the yellow glow sieving through the fog from the courtyard lights, she was beautiful.

Jane considered the glinting cognac in the bottom of her glass. She would leave the reckoning up of how much she owed the bar for another day. She looked at Harrison. For weeks she'd known and slightly despised him, as a boastful, vulgar, pathetic loser. He was a loser all right. He'd lost his wife and children to another man. His business hadn't worked. He had no home and no real hopes. All this had spilled out between the drinks, not in bitterness or anger, not even in self-pity. He was just puzzled by life. He couldn't understand how it had happened. She could. But she no longer despised him, any more than she despised herself. Loneliness can make even the best of people behave foolishly.

She looked at him. He must have been seven or eight years younger than she was, nearer to forty than fifty.

He still had time to make a difference to his life. If she reported him to head office, they would, she was sure, pursue him for the hotel bill he couldn't pay. But there were ways and means of hiding a bad debt.

"Look, you can forget the hotel bill," she said. "When you leave tomorrow, and you must leave tomorrow, just consider it paid. But you must never come back again."

"Thank you," he said simply.

Then very deliberately she put a hand on his and left it there. Perhaps, for once, if only for a night, two left-overs in love could find a place together now that the music had stopped.

She hadn't really been lying to him, she protested softly as she finished her coffee. Withholding her real name and profession were only minor sins forced on her by the circumstances. All the same, she was sorry she'd done it. He wasn't the sort of person who should be lied to.

Tim just smiled. "That's all right. I think I've been misleading myself for a lot longer." And he considered his keyboard on the other side of the room.

All his life music had been a companion. Only when he'd betrayed it by trying to make it do something he didn't believe in had that friendship faltered. Little wonder he hadn't been able to write.

Now, looking back at Amy as she slid comfortably down the bed, he played in his mind his new music, the music he'd been writing all day. He was happy.

"I thought you wouldn't like me."

Darrell was puzzled. "Why's that?" They were sitting next to each other on the edge of Shona's bed, drinking the wine from a shared plastic beaker.

"I don't know. I think I frighten boys. I put them off. I liked you straight away but I really thought I'd put you off tonight. Sometimes I say things I don't really mean. It's a syndrome. There's a medical name for it."

"We just call it silly talk down these parts."

"Yes. That's probably it. That's what I've got. The silly talk syndrome." She passed him the beaker of wine and watched while he drank some. "Aren't you going to kiss me?"

Darrell smiled to himself. He couldn't believe how confident and handsome he suddenly felt. He'd never felt this way before. "Is that the syndrome talking?" he asked. "Or do you mean it?"

Shona giggled in the darkness.

That was nice, too. He didn't usually make people laugh: not on purpose, anyway.

Taking back the beaker Shona helped herself to some more wine and then, putting it down on the bedside table, took off her shoes, swung her legs up and past Darrell and lay down on the bed. "You can lie down, too, if you want to," she said. "There's room. You must be dead tired. You've been on your feet all day."

Darrell did want to lie down. As she moved closer to the wall he stretched out awkwardly alongside her at the edge of the narrow divan bed.

For a few moments neither of them spoke. Darrell wondered what Barry Harrison would say he should do next.

"Shall I tell you something?" Shona said at last, then, without waiting for an answer, did anyway. "I've never had a boyfriend."

"Never?" Darrell found this hard to believe. A glamorous, exotic girl like Shona must have had stacks of boyfriends.

"Not a proper one. Not one for more than a night. Not one I was crazy about who was crazy about me. Actually, nobody's ever been crazy about me."

"I am," Darrell said. He was now leaning on his side, trying to see her features in the darkness.

"Honestly?"

He couldn't be certain, but it looked as though she was very pleased. "Honest!" he said.

"Well, you *have* to kiss me now," she said. "At the very least!"

Very carefully, because he was venturing into unknown territory, he rested his weight on his arm, leaned over and lowered his face to hers. Her eyes were closed.

Suddenly he stopped.

After a moment her eyes opened. "Are you all right? What's the matter?"

He was staring at something to the side of her right ear. "Don't move! By your head," he gasped. He kept on staring, rigid in fear. Lying on the white pillow in the glow from the outside lights was the head and part of the trunk of a long narrow snake.

278

Shona swivelled her head to look. "Oh, that's just Monty!" she said, and laughed.

Darrell still hadn't moved. "Monty?"

"As in python. But he's not really a python. He's just a pet. I've been wondering where he's been all day. I'll put him back in his case if you think he might put you off."

But the snake had already slipped back down the side of the wall and under the bed. Carefully Darrell sank down again alongside Shona, glad that he was well away from the wall.

"I knew you didn't really have Hitler's missing testicle in that box," he said at last.

He felt Shona's lips smile as he bent to kiss her. "Actually, I did," she said. "But Monty ate it."

She was sleepy now. Stifling a yawn, she looked around the room at Tim's computer and scattered sheets of music manuscript and remembered how he said he'd enjoyed himself writing all day. How similar his life must be to mine, she thought, and she remembered the first book she'd written, not for the fame or the money, but because she wanted to. And she wondered whether Amanda understood that emotion. Instinctively she knew she wouldn't, any more than Teddy understood why she sometimes cried when she invented setbacks for her characters. "How can you cry about characters and events you've invented and which exist only in your imagination?" he would tease. She didn't know how. She just knew she did.

She didn't tell Tim any of this. Stirring slightly she said, "You can't fall in love with me, anyway. This is a designated romance-free zone. Remember?"

Tim's arm was around her. "That was your description, not mine. And you were wrong."

Sleep was hovering now, but something was still bothering her. "Don't think I'm being provocative . . . because I'm not. But you didn't actually say why you don't want to make love to me."

"No, I didn't."

"And, having said you're in love with me, which I don't believe for a second, it does seem a sort of contradiction in terms, doesn't it?"

"Not really."

"No? OK! If you say!" She thought about that for a little while, but then decided she still wasn't satisfied. "So . . . I mean, well, why not? I'm just wondering, mind you, not encouraging you."

At her side, Tim became thoughtful. At last he said, "Shall we just say, I don't want to make love to you while you're thinking about somebody else?"

Amy smiled to herself. What had she been writing when Teddy had phoned her to say she was being watched by the reporter?

Given the choice, which would you prefer: that the person you love is making love to you and thinking about someone else, or that he, or she, is making love to someone else and thinking about you?

She closed her eyes.

CHAPTER
THIRTY-ONE

Overnight the fog had dissolved and now the sky was a whispy seaside blue as Darrell made his way across the little enclosed garden to the hotel building. It really did feel like spring, he thought: a wondrous day.

But how did *he* feel? Like he could never have imagined. Different. Happy, yes, but strangely more adult. He even felt taller, physically bigger.

He hadn't wanted to leave Shona. She'd looked so peaceful, seemingly amused by something in her sleep, her frizzed hair scattered haphazardly across the pillow, her bare, freckled arms and shoulders cradling her breasts close to her body. He should have woken her, and insisted she come to work. But he'd let her sleep on. She'd talked half the night, and the other half . . . well . . . she hadn't.

It didn't matter if she was late for work. She was only temporary staff, on a college placement, being paid hardly anything. The hotel could manage without her for another hour. He, however, had a responsible job. It was a Saturday. Saturdays were busy days in hotels.

So, slipping from her divan, he'd picked up his clothes from the floor and shaken them, because you never knew where a snake might have decided to make its bed. Then, dressing quickly, he'd gone back to his own room to wash and shave.

As he let himself into the hotel through the back door, Giles bounded up to him affectionately, and, putting its paws up against his chest, tried to lick his face. He didn't mind, or grumpily try to push the dog off, as he usually did. He didn't mind anything this morning. And he left the back door open for Giles to run outside.

Reaching the lobby he was surprised to find it still deserted. Usually Jane was already there, worrying over invoices and accounts, ready to chivvy everyone along. Not today. And though there was the smell of breakfast from the kitchen, there was none of the usual arguing. Peeping in, he found Domingos with a friendly arm around Agnieszka as she stirred a bowl of scrambled eggs. The day had begun far more happily than any other he'd known in his time in the hotel.

Going through into the loggia, which was to be used for breakfast until the ballroom could be turned back into the dining-room, he smiled as he began pulling down the Valentine decorations. Last night had been the best night of his life. Torquay United's draw with Manchester United didn't even come close.

So engrossed was he in his reverie he didn't hear the taxi until it was at the front door. Going to the window he looked out. A tall, clever-looking woman with crow-black hair was climbing from the cab and paying the driver.

282

He was puzzled. New guests shouldn't arrive until two at the earliest, and he hurried through to the lobby to unlock the front door as the bell rang twice.

A smiling, slightly cocky, metropolitan sort of woman in a black suit stepped inside. In her thirties, she was definitely pretty, but a bit terrifying. "Good morning. Sorry if I got you up," she said lightly, perhaps sarcastically.

"Oh no, I was just —"

She cut him off. "It's just that I'm looking for one of your guests — a Mr Fairweather? Tim Fairweather. He told me he was staying here."

Sensing the newcomer's arrival, Giles padded excitedly into the lobby.

"Oh yes. Mr Fairweather . . . that's room seven, the Exmoor Suite. But he'll probably still be asleep. We had a dance here last night. I'll just . . . Shut up, Giles!"

The dog had begun to bark excitedly, and was now bounding up and down the lobby.

"Quiet, Giles!" insisted Darrell. "I'll just give Mr Fairweather a ring to tell him you're here. Giles! Stop it!"

The woman's exaggerated expression of patience suggested that she was neither used to being kept waiting nor a dog lover.

"You're going out!" Darrell said, and grabbing the dog's collar he pulled him towards the front door. "I'm sorry about this. I won't be a minute. What name shall I say?"

But a minute would clearly have been too long. "I'll find my own way. Room seven?" The woman said and immediately began to climb the stairs.

At the front door Darrell was stranded as he tried to push the dog outside. "Actually, non-residents aren't allowed up to the bedrooms," he shouted, as, once again, Giles tried to come back into the hotel.

But, although she must surely have heard him, the woman made no attempt to stop.

Tim was awake when the phone rang. He had been for an hour, lying alongside Amy, both still dressed but covered by a blanket he'd pulled over them in the middle of the night. He'd been wondering about the person he'd fallen in love with who'd told him her name was Millie. Did it matter that she was actually somebody else, someone far richer and more successful than anyone he knew? And that her name was Amy Miller? Only that it put her out of his league. Soon she would be returning to her old life and her married lover who didn't deserve her, and that would be that. These moments with her sleeping alongside him he would remember for the rest of his life — a fragment of time that he would pluck from his past whenever he thought of what might have been.

Amy stirred with a slightly bewildered look as she heard the phone ring.

He picked it up. "Hello?"

"Sorry to wake you, Mr Fairweather. Front desk here. There's a lady on her way up to see you." Darrell sounded embarrassed.

284

For a second, Tim couldn't quite make sense of this. "Coming up here? What lady?"

"She didn't give her name. I'm sorry, I couldn't stop her."

At his side he could feel the mattress give and spring back as Amy began to move. She'd heard what he said. Almost simultaneously there was a knock on the door. He clambered off the bed.

Then came another, louder knocking.

Within a moment Amy was standing by the French windows. Sadly she tried to smile. Was this the way he would remember her? he thought. As she was at this very second, her hair tousled, eyes bleary, the dress she'd bought for the ball crumpled, holding her party shoes in her hands?

The knocking grew louder. "Tim! Tim!"

He didn't need to recognize the voice. He'd already guessed who his visitor was.

Amy unlocked the French windows.

"Mr Fairweather . . .?" Darrell was prompting down the phone.

"It's all right, Darrell. I'll deal with this." And, hanging up, he crossed to the door.

Swinging her leg over the balcony rail, Amy dropped down on to the narrow ornamental ledge with the low wrought-iron rail that connected all the balconies along the side of the hotel. Then carefully she began to edge along it towards her own room. Five days ago she'd never had to escape from anywhere in her life, now she was doing it for a second time. What was happening to her? She only hoped she'd left the door to her own balcony unlocked.

She didn't look down but kept her eyes on the wall as she reached the window of the suite between Tim's room and her own. At least the curtains would be drawn, she thought, remembering the teenagers she'd accidentally seen petting as she'd climbed down the side of her apartment building. She was only half right. As she passed the window she found herself looking through a small gap in the curtains into the honeymoon suite.

Lying curled happily together in the centre of the white-laced four-poster were Michael and Eleanor.

Quickly averting her eyes, she hurried on, clambering over the rail to her own balcony, and her mercifully unlocked French windows.

Tim stood back as Amanda entered the room.

"God, I thought you must have a girl in here at the very least!" she laughed. "You aren't even undressed. Don't tell me you worked all night again."

"No, I didn't work. I had a lot of thinking to do."

She put her arms around his neck. "Aren't you at least going to kiss me?"

Tentatively he kissed her lips. He'd forgotten how she smelled. Her perfume, once so familiar and welcome, now seemed too sharp.

"Well, I've had more enthusiastic welcomes!"

"I'm surprised to see you. No! I'm amazed to see you. I thought you were still in Denver."

"I came back. How's the head?" She was staring at his bandage. He'd forgotten about it.

"Fine. I told you it was nothing. Did the tour finish early or something? I mean, how did you get here?" He looked at his watch. It was hardly eight thirty.

"I quit. There were problems. You know how these big tours are. It got messy. So I flew home yesterday. I tried to get here last night. Got to Taunton but the taxi driver said it was too foggy on the moors. Didn't want to bring me. So I stayed there. And here I am, up with the badgers, to enjoy the weekend with the man I love." She hesitated. "It seems I missed the big dance."

He nodded. And, yes, he did know how these tours were. Everyone in music did. He knew Amanda, too, and it occurred to him that he was looking at a woman he'd thought he loved. But now he couldn't remember why.

Amanda was still talking. "Your messages sounded so bleak . . . stuck here by yourself. So, I thought, I know, I'll give him a nice surprise!" And then she added, so late it sounded like an afterthought, "Besides, I missed you."

Amy was already in the shower. I'm not crying, she told herself as the early-morning water heated from cold through tepid to hot. I've nothing to cry about. How could I be crying?

Perhaps a fleeting shadow at the window had disturbed Michael, but he'd woken to a new world. At his side he felt the warm, white skin of Eleanor pressed against his.

She was still sleeping, and he luxuriated in her very presence. So *this* was what married life meant. Closeness and contentment.

In the night he'd been amazed at how perfectly their bodies had fitted together. But this morning, this waking moment, made him happier. This was their future together, as naked as babies and almost as innocent.

Lying at the bottom of the bed was the book Eleanor had found, *The Ladder of Sex*. They'd laughed about it the previous night, and wondered whether they truly had been served love potions. He knew they hadn't. Their private ceremony among the ruins of St Gytha's had been all the love potion they needed . . . and, all right, perhaps a little encouragement from the Holy Ghost.

CHAPTER
THIRTY-TWO

Shona hadn't stayed in bed long. She wanted to be with Darrell. Just to be near him, helping him, accidentally on purpose touching his arm as they passed, and sharing little knowing smiles with him was a thrill. Life was suddenly dazzling.

"A degree in hotel management?" her father had laughed when she'd told him what she was going to study at university. "Whatever will these new places think of next? Oh, well, if that's what you want to do with your life . . ." She'd been hurt at the time, having half thought that for once she might be congratulated for her enterprise. But when she'd been laughed at, though her parents had tried to conceal their amusement behind affection, she'd just made a funny face and told a joke, and neither of them had realized. Last night, because he'd asked, she'd told Darrell about the course she was on. He'd been very impressed. "That sounds really good," he'd said. "Your parents must be proud of you."

"Mmm . . . well," she'd said vaguely. She hadn't had the heart to tell him that hotel management was not the academic course her parents would think a daughter of theirs should be taking.

"I'm proud of you, too," he'd then said.

"Really?" she'd asked.

"Yes, of course."

And she'd found herself disguising her tears of happiness, by pushing her face into her pillow.

Now she was busily helping set out the breakfast display in the loggia, with the Scottish hiking couple already down and looking at their maps again, while Darrell had been asked to take some coffee and toast up to room seven, the Exmoor Suite. Outside in the car park Giles was barking repeatedly at something, which was marginally irritating, but at least he wasn't jumping up and frightening Monty.

Quickly she went into the kitchen to give Agnieszka the Scottish couple's order. By the Aga, Jane was going through a list of requirements with Domingos. With her hair dishevelled and her make-up apparently hurriedly applied, she looked, thought Shona, as though she'd been slept in.

"And, Shona, when you have a minute could you see what Giles is so excited about?" Jane said as Shona passed on the order.

"Of course."

Jane smiled. "Good girl."

Good girl! Shona wanted to shake herself. What had come over the woman?

Room service had been Amanda's idea. Tim had been about to tell her that it wasn't fair on the staff to make demands after such a busy night, but, on reflection, he didn't want to parade Amanda before the entire hotel

290

either. Besides, she only wanted a round of brown toast and a cup of coffee.

Since she'd arrived she'd been edgy, and over-casually bored when he'd asked her how the tour had gone. He hadn't pursued the subject. He didn't care how it had gone. Actually, that wasn't quite true. He was pretty sure he knew exactly how it had gone.

Now munching her toast she was moving around his room, smirking disdainfully at the book on film music he'd bought, looking at the scraps of manuscript he'd rejected. He observed her as if from a distance, feeling somehow uninvolved.

"Anyway," she said at last, as though finally reaching a point in their conversation when it was probably polite to ask about work, "how's the piece coming?"

"It's coming," Tim replied without expression.

"Great! Actually, I thought I might be able to help you with it . . . you know, a fresh view . . . a new pair of ears before you submit it."

Tim didn't respond. He hadn't thought of the competition in two days.

Passing him, she ran a hand flintily across his shoulders then sat down at the keyboard and picked up some sheets of manuscript. "Is this it?" Quickly she read the music, then shook her head. "Oh, no, it can't be."

"Actually, it is," Tim said.

She laughed. "No, seriously. Can I see it? Or do you want to play it for me?" And she got up from the keyboard and left it for him.

"*Seriously.* You're looking at it . . . holding it. That's it . . . what I've been working on."

She looked at him as though still half believing he must be teasing her. Then she turned back to the manuscript and scanned the pages again. Finally, she looked back at him, as though still waiting for the joke.

There wasn't one.

"Tim . . ." she said at last, running her forefinger along the lines of notes. "This is pure romantic melody."

Tim nodded. "Yes. Quite a nice little tune, I think, don't you?"

Amanda was becoming impatient. "Well, nice it may be. But you'll be laughed out of the competition with a 'nice little tune'."

Keeping his eyes on her Tim smiled to himself. "I'm sure I will be," he said. "More coffee?"

When her new mobile rang there could only be one caller.

"Amy. I'll be with you in about ten minutes." Teddy was in bouncing form. "I got away early. Great run down the motorway. Just coming across Exmoor now. See you at the front door of the hotel. OK?"

"Er . . . yes." Amy had been sitting, dressed, watching the sea.

"Fantastic. Can't wait to see you." And he hung up.

Amy pulled out her bags, collected her belongings and began to pack. Her party dress was hanging over the back of a chair. Taking a sheet of hotel stationery from the desk she wrote a note for the room maid, and

292

placed it with the dress, her new shoes and new earrings on the unslept-in bed.

I won't need these any more, so if you would like them for yourself, or anybody else you know, please take them.

Then, signing the note *Amy Miller*, she picked up her laptop and bag and made for the door.

"Giles! Giles! Come here, boy!" Shona yelled.

The dog ignored her, tearing around the car in the corner of the car park, barking repeatedly and jumping up at the window.

Shona continued towards it. She was too happy to be cross. "Come on, boy! Here, Giles!"

When she was almost at the car, Giles turned to her, as if wishing to show her something.

That was her chance. Reaching down she grabbed the dog by the thick tuft of black fur on the back of his neck and felt for his collar. He struggled for a moment, pulling her closer to the car. "Hey! Stop that!" she insisted. Then, just as she was about to return to the hotel, she happened to glance inside the car.

At first she didn't quite understand what she was seeing, and momentarily she turned away. Then, puzzled, she stopped and looked back to make sure.

"You're behaving very strangely, Tim. Are you sure your brain wasn't buckled when you fell off your chair?" Amanda's voice had turned brittle.

Tim didn't reply immediately. "Actually, I think it might have been straightened," he said at last.

Amanda's dark brows knitted. "What do you mean?"

"That I'm seeing things more clearly than I was."

Amanda was still by the keyboard. "And?"

"Well, let's put it this way: I think I've been trying to be something I'm not."

"Your brain has definitely been buckled." There was just a touch of derision there.

"No. I don't think so. You've got me wrong, Amanda. Dead wrong! You want me to be someone else. And I can't be. I can't write the music you'd like me to, not anything that would be any good, anyway. I thought I wanted to. For you. For us. But I can only do what I can do. I'd never have a hope in the competition. You know that. I don't even like that stuff."

"But I *love* what you do, Tim." Amanda's voice suddenly softened. She moved closer to him and put a hand on his arm. "Forget the competition. What do those judges know, anyway? All I want is for you to expand your horizons, be more daring. Take risks. Can't you see? You could be so much more than you are, Tim . . . if you could just . . ."

Tim suddenly wasn't listening. He was hardly even seeing Amanda or hearing her ambitions for him. His mind's eye was filled with Amy. "I'm sorry, there's someone I have to talk to . . ." And walking past her, he hurried from the room and down the corridor.

"Tim . . ." Amanda's cry trailed after him.

294

★ ★ ★

"Yes . . . police and ambulance. This is urgent!" Jane was pink, as though she'd been running, shouting into the phone, staring back at the hotel car park as she spoke. At her side, Shona was nodding her head vigorously.

In front of the desk, Amy took her bill from a distracted Darrell, who kept glancing through the window, and keyed in the PIN of her credit card as Domingos and Agnieszka hurried through the lobby and out into the car park. Shona followed them out. "Thank you," said Amy as Darrell gave her a receipt. "Goodbye."

"Thank you," murmured Darrell, though his thoughts were obviously elsewhere.

Picking up her bag and laptop, Amy crossed the lobby and stepped outside, almost colliding with the newsagent and his stack of papers.

"Morning," he smiled. "Seems like there's something going on over there."

Amy looked across the car park. "Yes! I don't know what it is." The Scottish hikers were now approaching the car, too.

Normally she would have gone to investigate but at that moment, as the newsagent got back into his van, she saw Teddy's black BMW coming swiftly up the drive. With a last glance at the hotel, she walked down the drive to greet it as it skirted the car park and drew up beside her.

"Amy . . . love . . ." Teddy smiled as the door opened.

She climbed in.

The car accelerated away.

Tim watched the BMW leave from the hotel step, scarcely aware of the drama developing across the car park. Had he been a second earlier . . .? No. What could he have said? It wouldn't have made any difference. Moving forward, he gazed at the gap in the pine trees into which the car and Amy had disappeared.

So that was that. She was gone, out of his life. But he still stared down the empty drive.

Then suddenly he became aware of a squeal of delight behind him. "Congratulations! I'd no idea." The words were addressed to him. "I didn't even recognize her. Amy Miller! Here! This is wonderful publicity. Bristol will be delighted. Thank you *so* much." It was Jane, the hotel manager, blushing with excitement, holding a newspaper out to him.

Tim looked at it. At the bottom of the front page was a large photograph of Amy walking along the quay with him the previous morning, seemingly sharing a joke. **ROMANTIC AMY IN DISGUISE — KINKY WEEKENDS WITH SECRET FIANCÉ**, ran the headline.

"You naughty things!" teased Jane. "And now she's gone again! It's like hide-and-seek. Such fun!" For a moment, in her excitement, she seemed to have quite forgotten the evergrowing crowd building around the car, as now Grace pushed George past them to take a look. Then she was off again, back across the car park.

Tim didn't care about the car. He was staring at the newspaper.

So was Amy. It had been waiting for her on the passenger seat of the BMW, Teddy having spotted it when he'd stopped for petrol on the way down. "But it isn't true!" she gasped. "None of it."

At the wheel, Teddy was almost laughing in triumph as he drove quickly up towards the moors. "How about that for a pick-up?" he chortled. "Like clockwork. No one even saw me. Well done!"

"But, Teddy . . ."

"And you're looking wonderful. Truly wonderful! The sea air's done you good. I love the hair, too. Like spun gold. Burnished gold even! You're nothing like a platypus, even if you are engaged." And he laughed, foolishly.

Amy was shaking her head. "But I'm not engaged. You know I'm not. He just said that to put them off the scent. To make them leave me alone."

"So? Who cares? The papers get it wrong again. It happens every day. My, have I been looking forward to seeing you!" And suddenly putting a hand out, he stroked the top of her thigh.

She didn't like that. It wasn't affectionate. It was proprietorial. She studied the newspaper, turning to an inside page to read the main story and the suggestion of sexy games she was supposed to have played. "This is terrible," she murmured.

Teddy was still breezy. "Come on, it doesn't matter."

"What? *Doesn't matter!*" She stared at him. As usual, not a hair was displaced, his smooth face was tanned and healthy-looking, and his weekend clothes, the corduroy trousers, hound's-tooth shirt and cashmere navy blue sweater looked as though he was wearing them for the very first time. Everything about him suggested success and wealth. And self-satisfaction. An image of the shaggy Tim, his long hair and his bandage coming loose again, peeped at her from the previous night.

The siren of a police car travelling quickly in the opposite direction across the moor made her look at the road. A couple of hundred yards behind it an ambulance was following, its light flashing.

"What did you do back there before you left? Murder someone? Was it that boring?" Teddy joked.

Amy put the newspaper on her knee. "Teddy . . ."

He sighed. "Amy, OK! You had a holiday fling! You're entitled. It happens. You're a single girl. I do understand. Pity the papers got to know, but —"

"But it didn't happen. I didn't have a fling."

Teddy gave her a sideways, old-fashioned look. "Amy! Come on!"

"I *mean* it." She was almost shouting.

Teddy shrugged and smiled. "OK! I really don't mind. It doesn't matter."

"*Don't mind?*" Amy could feel herself going red with anger.

"It's worked. The papers are off our backs. There's no one spying on us any more. We're in the clear. In some ways this guy . . . whatever his name is . . . he's perfect."

That was it. "Stop the car!" Amy snapped.

"What?"

"Stop this car!"

"We're in the middle of the moor?"

"Just stop this bloody car!"

CHAPTER
THIRTY-THREE

The dash across the car park had now become a gentle stampede as Barry Harrison put his two suitcases down on the hotel steps and hurried over, passing the elderly ladies on the way. Even Michael and Eleanor, who was dressed today in an almost daring plum-coloured jacket, couldn't resist the temptation. Only Tim had no interest.

"Tim!"

He looked round.

Amanda was holding a newspaper she must have picked up at reception. "Why didn't you tell me?"

He didn't answer.

"This is sick!" She began to read. "*According to her fiancé, Tim Fairweather, the couple meet regularly in out-of-the-way hotels for sex, pretending to be strangers.* Is this true? No. Don't try to lie. Why else would you be in this godforsaken dump? Christ! Amy Miller! There's an overpaid, over-rated, chick-lit tart if ever there was one!"

Tim had never hated anyone. He rarely actually disliked anyone. But at this moment Amanda was coming very close to being the first.

She hadn't finished. "Well! Say something! How long has it being going on? How long have I been wasting my life on you . . . doing everything I could to help your career . . . introducing you to new music . . . new ideas . . . new people who could offer you new possibilities . . . when all you want to do is write mushy, trite little melodies to match Amy Miller's pathetic little stories."

The sound of a police car and ambulance entering the car park interrupted her venom.

"Well? Can't you say *anything*?"

Tim could have said so much, mainly that for the life of him he couldn't imagine why they'd ever got together in the first place. He didn't. There was no point. "I think it's time we both tried other see-saws," he said.

Amanda pulled a face, her beautiful, classical, clever features twisting into a sharp slice of bitter derision. She looked almost ugly. "If that's some kind of cryptic riddle . . ." she spat.

But he wasn't listening. Turning away, he walked across the car park to the crowd and watched as the police conferred, the ambulance waited and a fire engine arrived. Everyone was there. Jane was supervising, while telling the police officers that Amy Miller had just been a guest; George and Grace were watching bemused, and Darrell was standing gallantly alongside Shona, who appeared once again to be feeding something under her shirt. Beyond them, Michael and Eleanor were hand in hand; the white-clad kitchen staff had their arms around each other, and

Barry Harrison was back in his brown suit, leering fruitily.

Peering over Harrison's shoulder, Tim looked at the car. It was the reporter's Porsche. Shifting his position he got a better view. Inside he could make out the bare cheeks of Abbott's bottom, framed by the two jack-knifed thighs and knees of his pretty photographer, who appeared to be wedged under him. With one foot stuck in the spokes of the steering wheel, she wasn't looking quite so cute today.

Harrison was smiling. "It's St Valentine's Revenge," he whispered over-loudly. "They must have been there all night. Looks like he's been clamped." And he chuckled smuttily to himself.

A sudden flash made them both glance round. And then another. No one had noticed a local photographer appear on his motor cycle. Some newspaper would pay handsomely for photographs like this.

Tim had seen enough. Backing away, he ignored the hotel, where Amanda was still waiting, and set off across the car park and down the path towards the town. There was only one person he wanted in his thoughts, and she wasn't here. Everything else was just getting in the way.

For some reason, though numb with cramp, Abbott was thinking about Polly, the neighbourhood snitch in the helmet with the *South Park* transfer, who'd got him into Amy Miller's apartment block. She'd got a crush on him, believing his profession to be glamorous and exciting. And he'd used her to help him get what he wanted. Would she still have a crush on him when she saw the photographs of his backside on newsstands across the country tomorrow morning? Would she still want a tour of the newsroom? And would Jenny, his wife, be thrilled? And the boys?

If he could have sighed he would have done. What was it, he puzzled, that drove reasonably sensible, intelligent men and women to mate as promiscuously as bonobos whenever the opportunity presented itself? Were some people like him built with a design flaw, something that dictated that no matter how happily married they were, and he and Jenny were very happily married, they just couldn't turn down the opportunity of a quick extra-marital adventure?

From the angle at which he was stuck he couldn't see Suzy's face, just her ear and the dark roots in her thick, bleached hair. They'd stopped talking, blaming each other, hours earlier when they'd given up trying to move. They'd never had much to say to each other at the best of times. But now, as indignity was added to the hours of cramp and pain, he felt ashamed. In her own sexy way she'd been affectionate and kind. She didn't deserve this.

Out of the corner of his eye he now saw the sparkle of a fireman's acetylene cutting equipment approaching. It looked like a firework, but it was hardly the best way to celebrate the end of a dirty weekend.

Teddy had pulled the BMW off the road into an Exmoor picnic area. From the passenger seat Amy looked out on a light scatter of litter around a rubbish bin, cigarette butts, chewing-gum paper and part of a Mars bar wrapper. There was even a used condom lying in the dust. Human beings were such untidy animals, she thought. Her life was untidy.

"Amy?" Teddy waited.

She was hunched up against the passenger door. "It just won't work any more," she said. Perhaps she should have had tears in her eyes, but she couldn't feel any.

Teddy was confused. "What?"

"I'm sorry."

"But why, Amy? What are you saying?"

She shook her head. She couldn't explain.

"Amy, think about it. It'll be all right." He took the newspaper from her. "Don't worry about this. It means we can still see each other. In secret. And if you want to, you know . . . continue with . . ." He indicated the newspaper and the photograph of Tim. "Well, you know, I'm married, I'm not the possessive type."

"That's the point," Amy burst out. "What's wrong with the possessive type?" He still didn't believe her. "I *am* the possessive type, and I *want* the possessive type."

Carefully he put a coaxing arm on the back of her seat. "I'm sorry. I didn't mean that. Look, just come and see the cottage. Sleep on it. We'll talk about it later. You've had a tricky time. I'm sorry I got you to come down here. It was a mistake. My mistake. It's muddled you. You'll feel different tomorrow." The smooth talk spilled out of him like honey from a broken jar.

304

Amy watched as a small pack of ragged-coated Exmoor ponies made their way slowly across the picnic area. "I can't," she said.

With the skill of the interviewer, Teddy suddenly changed tack. "This music teacher guy . . .?" He was about to probe.

She stopped him. "He's been reclaimed."

"Ah!" He watched her. He was, she knew, hoping she would break down so that he could comfort her.

She didn't. In the distance the blue and cream outline of a bus had appeared over a hill. That decided it. "Look, thanks for coming down all this way. It was sweet of you," she said. Then with a sudden deft kiss on his cheek, which he wasn't expecting, she opened the car door, pulling her bag and laptop after her.

"Amy! Amy, wait! Where are you going?" He was too surprised to stop her.

"There's someone I need to see," she said, then added, "I'll still watch your show."

And slamming the car door she hurried back on to the road, waving to the approaching bus to stop.

The last she saw of Teddy Farrow was as she clambered along the inside of the bus. He was standing by his car, gazing in astonishment after her.

"Isn't that Teddy Farrow?" a fat lady in a yellow raincoat, off to town to do her shopping, remarked to her thin friend as the bus pulled away.

"No. Nothing like him. He's much taller than that," the friend replied. "What would he be doing here, anyway?"

Only now, sitting alone on the back seat as she watched the ponies make their lugubrious way across the moor, did Amy's tears begin to leak. Exactly what or who the tears were for, she wasn't certain.

As the doors of the ambulance closed and the firemen put away their equipment, ending the tragi-comedy of the now roofless Porsche and its driver and girlfriend, the audience of guests and staff began to disperse.

Jane was the last to leave the scene, watching until the hotel car park was free of outsiders. Waiting for her in front of the hotel was Barry Harrison.

"I just wanted to say thank you," he said. "I'll pay you back when I get straight."

Jane shook her head. "No. There's no reason to. It's dealt with. The account is clear."

He nodded, then shook her hand. So formal now.

She watched him as he loaded his bags into his Toyota. He wasn't a lover she would have chosen if she'd had any choice. He wasn't a looker, or a great conversationalist. He was a loser. But he wasn't a bad man, and a lover he had become: a lover she'd enjoyed. Sometimes a girl just had to take her pleasures where she could get them. It had happened before. Hopefully it would happen again. And she couldn't help noticing that he seemed to have been quite grateful, too. Even again this morning.

His car pulled away. He waved from the window. She waved back. It had been a good night.

Had it had anything to do with Domingos' love potions? Quails' eggs, crushed walnuts and vodka? She doubted it very much. But they were a token. And if Bristol allowed her to stay on at the North Devon Riviera she'd make jolly sure she served them again at next year's Valentine's Ball.

"The answer is yes, by the way," Darrell whispered as he and Shona reached the hotel to return to their chores.

"Yes?" Shona enquired.

"Yes, I would like to go around Hungary with you after Easter and stay in hotels and everything."

She touched his hand fondly, bright with pride. "That'll be just brilliant, Darrell. Boyfriend and girlfriend. You won't be disappointed."

CHAPTER
THIRTY-FOUR

Tim only noticed the taxi after it had passed him. He didn't see the passenger's face, but he recognized the angular scythe of black hair in the back seat. Amanda didn't turn to look at him, though she must have seen him. He was glad.

He walked on. It was a pleasant day and he looked out at the sea right across to South Wales, and watched the little waves breaking. Then on a whim he suddenly climbed down to the beach and made tracks along the wet sand where the tide had receded. He needed to think, and this was where he'd seen Amy walking that first morning. Just being here, seeing what she'd seen, he felt closer to her. For a couple of brief days he'd lived a little fantasy, away from the uproar of school, the rattle of the bars where he played so anonymously and the dampness of his flat. But now it was over. And finding a large rounded boulder, he climbed on to it and thought of what had just been.

They'd taken a stroll along the front every day, so Amy knew where to find them, Grace and George, sitting on the otherwise deserted promenade.

Grace laughed when she saw her get down from the bus. "We thought you'd left," she said. "You missed all the excitement."

"I remembered there was something I needed to ask you."

Grace chuckled. "It's over-rated, you know, this wisdom-of-the-elderly thing. We've forgotten anything useful we ever knew. We've all got galloping Alzheimer's. You'd get as much sense out of that seagull." And she pointed to a very large gull, which was sitting on the tubular iron railings of the promenade watching them.

Amy shook her head. "I don't believe you. Yesterday you said that love only worked if you believed in it, like Tinkerbell in *Peter Pan*. That love was a decision. That that was half of it, anyway."

Grace became mischievous. "I said that? It must have been one of my better days. Usually I just moan on about my rheumatism and what it was like during the war."

"Yes, you did. But you also said that there was something else, another half, which I should ask you about some other time. I was wondering if now might be the time."

"Well, George," Grace teased merrily, "shall we tell her? What d'you think? Can she be trusted?"

If he could have done, Amy was sure the old man would have smiled.

Tim wasn't aware of her approach, so quietly did she tread across the sand, so muffling the sound of the sea. He was thinking about her. Of course he was.

"Do you mind if I share your rock?"

She looked so casually pleased to see him and he was so surprised that words left him.

"I mean, it's the only dry one around here. Could you budge up a bit?"

He moved over. She scrambled up and joined him, and for a long moment they sat together, exchanging smiles.

At last she said, "You remember how we thought Grace and George must know some secret because they seemed to be so happy?"

He nodded. His bandage was coming undone again, and he could feel it flapping down the side of his face. He ignored it.

"Well, according to her, the secret is to make your friend your lover and your lover your friend. If you can."

"It's that easy?"

"Seems like it. Anyway, you and me . . . we're pretty good friends, aren't we?"

"I hope so."

"I know we are. And well . . . I was thinking, after what you said last night about being in love with me, which I didn't believe then, though I wanted to, and I really want to believe now . . ."

"It was true then and it's true now. Even truer."

She dimpled with pleasure. "Good. Because that's how I feel about you, too."

"No!" That he couldn't believe.

"Yes. I'm afraid so. So perhaps we should, you know, see if we can balance the equation."

"Balance the see-saw, you mean."

"Exactly! The Lovers' Law of the Eternal See-Saw. Finally in balance . . ."

"By being lovers and friends, friends and lovers."

"And never thinking of anybody else when we're making love."

He pretended to frown. "Why would we ever want to do that?"

"We won't."

They looked at each other. "Are you by any chance trying to get off with me?" he teased.

She giggled. "I'm trying very hard to get off with you."

"Good," he said, and putting his arm around her he felt the comfort of her warmth.

Suddenly she pulled away. "Just a minute. If you're going to kiss me, and I hope you are, there's something I have to do first." Then very carefully she began to undo the bandage from around his head, letting it fly like a streamer in the breeze as it fell away. "It seems to me," she mused as she parted his hair and examined his scalp, "the wound has healed now. You won't need this any more." And rolling the bandage into a ball she put it in the pocket of her coat.

There really ought to have been music to accompany them, Tim thought, as he held her, and they kissed, and as, for the first time in days, he felt the draught around his forehead and ears where his bandage had been. Something by Francis Lai or one of those other famous film composers was what was needed.

But as there wasn't, he'd just have to write it himself.

311

CHAPTER
THIRTY-FIVE

They could have gone back to London, but where was the hurry? A double suite at the North Devon Riviera Hotel for a few days more seemed a better idea, somewhere that Tim could work at his keyboard and Amy at her laptop. Sometimes she would watch him as he worked, and sometimes he'd watch her. Then sometimes they'd break off and not work at all. And afterwards they'd just lie there and plan a future together. There would be a future together, they never doubted that. Who knew where it might lead? Lovers and friends. Together their worlds would be reconfigured.

But Amy still had her book to write. And now as Tim played in the background the ideas flowed.

Whatever it is, or why ever it is, young love, old love, shared love or unrequited love, half-remembered love or never forgotten love, first love or second-hand love, a chaste afternoon of still wet-behind-the-ears, walk-in-the-park love or raunchy, nine-times-a-night, deep-down-dirty love; a night's love or a lifetime's love, his love or her love or their love, your love or my love or our love, the truth is no part of romantic love is really essential to life.

But when we experience it, when we feel it, somehow everything in the world becomes more beautiful, everything we do more worth the doing. And life itself seems to become more alive. We know that biologically human beings could go on reproducing for eternity without love. We could. We really could.

But who wants to live in a loveless eternity?

Also available in ISIS Large Print:

I Did a Bad Thing

Linda Green

Sarah Roberts used to be good. Then she did something bad. Very bad.

Now, years later, she's living a good life, working as a local newspaper reporter and living with her saintly boyfriend Jonathan. She has no reason to think her guilty past will ever catch up with her.

Until Nick walks back into her life. And suddenly what's good and bad aren't so clear to Sarah any more.

ISBN 978-0-7531-7912-3 (hb)
ISBN 978-0-7531-7913-0 (pb)

Kissing Toads

Jemma Harvey

Delphi, garden programme presenter, and Roo, TV producer, have been best friends since childhood. As different as night and day, they've been there for each other's every merciless heart-break, every evil critic and knotty wardrobe choices. But now, Delphi's career seems slightly stuck and the spectre of the has-been garden presenter looms large on the horizon, while Roo's long-time boyfriend has secretly gone and married his long-time Romanian girlfriend. They decide to ditch their life of urban glamour (Delphi) and overworked late nights (Roo) and sign on for a garden make-over programme in Scotland. Draughty castle, craggy rock star with ambitions to be the laird and a cast of very strange characters included — the two are in for a big surprise.

ISBN 978-0-7531-7868-3 (hb)
ISBN 978-0-7531-7869-0 (pb)

Elissa's Castle

Juliet Greenwood

When Elissa Deryn buys a dilapidated castle in Snowdonia, with the intention of turning it into a B&B to support her in her old age, she has no idea just what she is letting herself in for.

Far from fading away into obscure old age, Elissa suddenly finds herself eminently desirable. Suitors appear at an alarming rate. But is it Elissa's charm, or her castle and its unique Elizabethan garden, that is desirable? Can she find one amongst them all who will love her for herself alone, and not for her assets?

Or is she having far too much fun as she is?

ISBN 978-0-7531-7738-9 (hb)
ISBN 978-0-7531-7739-6 (pb)

The Cinderella Moment

Gemma Fox

While off to seek her fortune, Cass meets Prince Charming in a carriage — a railway carriage, that is. That chance conversation, and apparent good luck of finding a mobile phone, turns her whole life upside down. But what if Prince Charming turns out to be the Big Bad Wolf after all?

A summer job in Brighton, an ex-husband who makes pumpkins look bright and a very unlikely pair who double as fairy godmothers, when not on the pull or drinking themselves into a stupor, take Cass on an adventure which is almost more nightmare than fairytale. So when midnight strikes, will everything vanish, or will the real Prince Charming be revealed?

ISBN 978-0-7531-7666-5 (hb)
ISBN 978-0-7531-7667-2 (pb)

Babyville

Jane Green

Meet Julia, a wildly successful television producer who appears to have the picture-perfect life. But beneath the surface, things are not as perfect as they seem. Stuck in a loveless relationship with her boyfriend, Mark, Julia thinks a baby is the answer . . . but she may want a baby more than she wants her boyfriend.

Maeve, on the other hand, is allergic to commitment. A feisty, red-haired, high-power career girl, she breaks out in a rash every time she passes a buggy. But when her no-strings-attached nightlife leads to an unexpected pregnancy, her reaction may be just as unexpected . . .

And then there's Samantha — happily married and eager to be the perfect mother. But baby George brings only exhaustion, extra pounds and marital strife to her once tidy life. Is having an affair with a friend's incredibly sexy husband the answer?

ISBN 978-0-7531-7616-0 (hb)
ISBN 978-0-7531-7617-7 (pb)

ISIS publish a wide range of books in large print, from fiction to biography. Any suggestions for books you would like to see in large print or audio are always welcome. Please send to the Editorial Department at:

ISIS Publishing Limited
7 Centremead
Osney Mead
Oxford OX2 0ES

A full list of titles is available free of charge from:

Ulverscroft Large Print Books Limited

(UK)
The Green
Bradgate Road, Anstey
Leicester LE7 7FU
Tel: (0116) 236 4325

(Australia)
P.O. Box 314
St Leonards
NSW 1590
Tel: (02) 9436 2622

(USA)
P.O. Box 1230
West Seneca
N.Y. 14224-1230
Tel: (716) 674 4270

(Canada)
P.O. Box 80038
Burlington
Ontario L7L 6B1
Tel: (905) 637 8734

(New Zealand)
P.O. Box 456
Feilding
Tel: (06) 323 6828

Details of **ISIS** complete and unabridged audio books are also available from these offices. Alternatively, contact your local library for details of their collection of **ISIS** large print and unabridged audio books.